For all the love and support you always showed me,
this is for you Grandma.

THE DREAMSCAPE MURDERS

To Sydnie
Thank you for the support. Enjoy!!

Heather.

THE DREAMSCAPE MURDERS

H.M NEWSOME

BROWHILL PUBLISHING HOUSE

Prologue

August 2026

Brian and Amara Adebayo lounged in the hot tub they had created in their dreamscape, sipping on champagne, as the water fizzled and the jets pulsated with a gentle roar. They were continuing their celebrations from the evening dinner with the recent buyers of the two and a half million dollar condo in Manhattan overlooking central park. Brian had been facing a slump in sales recently and this sale marked a turning point for them.

Since they had their chips installed, they had enjoyed their extra time together in their sleep, and that night was no exception. They both led busy lives, and not wanting to diminish their intimate connection when they were exhausted from a long day, they connected in their dreams.

"I'm so proud of you darling," Amara said to her husband. She slowly ran her hand down his naked torso and leaned into him for a kiss. Brian pulled his wife closer and began exploring her body. They felt safe in their dreamscape, alone, just the privacy of the two of them.

Amara's body gave a sudden jolt that Brian felt and he released her from his embrace. Something was wrong. He pulled away, only to see a surprised look in her eyes and blood pouring down her chest. A moment later, he felt hands on his shoulders from behind him and the pinch of a knife as it sliced into him. The last thing he saw was a man with a grey beard standing behind where his wife had been, watching him slump down into the bloodied water.

One

*They say that if you meet someone in your dreams,
they are dreaming about you too.*

*BREAKING NEWS - Los Angeles - April 12th, 2022.
DreamScape Ltd. has launched their brain-implanted
chip so that you can connect with people in your dreams.
CEO Walter Dumas believes this to be the "easiest and
safest way to connect with those you love. Without
taking time out of your day, you can enjoy time with
them while you sleep." The chip is currently exclusive to
those who can afford the $7,000 price tag, but interest
keeps growing, and the company states that they are
fully booked as of launch day.*

Meeting someone in their dreams was now real. The
only difference was that you could schedule who and
where you wanted to meet. At first the new technology
was feared and seen as an invasion of privacy. Putting

a chip in your brain—people thought it was insane. Of course the rich and tech-savvy did it first; they wanted the newest, rarest, and best technology available. Then everyone wanted to be part of the crowd, triggered by the fear of missing out, and so the demand for the implant grew and DreamScape Ltd. had to make them more available.

Twenty-four-year-old Ada fell into that group. She couldn't wait to create her own dreamscape, but felt ashamed of wanting it so badly when her family was against it. However, when they called her name, in the waiting room at the Nottingham DreamScape clinic for her noon appointment on August 24, 2026, saying, "Next is Ada Carpenter," she was so pumped! She stood up from the white faux-leather chair in the corner of the waiting room and headed over to the nurse standing by the white marbled reception desk with her clipboard. Ada smiled at her and said, "I'm here." The nurse gave a half-smile in return and led her into a room in the back.

The procedure didn't take long at all. With the medical advancements over the past years, it was now only a couple of hours that you had to stay at the clinic. The DreamScape Clinic used a machine that cut a small hole in the top of the skull and inserted a long needle with a little chip on the end to get as close to the hippocampus as possible. The chip, when activated, then started wiring into your neurons to send and receive signals. Ada decided that she was going to have to sport a ponytail or hat for the next few months to cover the small bald patch, but she knew she could get away with it. The coolest part, she thought, was that it could all be controlled and charged with an app on your smartphone. "I will be able to download my dreams and memories to have them forever," Ada whispered to herself.

The DreamScape Clinic in Nottingham had only opened up the previous year. Before that, they only had one clinic in London for all of the United Kingdom. However, as the demand grew, smaller clinics started branching out into other cities and the price went down so that it was more accessible to the so-called regular folks. Ada had been saving for the last two years for her chance to get the chip, and now that the price had dropped to £1250, she finally had her chance. Her mother, Helen, and her two older brothers, Davey and Craig, had always been against the implant, but at 24 years old, she knew she could make up her own mind, especially seeing as she was using her own savings to get it done.

Many people, even her eldest brother Craig, in his thirties, feared this technology still, but Ada had pleaded with him over and over. "Just think what it will do to help people with Alzheimer's and dementia. They can literally watch their memories forever." Of course not every story was a success for DreamScape Ltd. Part of the fearmongering in the media was about the few people who had suffered strokes or seizures after getting their implant, but the chances had been outlined in the pamphlet and online as slim. The majority of people were walking around and loving their lives with the new technology in their brains.

So far, not even half the population of the world had had the chip implanted. The last statistics released stated that over two billion people had made the choice to get the chip. There were many still out there thinking it was a big conspiracy, and that the government was going to control and monitor the population with GPS, and yet they all had smartphones that basically did the same thing. Helloooo, GPS on your phone, guys! Ada always thought.

Ada's boyfriend, Frederic, 26 years old and originally from Paris, had gotten his implant one month earlier and had been waiting for Ada to get hers. It's done now! she thought. I wonder how I can surprise him. I didn't exactly tell him I was going to get it today. I just lied and told him I wasn't feeling well and called in sick to work.

She had actually taken a vacation day from the publishing office where she worked, The Brow House on Main Street, but they didn't know the reason either. For a technology that was so advanced, it was really all kind of hush-hush. You never knew how people would react and treat you if you told them you'd had the chip implant, but how else would you know who you could link with if you didn't say anything? It had become a sort of secret society: one person told another person, and then they would let you know of someone they knew that had it, and it spread from there within the Dreamcaster society. That's the name they had chosen for themselves: Dreamcasters.

Two

"Ada, where have you been?" was the first thing she heard on the other end of her mobile from her brother Davey. He was 29 and still living at home with Ada and their mum in their small three-bedroom cottage-like house with its grey stone walls and green shutters on the windows in the front.

"I've been out visiting Kira, I'll be home soon for dinner," Ada said. Kira, whom she had known since they were eleven years old, was on the waitlist for her chip as well, so they had it planned that Kira would back her story up when she went for her appointment.

"Well, you'd better get home quick. Mum is in one of her moods and if you're late for dinner, she will throw a fit. Get home now!"

"All right, Davey, I'll be there in fifteen minutes," she sighed.

It was always a drama for some reason or another. Ever since her dad had left four years earlier to move in with his new wife in London, Ada's mom had been thinking that she had to do it all. Meanwhile, she had two adult children who worked full-time jobs living with her and helping with the bills. Her other son, Craig, married to Elaina, lived in London with their beautiful daughter Charlotte. They weren't children anymore, and had their own lives, but Ada's mum felt the need for control. Maybe it's her way of showing that everything was ok, Ada thought.

As she rushed home, she forgot to tie up her long, slightly wavy, chestnut hair to cover the bald spot and ran in the door to please her mother. Thankfully, at five feet seven inches she was taller than her mum, so she couldn't see anything, but Davey, who was hovering in the kitchen, was four inches taller than his sister and started giving her a strange look. Ada then realized what she had forgotten to do. She quickly took the elastic band off her wrist and tied up her hair into a ponytail. She knew Davey wouldn't dare say anything in front of their mum—Helen was already too fragile—but she was sure she'd hear about it later.

After a nice warm dinner of chicken, potatoes, and some terribly boiled carrots, Helen went into the den to watch her shows.

"What the hell was with that patch of hair missing, Ada? What did you and Kira get up to today?" Davey said accusingly.

"We were trying out her new hair straightener, and we left it on that part too long. It kind of burns a bit, but it will grow back," Ada lied.

Davey squinted his eyes at her, telling her subconsciously that he didn't believe her, but that he was letting it go for now. After he left the kitchen, Ada started to clean up the dishes from dinner and took a moment for a long deep breath. That was close, she thought.

Ding, ding, Ada's mobile chimed with a message from Frederic, checking in on her to see if she was feeling better. "Once I surprise him, I won't feel so bad about lying to him, but today feels like all lies," she muttered to herself. She texted him back once she was done with the dishes and let him know that she was feeling much better and asked if they could meet that weekend. "Of course! Xo," he replied. Now to plan the big reveal for him, she thought, and knew she had to figure this chip out first. Some people said they had a hard time accessing it in their sleep, while others had no problems. The doctor at the clinic had suggested a guided meditation, and sent her the link to listen to it in bed as a way to help her access the chip. I'll give that a try first before reaching out to other Dreamcasters to hear about their tips and tricks, she thought.

Ding, ding, a text came in from Kira, checking on how she was doing. "I feel great! No issues, but Davey is suspicious," Ada replied.

"Can I call you? I have interesting news," Kira said.

"Sure, let me just get up to my room and I'll give you a ring," Ada texted back.

As soon as Kira answered the phone, she was already amped up about something.

"Hey darling, did you hear about the couple in New York that died in their sleep?" she said rapidly.

"What? No. Don't people die in their sleep all the time, babes? What's so special about this story?"

Kira continued in rapid-fire reply. "They were both chipped and died in their dream together!"

"Wait, what? How would anyone know that, Kira?"

"Because the medical examiner saw that they were chipped when they ran their DNA and tried to download the most recent dreams. Did you know that your DNA is now linked to this chip identification? Did they mention that at the clinic, Ada?"

"Well, there were some long forms to read and agree to, and they took some blood," Ada said, "but I didn't read it all thoroughly."

"Okay." Kira paused. "I did some research, and it appears that you have to agree to the DNA sample, which you likely did by signing the form and ticking the boxes without reading it. The blood sample is then stored in a database for DNA sequencing, and linked to that, in your file, is your chip identification. Basically, they have access to all of you now!"

Ada had to stop and think for a moment. She hadn't heard of this before today. Perhaps she should have read the five pages of forms that she was signing.

"So," Ada said, "they can clone me and download my dreams and memories now, great. Well, I'm not overly worried, Kira. Two billion people have this chip, and this is the first I'm hearing of anything bad about it, aside from the small percentage that had issues with seizures or strokes."

"Oh, I'm not trying to scare you, darling," Kira said. "I just didn't know if you knew. Back to the story about the couple in New York."

"Right, of course, what did they find in the download?"

"That's just it, they aren't confirming, but some sources mentioned it was deleted!"

Three

BREAKING NEWS - New York City - Millionaire real estate mogul Brian Adebayo and his wife Amara died last night in their sleep. Police are releasing few details about the deaths, but sources in the medical examiner's office have leaked a link to the couple's DreamScape chips. Information is being downloaded to see if the NYPD can determine the cause of death.

"I've always heard that if you die in a dream, that you die in real life too, which is why when you're about to die in a dream, your body wakes you up. I guess that didn't work for them," Kira hypothesized.

"How would they both die in their dream? It's probably just the fear media trying to get the conspiracy nuts to go all out on the chip. They probably died of natural causes in their sleep, and just so happened to have the chips implanted. C'mon, Kira," Ada replied.

"Both?" Kira asked. "Both just die of natural causes in their sleep at the same time? I don't think so. Something is going on. But who knows? I'll keep you updated if I hear more."

After they ended the call, Ada started to feel the fear of the story. The what-ifs started swirling around in her mind. It just didn't seem to make any sense. Four years the company had been in business and this was the first anyone had heard of something like this happening. Ada decided to stick with her fearmongering media idea. They were always trying to depict the worst. She made the choice not to look up anything on the internet about the story and just leave it alone. It was time for some self care tonight after the half day she'd spent at the clinic. A nice bath and a good book always did the trick for her, so that's exactly what she had in mind.

After her nightly video call with Frederic, she headed to bed wondering how soon they could connect in their dreams and what his reaction to her surprise would be. She hoped this would add a little more interest to the relationship. She still had her headphones connected to her mobile from the video call and decided to click the link for the guided meditation that the doctor had given her. She wasn't a professional by any means when it came to meditation, but she had done it enough times to be able to get the gist of what she needed to do. She really hoped it wasn't some weird voice. Those were always the worst when trying to relax, but the person's voice was irritating to hear.

"Welcome to the DreamScape meditation for ease into sleep and deep connection to your dreams. Listen to the sound of the waves gently rolling onto the distant shore. Let the melodic overtones relax your body. Focus on your facial muscles, release the tension in your brows, take a deep breath and feel your jaw relax. Inhale deeply ... and exhale to release the tension in your neck ..."

Sounds pretty normal, Ada thought as she lay comfortably on her back with her arms at her side. She did her deep breathing in and exhaled out to relaxation, releasing the tension in her body as instructed. Her eyes became heavy as she continued to listen.

"... hear the waves get softer and the flowing water trickling. Picture your ideal place in your mind. Focus on your surroundings there. Imagine touching the things around you in your safe place ..."

As Ada drifted off into sleep, she didn't hear the rest of the meditation, but it was still playing in her earbuds. She fell into a deep sleep immediately and eventually went into REM sleep, where she found herself in the most beautiful forest grove. There were wild flowers of purple, yellow, and white surrounding her on every side and trees as tall as buildings. This must be some ancient forest, she thought, as she had never seen such large trees before, but then she remembered that this was a form of what she had imagined. The meditation came back to her: "Picture your ideal place ..." Of course—being surrounded by trees was her ideal place. She had grown up escaping to the forest any time she could because it brought her a sense of calm. Nature brought her peace, and now here she was in the middle of the most wonderful dream forest.

She danced around the grove, skipping and swinging her arms, and occasionally rolled in the grass like she used to when she was younger. She sat by the trees and listened to the sounds of the birds and the wind rustling the leaves of the trees. Peace, freedom, she thought. She heard a distant melodic tone, but couldn't place it. It was a frequency that seemed to soothe her even more, but it was strange to hear it in the forest. As odd as it seemed, she dismissed it because it was a dream and it was her dreamscape that she had created, so anything was possible. Suddenly she heard a loud *snap*, like a twig breaking. As she jolted out of the calm in her dream, she also woke herself up, breathing heavily as if she was frightened.

Four

In Toronto, Ontario, Canada, twenty-nine-year-old Ramon Díaz had just left the downtown DreamScape Clinic on Yonge Street, feeling unsure of his decision now that it was too late to change his mind. The majority of his friends had already done it, but he hadn't been sure about putting something in his brain. Needless to say, he had started to feel the peer pressure from them and decided to go ahead and do it. It wasn't as if he couldn't afford it, as he was a lawyer at one of the top firms in Toronto, Cauldwell & Barnes. He was making a good salary for only being a few years out of law school, but that had more to do with his father having connections in the legal field. Ramon's friend group were all very open about their decisions to get the chip, and they knew what day he was getting his, so they planned a little after-work gathering at Michaela's penthouse on Queens Quay.

When he arrived, they all immediately peppered him with questions.

"Sooo... Did it hurt?"

"How long did it take? Mine was a whole day thing."

"Do you feel liberated now?"

"I bet you can't wait to try it out. We should connect one night."

Ramon smiled and started to answer the questions as they were shot at him.

"No, Caitlyn, it didn't hurt."

"It only took about three hours, Brooks."

"I'm not sure I would call it feeling liberated, Ryan. I don't really feel any different."

"I'm a little nervous about using it for the first time, Michaela, but they did give me this guided meditation to help me connect, if I want to use it. Especially the first time."

Ryan poured him a glass of Jack's and Ramon drank it down in one gulp. "Damn, you must be stressed," Ryan said. "Here's another, but sip this one, man, we have work tomorrow."

Ryan and Ramon had graduated from the University of Western Ontario and both had started working for Cauldwell & Barnes after some negotiating with Ramon's father. Ramon told his father that he wouldn't take the handout if he couldn't bring Ryan along. They both had excellent grades and Ramon wanted to give Ryan a chance at something better, since they hadn't grown up in the same social strata.

"Yeah, sorry, Ry, I'm just a bit out of sorts with this. The whole thing still seems crazy to me," Ramon said, letting out a sigh. "Did you jump in right away when you got it?"

"It was right after we got that huge bonus for signing that big tech company," Ryan explained, "so it's been a couple years now, but I did try to connect right away. I wasn't successful for a few weeks. They didn't give out that guided meditation to help back then."

"Have you tried meditation before, Ramon?" Michaela asked. "I had and even though they didn't give that out last year, I found I was able to connect easier because I could bring myself to that space."

"I've maybe tried a handful of times, without much success, so it'll be interesting tonight for sure. What do you guys do when you connect? Do you meet each other, or other people?" Ramon asked.

Caitlyn chimed in, her glass of pinot grigio almost filled to the top. "I sometimes meet these losers ..."— she fanned her hand around the room at the group, and they all laughed—"... but usually I wander in my own mind and sometimes I meet new people, or people I've run into in the street or at meetings. It's kind of weird because before the chip you'd dream, and sometimes a weird person's face would appear in your dream and you'd think, I don't know them! However, your brain inserted their face subconsciously from seeing them that day. Now, sometimes, you'll actually meet them in your dreamscape because you're thinking about them."

"I'm not going to lie, Caitlyn, that sounds pretty damn terrifying," Ramon said, with worry in his eyes and his brow furrowed.

The five of them laughed and drank until about 10 pm, when they all decided they needed some sleep before their busy days the next day. Ramon went home to his condo on Blue Jay Way, just opposite the Dome, which was closed tonight due to the chance of rain. It was quiet and a real bachelor pad, with sparse furniture, a big screen TV, no family photos on the shelves or tables, and only a few pieces of art decorating the walls. It definitely looked like a single guy lived there, not to mention the gaming console tucked onto one of the shelves under the TV. He took a hot shower and decided to go to bed to attempt the guided meditation he'd been given. Normally he would sleep naked, but somehow he feared that if he was naked, he'd show up and meet someone in his dream and still be naked. Better not take that chance to start, he thought. Putting on some basketball shorts and a T-shirt, he got as comfortable as he could in his queen-sized bed. He clicked the link they'd sent him and the meditation started.

"Welcome to the DreamScape meditation for ease into sleep and deep connection to your dreams. Listen to the sound of the waves gently rolling onto the distant shore. Let the melodic overtones relax your body. Focus on your facial muscles, release the tension in your brows, take a

deep breath and feel your jaw relax. Inhale deeply ... and exhale to release the tension in your neck ..."

Ok, Ramon, you can do this, he thought. Inhale deep, exhale slow; inhale deep, exhale slow ...

"... feel your breathing equalize. Listen to the calm and hear the waves get softer and the flowing water trickling. Picture your ideal place in your mind. Focus on your surroundings there. Imagine touching the things around you in your safe place and feel them with your hands. Let the textures and the smells guide you into your space. Feel your body relax into your surroundings with each breath ..."

Ramon found himself in front of a log fire, sitting in a large comfy green chair. He could feel the suede fabric under his hands and the warmth of the flames on his face as he leaned closer. As he glanced around the room, he realized he was in a log cabin, one that looked oddly similar to the one he used to stay in with his family when he was younger. He sat back and relaxed in the chair as he watched the flames dance around on the logs. He was alone, and he felt strange, but wasn't quite sure why. He closed his eyes and wished for some company around the fire, and in the next moment there was a knock on the door to the cabin. He got up and opened it. It was Ryan. "How ...?" he began.

"It's like you called for me, man. I was in my space and then I started walking and there was your cabin, so I came over," Ryan answered. "It's ok, Ramon. Let's just sit down. I know it's still new for you."

Five

Ramon didn't use the guided meditation to access his dreams for the rest of the week. Meeting Ryan in his dream had freaked him out. What have I done? he thought. He headed over to his parents' Rosedale house, what some would call an old mansion, in one of the wealthiest neighbourhoods in the city. He tried to visit every other weekend for dinner when they weren't hosting some sort of party or other. This weekend his mother was happy to receive him and planned a nice dinner that their cook was making for them.

"Oh, honey! It's so wonderful to see you! We're having your favourite tonight, green enchiladas, and churros con cajeta for dessert. Did you change your hair? It looks different." His mother, Gabriela, always greeted him this way, with affection, hugs, kisses, and questions.

"Sounds wonderful, mom, thank you. It's great to see you too." He smiled and hugged her again. "I heard that if you keep your hair parted the same way too long, it can cause early baldness, so I thought I'd try something different." In reality, he was covering his small bald patch by parting his hair to the other side. "Dad! You're home, I wasn't expecting you until later. You didn't have to work in the office today?"

His father, Carlos, was a top criminal attorney and frequently worked all hours of any day of the week. Aside from the odd vacation or getaway to the log cabin up north, Ramon didn't have a lot of memories with his father, but he always knew that his father had his best interests at heart and encouraged him in his studies. Because of which, he ended up landing him the job with Cauldwell & Barnes practising corporate law. As much as Ramon admired his father, he didn't want to follow in his footsteps completely and become a criminal lawyer. He didn't want the lifestyle of working 24/7.

"Mi hijo! It's so good to see you. How's the firm treating you? Do I need to talk to anyone over there? Is Ryan settling in well?"

The small talk was always work-related, but Ramon didn't mind. He knew it was his father's way of showing he cared.

"Ryan's doing great. He'd love to come and visit sometime soon. Maybe I'll bring him next visit." Ryan had become like a second son to Gabriela and Carlos over time. He was over visiting so much as the two boys grew up that Ramon's parents just treated him like part of the family.

"Oh, that would be lovely, my dear," his mother said.

Throughout the visit and the delicious dinner that the cook had made, Ramon was peppered with the usual questions that were normal conversation in his parents' house.

"How's work?"

"How's the condo?"

They were always making sure his life was good. They paid for the condo that he lived in; he only had to pay the fees, monthly bills, and expenses. The conversation eventually moved on to the dreaded questions that Ramon knew were coming.

"Have you met anyone?"

"You should find a nice girl to settle down with, Ramon. We want to be agile enough to run around with our grandchildren," his mother said.

"No, mom, I haven't met anyone recently. Don't worry, I'll get you some grandchildren one day. I'm just really focusing on my career right now." Ramon gave the basic answers, as always.

"My friend Marie has a beautiful daughter, and she's coming for a visit soon. Perhaps I can set you two up and you can show her around the city, honey," Gabriela suggested, as she tended to do.

"Thank you, mom, I appreciate that offer. How about you let me think about that and we can talk about it when it gets closer, okay?" Ramon hated to tell his mother no, but preferred to just push her off until the next conversation.

After he left his parents' house, Ramon took an Uber to meet his friends for some drinks. Caitlyn arrived at the same time he did and they went into the bar together to find the rest of the group, walking through the glass-walled entrance and glancing around at the tables of people.

"So, Ramon, how's the chip? Have you explored your subconscious yet?" she pressed him as they snaked their way to the back of the bar.

"I did the first night, but I haven't since. Maybe tonight I'll try again." He paused. "Ryan showed up the first time, which kind of freaked me out. Have you been hanging out with anyone in your dreams?"

"I've met with Ryan and Michaela a few times," she replied. "It's like we hang out and then go home and then hang out again. It's been great fun! Just give it some more time and you'll love it."

They saw the rest of the crew, half of them sitting and half standing around a bar-height circular table, and drinks were shared all around. Ramon took in the moment and enjoyed their company and the laughs for the next few hours until they all decided to leave. He and Ryan left at the same time to share an Uber home. They lived near enough to each other that he could drop Ryan off before heading back to his condo. As they waited for the ride to show up, Ry asked, "So I haven't met with you since that first night, man, everything okay?"

"Yeah, I just wanted to take it slowly, I'm going to try again tonight and see what happens," Ramon said as he stared up the street for their car.

Ryan nodded. He knew Ramon liked to keep it safe and easy. "I get it, man, ease in slowly. However, if you want some company, just think of me and maybe I'll show up again. Can't make any promises, though. I met this really hot blonde last night, out of nowhere, in my dreamscape. Not sure if she's a figment of my imagination, or actually another person with a chip. So I might be occupied, if you know what I mean." He nudged Ramon, and they laughed.

The Uber pulled up to the curb where they were standing and they headed home, not daring to talk about the chip anymore.

"Hey, Ry, my parents would love to see you. It's been a while since you visited. How about we go for dinner in two weeks? They have a great new cook. Had the best enchiladas today."

"Oh, a home-cooked meal at your parents' place! Count me in. Just let me know when," Ryan said.

Ten minutes after dropping Ryan off, Ramon was home and exhausted from a long day. Aren't weekends supposed to be for relaxing? he thought. He hadn't done much but socialize the whole day and it still felt like a lot. He was happy to be home and in the peace of his space. After a long hot shower to wash the day away, he crawled into bed, still feeling the effects of all the wine he'd consumed. Ready for another try, he clicked on the link, got comfortable, and started listening to the meditation again.

"Welcome to the DreamScape meditation for ease into sleep and deep connection to your dreams. Listen to the

sound of the waves gently rolling onto the distant shore. Let the melodic overtones relax your body. Focus on your facial muscles, release the tension in your brows, take a deep breath, and feel your jaw relax. Inhale deeply ..."

Ramon fell asleep right away this time. He didn't really follow the instructions, but with the calming tones and the amount of alcohol he had in his system, the connection was almost instant. He was back in his log cabin again. Hmph ... I didn't even have to try this time, he thought. The fire was already burning, the warmth surrounding him and lighting the room, casting flickering shadows on the walls and ceiling.

"Would it be weird if I just napped in front of the fire, in my dream?" he asked himself. "Seems like that would defeat the purpose."

He decided not to waste this opportunity and got up to look around. Everything was as if he was in the actual cabin from his childhood. All the dishes were in the correct cupboards, all the drawers were neatly organized, as they always had been. His mother was meticulous about that sort of thing, which was probably where he'd got it from. Everything had a place. The family photos, he noticed, were the only thing that were different. The childhood cabin had many old photos from when he was a child, and his grandparents and parents were in them, but these photos were now all of him. As an adult. "Weird," he said aloud. He finally concluded that, because it was his subconscious, the pictures represented his memories. They weren't even pictures that had actually been taken, just snapshots of moments in his life.

Now that he had explored all the rooms in the cabin, he decided it was time to take a look around outside. He opened the door and stood on the porch. He was expecting it to be cold outside because the fire was blazing inside, but it wasn't. Right ... I can climate control my dreams; it makes sense, he thought. He looked down at himself and noticed he was wearing long pants and a light down-filled black jacket. On his feet were some tan-coloured ankle high boots that he obviously hadn't gone to bed in. He didn't recall wearing a jacket inside the cabin, but realized that his brain was making sure he was prepared for whatever environment he was in.

He wandered down the path towards the lake where he used to swim or canoe in the summers when they were there. Through the bushes that surrounded the path, he could see the moon glistening off the water. He stood on the dock and looked around at the trees that surrounded the rocky shores of this small lake. Memories of his childhood came to him, and he sat down at the edge and looked out over the water. The wind was rippling the water just enough that the moonlight shimmered. This is so peaceful, he thought. He smiled as he kept looking around the lake and remembering.

Off to the right in the distance, there were more ripples on the water than on the rest of the lake. He focused his sight on that area and started to see the outline of a canoe. "What the hell?" he muttered aloud.

Deciding to dismiss it as a mere memory of his time on the lake in the canoe, he went back to enjoying the peace and tranquility of sitting on the dock. What felt like thirty minutes later, although dreams don't really count time, he noticed that the canoe was closer to him now and there were two people sitting in it. Adult-sized people. It can't be a memory, I was only a kid, he thought. As he focused harder on the canoe, he saw that someone was paddling it in his direction, and he caught a glint of glass reflecting the moonlight for a moment. Are they spying on me? Are those binoculars? His heart was pounding in his chest and the darkness that surrounded him suddenly seemed to reflect his fear. He woke suddenly, sweating, and turned on the light beside his bed to orient himself again to reality.

Six

For the rest of the week, Ada tried connecting to her dreams without meditation. She managed once and enjoyed her forest grove for a short while until she found she was bored being there alone with nothing to do. During the rest of her sleep she didn't remember dreaming about anything else. Maybe I need more practice, she thought, dismayed. I don't see what the big deal is, but maybe once I tell Frederic today, it will get better and we can connect in our dreams.

She and Frederic were going to meet at the pub for a quick bite to eat before going back to his flat in the Lenton area of Nottingham, where it was mostly a student population. He had been in that area since his student days at the University of Nottingham and felt comfortable there, so he'd stayed and got a better flat on his own.

They had become regulars at the Crown and Table pub, and seemed always to get about the same seats for their date nights.

"We should really branch out and do something else for our next date night. We've become an old married couple," Ada laughed timidly.

"But this is our spot, Ada. It's where we met. That has to mean something, right? I mean we can go somewhere fancier if you like. I just thought you liked it here."

Frederic was no romantic, but he could tell that things were becoming a bit stale between them.

"I just want some new memories and experiences with you, hon." Ada tried to smooth out the conversation, but it still remained a bit awkward.

She decided to change the subject. Now was the time for the surprise. Maybe this would spice things up in their relationship, or so she hoped. Slowly she started, not really knowing how to say it. "I ... um ... have something to tell you."

Frederic's face became worried and it felt like a wall had just gone up between them.

"It's not bad!" she blurted out. "I ... um ... wasn't sick earlier this week when I said I was. I ... uh ... finally got my chip done." With a halfway enthusiastic smile she added, "Surprise."

Way to go, *Ada*, she thought, not much of a surprise when you sound so ashamed about it. There was silence between them again. Have I done something wrong? she wondered, as she waited for Frederic to say something, anything.

"Wow, that's great, Ada," he finally responded, "but why didn't you think you could tell me?"

Here we go, she thought, and then said, "I wanted to surprise you, and honestly thought it would be different than how it just came out. But now we can talk about it, and we can meet in our dreams together. That'll be a new kind of date night!" Ada was trying to salvage the conversation and the good time they were supposed to be having.

"I see," he said emotionlessly, "though I still don't get why you wouldn't just tell me, but this should be interesting to try. Have you been inside yet? Did you create your dreamscape?"

They continued talking in hushed tones as they ate their meal. Frederic shared what his dreamscape looked like and Ada shared hers. He explained that he'd used the meditation for a week straight until he was able to get into his space without it. He had also met with some family members who were still in France in his dreams, and it was great to see them. Sometimes it was in his dreamscape, and other times it was in theirs. Ada didn't realize that you could travel to someone else's dreamscape to meet them, but she was still new at this. Aside from that random twig snapping the first night, she always felt alone in her dreamscape.

They headed back to Frederic's flat after another round of pints to watch a movie on Netflix and talk some more about how they could meet that night in their dreams. At the flat, which still looked like Frederic was a student in a dorm with hand-me-down furniture, they fell into their normal routine. Ada had some clothes there for staying overnight, as she did frequently, and all her toiletries. They both changed into something more comfortable before deciding on a romcom for their movie. As they snuggled closer together on the sofa, laughing and watching the film, Ada wondered why the movie industry made scripts like this, full of a type of romance that she'd never experienced before. After the soppy ending to the film, she asked Frederic how they were going to link in their sleep.

"Well, if we each think of the other person then it almost calls to them to show up," he replied. "As you fall asleep, picture your dreamscape and imagine me being there with you. What is your dreamscape like, anyway?"

Ada tried not to let this last question irritate her. They had just discussed her dreamscape at the pub. With a controlled breath, she decided to describe it again for him. "It's a forest, with ancient tall trees and a grove filled with wildflowers," she answered a bit glumly.

"Okay, I'll add that to my image and think of meeting you there," he said. They got ready for bed, closed their eyes, and opened their imaginations.

Ada imagined seeing Frederic on the other side of the grove waiting for her. She imagined him being as amazed by the atmosphere of tranquillity as she was the first time she created her dreamscape. Frederic imagined a forest full of trees and walking with Ada down a path. They both drifted off to sleep eventually, and before Ada knew it she was in her grove. She looked around for Frederic, but couldn't see him. She walked through the purple heather that was growing in the grove and spun around in all directions. Still he wasn't there. Damn, she thought, it didn't work.

She thought about Frederic some more and walked back into the trees and sat on her favourite fallen tree. She concentrated hard and closed her eyes, calling out to him with her mind.

"Wow, this is like your own private dwelling here, Ada!"

As soon as she heard Frederic's voice, she opened her eyes. He was standing at the edge of the grove.

"You should alter it as you go and maybe add a little cottage or something, so you're not sitting on a log."

"It worked!" she said. "How do I alter it? Just think of it and picture new things?"

"Yes, it's your mind, so you can have whatever you want here—a waterfall, a cottage, a Ferris wheel, if you like. It's all up to you. I change mine all the time," Frederic explained.

Ada imagined a large hammock swing big enough for two people so that they could lay in each other's arms and be comfortable. She concentrated hard, and when she opened her eyes, there, in the middle of the grove, was the large hammock swing for two.

"How about that!" she exclaimed.

They maneuvered themselves into the hammock and she snuggled right up next to him. This is peaceful, she thought. Frederic was tall, almost six feet, and had a husky build, so he took up more room than she did. Ada noticed that he was dressed in faded blue jeans, loafers, and a soft black turtleneck sweater that contrasted with his white skin and dark brown curly hair. Even though they were outside in this grove, it didn't feel cold. She looked at herself and noticed that she was wearing a leopard print dress that came just below her knees. Ada always preferred to stand out in her style, but she didn't even own anything like this in her wardrobe. She concluded that this must be how she saw herself and thus had projected it into her dreamscape.

They both talked and were silent, enjoying each other's company in the dream. Frederic suggested darkening the sky so they could see the stars as they lay there, so Ada closed her eyes and thought really hard. When she opened them, the Milky Way was shining brightly above them. The rest of the night was a blur for her, but when they woke up in the morning, they talked more about what she could do in her dreams. For the first time, Ada was excited to go to sleep at night. She couldn't wait to play with her dreamscape and she felt confident about exploring within it now.

Seven

Over the next few nights, Ada expanded her dreamscape. She created a quaint little stone cottage with a large fireplace and stone mantle above it, as well as two big, comfy red armchairs. She decorated it with flourishes as she would decorate her own place if she ever moved out of her mother's house. One wall had a brocade wallpaper in ivory and grey, and there was a fluffy faux-sheepskin rug, large enough to sit under the chairs and cover the surrounding area.

Outside, she created some pathways of stone from the cottage to the grove, and removed the hammock she had placed there when Frederic had visited. She added a white marble two-tiered fountain in the middle of the grove with some benches so she could sit there and listen to the calming sounds of the water. She did all this with a fierce determination to make her dreamscape her own personal haven. This is better than meditation to bring me peace, she thought.

Once she had completed the benches, with their added large pillows for comfort, she decided to sit and enjoy her creations. As she sat there in peace and calm, listening to the gurgling fountain water, she closed her eyes to take it all in. When she was in her dreamscape she couldn't account for time, so she had no idea how long she'd been sitting there with her eyes closed when suddenly she felt a shiver run down her body. She opened her eyes wide and sat up straight for a moment, just listening. I never feel cold here, she thought. Why would I shiver?

She knew immediately that something was off. She stood up and walked around the grove, scanning the forest to see if she could figure out what had triggered her sudden alertness.

****

Peering through the trees from a distance, they could see her. They weren't sure what had alerted her to their presence, but knew that they couldn't linger much longer where they were.

"She sees us," the man with the grey beard messaged telepathically to his young companion.

They slowly backed away out of Ada's forest and grove, treading carefully so as not to break a twig again like the last time.

"Let's move on," the older man ordered the younger one. "Time to find another."

"She's done so much in such a short time. She's creative and unique," the young man with shaggy brown hair messaged to his leader.

"Let's leave her to it for now, and reenter next time a bit further away." The older man said as they exited Ada's dreamscape.

****

Ada continued to look around cautiously. Something had spooked her and she knew it. With so much time and concentration on building her dreamscape up, she hadn't been paying attention to her surroundings. This is my dream, and my space, and I shouldn't have to be cautious, she thought. Enough for tonight. With that she exited her dreamscape and fell into her normal sleep pattern.

When she woke up in the morning, she was more tired than she'd thought she would be. She had noticed this over the course of the week, and started to think it was because she was taxing her brain and energy in her dreams. I won't do it tonight, she told herself as she yawned and stumbled into the bathroom for a shower to wake herself up.

Ding, ding. A text came through from Frederic. "Good morning! I tried to call you to my dreamscape last night, but I guess you weren't active with the chip. Maybe tonight?"

Huh, she thought, maybe I was so focused on my own self that I didn't feel him calling to me. "Sorry, hon, I've been building all week in my dreams, you should see it now! I'm actually going to take a break tonight, I feel like I haven't slept," she replied.

Ada really liked Frederic, but she knew, not enough; she always felt like something was missing between them. They enjoyed time together, and the sex was great when it happened, but there was still something missing, and she couldn't put her finger on it. He seemed like a great guy, but did she really see a future with him? This was a question she asked herself weekly.

Ding, ding. Another text, this one from Kira. "Are we still on for tonight? Drinks after work? You have to fill me in! xo."

"Yes! Of course we're still on, babes! I wouldn't miss catching up with you for anything xo," Ada replied.

Thanks for the reminder, she thought. Now I have to plan a work and a going out outfit. She threw her long chestnut-brown hair up into a messy bun and picked out a jade green retrofitted A-line dress that could pass for work and drinks later. After she had applied her make-up, she headed down for a quick breakfast before catching the bus to town for work. Her brother, Davey had already left, but her mum had made her a travel mug with fresh tea ready to go.

"Thanks mum, love you!" she said, as she darted in and out of the kitchen, grabbing the tea, a muffin, and an apple before heading out the door.

The morning at the publishing house went by so fast. Ada was feeling exhausted and was already on her third tea when Joel, her co-worker, came knocking at her door.

"Ada, lovely, we should go grab a bite for lunch, what do you say?"

Joel, slim, tall and blond, with vibrant blue eyes, always caught the ladies' attention, but unfortunately for them, he was happily married to Arthur. Arthur was slightly older, wealthy, and eccentric, but he and Joel just fit so well together.

"That's the best offer I've heard today, Joel. Let's go." They headed down the main street to the Garden Bistro for a light lunch and some gossip.

They both ordered their usual, as they were on a time limit for their lunch break. Ada had her tandoori chicken wrap with a side salad, and Joel ordered his vegan protein bowl.

"So," Joel jumped right in, "I'm not sure where you stand on the whole chip thing, but Arthur and I have them." He looked quizzically at her to see if she would object to this conversation.

Ada smiled and said sarcastically, "And how's that working for you guys?"

"Oh, luv, I'm so glad you're not one of *those*. Listen to this," he continued in semi-hushed tones. "Arthur decided it was best if we had a shared dreamscape, not each having our own. It's been wonderful, a mansion on the cliffs of Santorini, the most amazing infinity pool, basically anything I could dream of. But when you live with someone, and then you have to spend your dreams together as well? It's a bit much. So I don't know how to get some me time without offending the bugger. I think I'll just create a special wing on the mansion and say it's my study or something, so that I can get some alone time. What do you think?"

Ada was a bit shocked. Not at the extravagance of the place, but that they had a shared dreamscape that they'd built together. "Joel, he can't really expect you to be together the whole time. That would be like hijacking your dreams every night. I'm sure he'll understand."

As she mentioned hijacking, she remembered the strangeness of her dream the previous night. "Joel, have you ever, I don't know, felt someone watching you in your dreamscape? Besides Arthur, I mean?"

Joel thought about it for a moment. "What do you mean, lovey? Like someone you don't know?"

"Yes. Last night I felt like someone was watching me. It really creeped me out. My dreamscape is a forest that I love and keep building up, but one time I heard a twig snap, and last night I just knew someone was there. Oh, I have the chip, by the way."

Joel's eyes were wide, and the smirk on his face said it all. "Why didn't you tell me? I'm actually quite surprised that little bookish Ada took a step towards technology. Oh my ... this explains your hair all wrapped up in a bun these last couple of weeks, doesn't it?"

Ada smiled sheepishly and nodded as Joel continued, "I can't say that I've felt anyone watching me or noticed anything odd, but I already know that someone *is* there with me, so I'm probably not as alert as if I was alone. And people can appear in your dreams, I've heard. Whether you invite them in or they just show up, I'm not entirely sure. Did you actually see anyone?"

"No, I haven't seen anyone, it was just a sense, a shiver, an awareness, you know?" Ada flagged the wait staff for their bills. She didn't want to talk about this anymore.

On the way back to the office Joel said, "Stay alert, luv, but it's also likely your mind just playing tricks on you, right?" He had a point. She hadn't called for any-one to meet her there, and she was so busy creating she wasn't thinking about people, so how would they be there? Made sense.

"You're right, Joel. I'm still learning how to adapt to it, so it's likely just my own brain doing weird things."

Eight

The grey-bearded man, Gustav Lindenholst, sat in his abandoned house with its blacked-out windows that he'd taken over in Detroit after the economic crash. He stole electricity from the city and a friend in a telecom company set up his internet access for his communication room, which sported ten computer screens and multiple operating systems. He had worked in IT prior to being fired for stealing corporate information. He had done it many times before at companies he worked for, but had never been caught. Now people paid him for finding information. Before he was in IT he had been in the army, where he was sent on special ops missions after helping to provide the intel to the teams.

Gustav was nearing fifty and had no family that he was in contact with. He enjoyed his solitude and his work. Although he had lots of money, he preferred to live off the grid without anything lavish while hiding his money in offshore accounts.

Andrei Kuzmenski, his young apprentice, came in through the back door, as Gustav didn't want anyone coming in the front that might suggest the abandoned house was lived in. Andrei was 24, tall and lean, with shaggy brown hair that Gustav was always telling him to get cut.

"Why do you insist on living in this shithole, Gustav? You've made a ton of money. Why don't you get somewhere nice?" Andrei casually asked his superior.

"Fewer eyes to see our business here, Andrei. Why have a flashy place to show off my money when the government thinks I'm unemployed?"

Andrei shrugged his shoulders and shook his head.

This younger generation is all about flash and showing off, Gustav thought.

"Who are we monitoring tonight, Gus?" Andrei inquired.

"There's an Italian couple, wealthy from family money, in Naples—the Espositos. I already have Charmaine in place there to enter the house once we're done. We'll watch them for the next two nights to get the floorplan."

Gustav was the mastermind behind the hacks, but it was never his idea to start them.

"Did the *Man* give a reason for this one? Or are we just taking the extra afterwards?"

"Andrei, you ask too many questions. A job is a job. Are you not happy with your cut?" Gustav asked.

"No, no, it's cool. Sometimes I just wonder who the person is when we're given a name, you know?" Andrei held up his hands in surrender. Gustav shook his head and turned back to his monitors. It was almost night time in Naples.

"Just get something to eat, and be ready to help me with the codes. Once we're in, we'll work telepathically as normal. There's a lot on the line."

Nine

A couple of evenings later, the Espositos, Flora and Carmine, waved goodbye to their dinner guests and left the staff to clean up from the gathering that night. They took the remainder of the champagne and two glasses out to the balcony that had a perfect view of the Bay.

"Flora, darling, you were fabulous tonight, and so stunning as always," Carmine said as he kissed his wife and they toasted to their successful evening with the new investors.

"Thank you, my love. We make a great team." Flora smiled broadly at her husband's loving gaze, her red lips accentuated by her pearly white teeth.

Even after 26 years of marriage, they still loved each other as if they were newlyweds. Flora was a big part of Carmine's business dealings and she supported him always. With the mansion full of their staff, they still felt alone sometimes now that their children had all moved on to their own projects and homes. They enjoyed each other's company, and the romance had not died in all those years together. Carmine played *Vivo per Lei* by

Andrea Bocelli on the outside speakers and they danced on the balcony. Their closeness was evident to anyone who knew them.

Once the staff had departed for the evening, the Espositos carried on their joy of the evening into the bedroom. With so many years together, they knew every aspect of each other's bodies and how to please one another. Their love was real and enduring. After tiring each other out and being fully satisfied, they held each other as they fell asleep in each other's arms, their clothes still strewn all over the floor and the gas fireplace still burning in the corner of the room. They knew it wasn't the end of their night, as they would meet again in their dreamscape for another round of lovemaking.

****

Gustav saw the signal turn green on the monitor. "Finally they're asleep and activating their chips," he said. He began typing furiously on the keyboard to enter their dreamscape. He and Andrei wore their headgear that connected their chips to the system so they could operate while fully awake in order to complete the mission given to them. They remained in the dark corners of the house that was the couple's dreamscape. It was very similar to their own real-life home. Not very imaginative, he thought, and Andrei nodded.

They knew why the Espositos didn't need an alternate reality, because they were already living a dream. Gustav and Andrei quietly crept through the house until they got closer to the couple. They heard them having passionate sex in one of the upstairs rooms and crept into another room down the hall to wait it out. They didn't talk, didn't mention anything, they just waited. Knowing they had a job to do, Gustav was getting in the mindset to do it. He didn't like mess, so it had to be as clean as possible, and then he would remove the memories from the chip like he did with the couple in New York.

After what seemed like an eternity, the noise in the other room settled down to soft whispers.

"I guess you can have more stamina in your dreams," Andrei sent to Gustav with a wink. Gus just shook his head at the immaturity of the statement.

"We are here for a job, get your head on straight," he sent back with a stern look.

Gustav slowly went to the door to listen better. He would take the man out first, and Andrei was to grab the wife. He crept out into the hallway, not making a sound, to get a better look into their room. The door was ajar and he could see them, naked, sitting together looking out the window at a view that appeared to be a sunset. Their backs were to the door, and they were close enough together for the job to work out smoothly. Gustav motioned for Andrei to come closer.

"I will go first, but be right behind me to get the wife. Do you have the rope?"

Andrei nodded his understanding. They both took careful and slow steps into the room so as not to be heard and crept up behind the couple, who were still enjoying themselves. Gus snapped Carmine's neck with one quick twist. Andrei wrapped the rope around Flora's neck and crossed it at the back, pulling hard until she couldn't breathe anymore.

Quickly and efficiently, they exited the dreamscape and pulled their headgear off. Gustav texted Charmaine that she could enter the residence and make it look like a robbery by actually robbing them. He also instructed her to make their deaths more visible than just dying in their sleep. Gustav didn't want any connections to the couple in New York to arise. After that, he hacked into their chips to delete the last moments of their lives. If anyone downloaded the information from their chips, they would see their last moments as them peering out the window together.

"All right, Andrei, send a message to the *Man* to let him know the job is done, and that we expect immediate payment."

Andrei understood, and connected to the untraceable server they used for their communication with the *Man*, as they called him. It wasn't as if he had given a name. He only went by the screen name of *theVoyeur*.

Once the payment was received and Charmaine was out of the house, they celebrated a job well done with some vodka and takeout, which Gus sent Andrei to go and pick up. Charmaine could have done the job without a trace, but the idea was to have it look like a burglary gone wrong. She had added some flourish and broken some items. She also reported to Gus that she had pulled Carmine's body off the bed and tossed him down the stairs to make it look like he caught the intruders in the act. She also slit Flora's throat for good measure. That should eliminate any links the authorities could think of to the New York murders last month. Gus was confident in the job. Everything had gone as planned, so for the next few days he would watch the news to see how it unfolded, but he wasn't worried about anything. He knew it was a job, but he always felt a bit of guilt afterwards. He had preferred just watching people silently, as he had been doing for years since the chips were launched and he had figured out how to hack in.

People interested him, and he enjoyed watching them. Later he would return to his monitors and see who interested him tonight to watch what they were building or doing. Andrei had a few people that he enjoyed watching too, but they would go in together for safety as one of their rules. Andrei had taken a liking to a young woman named Ada in Nottingham, so they checked in on her regularly, but not tonight. Gustav just wanted something easy, maybe even to find some new people to pique his interest. There were billions to choose from and it was easy to step in and out of people's minds. After a few drinks he would get Andrei and himself connected and take a look at who was in their chips.

Ten

That same night, Ramon decided to go to bed early. It had been a long day at the office, his caseload had recently been growing, and he just wanted to go to bed. It was only 9 pm, but he didn't mind ending the day early. He fell right asleep and went to his cabin to unwind.

This is almost better than unwinding at home in the condo, he thought.

The fire was blazing, as it always was when he entered. He had a glass of whisky in his hand and sat in the armchair to the left of the fireplace. Once he felt calmed down, he grabbed the down-filled jacket by the door and went out for a walk. He had seen the lake many times now, and decided to go out into the forest to see what was out there.

It's probably just endless trees, he mused.

Having found the entrance to a path into the forest, he began to walk and look around to either side of him. He felt like he had been walking for ages, trees on either side, going on and on forever.

This can't be all there is, he thought. There must be other cabins or something.

The path kept going and he followed it, but as he did, he noticed that the trees were getting larger and larger.

"I've never seen trees like this before."

They were the tallest trees he had ever seen. Ramon knew that there weren't any trees like that in the forest by the cabin he had gone to as a child. It felt like this forest was just a vast space that kept changing as he went. Eventually he heard the trickling sound of water flowing nearby, so he headed in that direction, thinking that maybe there was a stream he could follow.

As Ramon got closer to the sound of the water, the forest area got lighter, and he could see an open space ahead. He decided to slow his pace because he didn't know what was in front of him, having never explored a place like this before. He stopped behind one of the largest trees near the edge of the clearing and peered around. All at once, he saw a beautiful grove filled with wildflowers, a two-tiered fountain, and some benches.

This is amazing, he thought. Where did this come from?

He walked slowly around the grove, staying just inside the tree line and trying to keep to the larger trees for cover.

"How would a fountain be in the middle of a forest?"

Ramon knew he was in his dreamscape, but didn't know why he had created something like this. He just couldn't understand—that is, until he had completed about half the outskirts of the grove. He stopped, amazed and curious about what he saw. On the other side of the fountain, on a bench, was a beautiful girl with long brown hair, wearing a summery dress with blue flowers on it. She was reading a book and hadn't noticed him. Ramon wondered if he should approach her, but worried he might frighten or disturb her, no matter how drawn to her he was.

****

Ada had been in her dreamscape for most of the night. She had gone to bed later than usual, but really wanted some alone time in her tranquil place. She had been re-reading one of her favourite books, Dante's *Inferno*, and just relaxing. Tonight she hadn't gotten any creepy vibes that someone was watching her and felt completely at ease. After a while, she stood up and walked closer to the fountain, closed her eyes, and thought about purple water. When she opened them again, the fountain was flowing with purple water that matched the wild heather growing in the grove. She started to lean forward to see her reflection when she heard a kind of gasp and quickly turned around.

"Who's there?" she shouted, with her back to the fountain, gripping the edge in sudden fear.

"Hi," Ramon said back to the shout as he stepped just past the forest line with his palms raised to show he was harmless.

"I'm sorry, I didn't mean to disturb you ... I ... I don't even know how I got here. Was that magic you just did?"

Ada was shocked that there was someone there—here—in *her* dreamscape, and wondered why she hadn't felt it the way she had before, with a weird sensation.

"Stay there," she said. "What's your name, and why are you here in my space?"

"My name is Ramon, I live in Toronto. I apologize, I didn't know this was your space. I was in my own dreamscape and went for a walk in the forest, and then the trees started to change and I ended up here. Where is 'here,' anyway?"

Ada was so confused. He seemed harmless, but how had he entered her dreamscape? Just by walking?

"My name is Ada, I'm from Nottingham, and this is my dreamscape that you seem to have walked into. I don't fully know how that's possible. Why don't you come sit down?"

She motioned him over to one of the benches nearby and, as he got closer, she saw that he was wearing a big jacket, long pants, and boots. Ada looked at him quizzically and he stopped.

"What?" Ramon asked.

"Why are you dressed for winter? It's not exactly cold," Ada replied.

Ramon looked down at his jacket and realized he was feeling a bit warm, and didn't need it in here.

"So how do I change to more appropriate clothing, Ada?"

"Oh, you don't know? I find that closing my eyes and thinking about what I want helps. Like I just did with the water," she answered.

Ramon closed his eyes and imagined himself in jeans and a grey dress shirt with white cuffs and collar.

"Better?" he asked as his clothes changed accordingly.

"It'll do for now." She smiled and shook her head.

He was all the typical things that women talk about: tall, dark and handsome. Check, check, and check. He had green eyes like her own, striking in contrast to his darker Latin features, clean-shaven, with his almost black coloured hair worn a bit longer on the top and shorter at the sides. He took a seat on the bench near Ada.

"Have you seen me before?" Ada began.

"Never. I mean, we live in different countries, and this is the first time I've been here in your dreamscape. Sorry again."

Ramon felt so bad for intruding, and was confused how this had happened.

"I only asked because sometimes I've felt like there's someone in the forest watching me, and it feels a bit creepy. I wasn't sure if it was you, but maybe it's other people just wandering in here without me knowing it. So weird," Ada said.

"No, this is my first time," Ramon said, "but now that you mention it, I did see two people in a canoe on the lake one night in my dreamscape. I guess if you have similar scenery, they can overlap. I'm not overly familiar with all the details yet. I didn't even know you could change things, like you've shown me. So thanks for that!"

He and Ada talked about their dreamscapes, and how Ramon's was just his childhood cabin and lake, but now he was going to be making some changes. They talked through their job situations, their families, and wondered together how they had just met. Theories were jokingly thrown around about fate, a glitch in the system, or some master puppeteer. Ada couldn't remember when she had smiled and laughed so much, and with a complete stranger who had intruded on her dreamscape. Ramon was no different; she could see on his face that he was at ease and happy to be here with her. She felt confused. She'd never felt anything like this before, never experienced this kind of chemistry. She wasn't sure that, because she was in her dreamscape, she wasn't making all this up in her head. Just as she asked Ramon, "Are you real? Like a real person, or am I making this up?" her alarm went off, startling her into reality. The dream was gone, Ramon was gone, and without an answer. She rolled out of bed to get ready for another day of work, groggy and confused. Thank goodness it's Friday, she thought. Just gotta make it through today.

Eleven

Ramon woke up suddenly. It was 2 am. He looked around his room, still filled with the darkness of night, and rubbed his face. He couldn't believe what had just happened. That last question before the abrupt wake-up call—he'd been thinking the same thing.

Did I imagine that? Did my mind make her up? He got out of bed for a glass of water and to shake off the dream. He still couldn't understand how he had gotten there, or if she was even real. All he knew at that moment was that he had an 8 am breakfast meeting with a client, so his alarm would be going off in just under four hours.

I have to try and sleep, he thought. He crawled back into bed, and couldn't manage to shut his mind off. He kept thinking about Ada: how beautiful she was, how smart, funny, and so easy to talk to she had been. He tossed and turned and checked his phone. 3:30 am. "Ugh, come on man, just go to sleep!" he cursed at himself.

Eventually he fell asleep just before 4 am, and his alarm went off two hours later. He moaned and slumped out of bed, exhausted. This is going to be a rough day, he thought. Even as he showered to wake up, he still couldn't get Ada out of his mind. Is she real? he kept thinking.

He texted Ryan to meet him at lunch. "Tapas?" Ryan texted back.

"Yes, the usual place just off Bloor Street," he responded.

Ramon then set off to his morning meeting with his client. He remained as attentive as he possibly could during the breakfast and dealt with all the paperwork before heading into the office. Once there, he found that time was dragging until his lunch with Ryan. He couldn't focus. He desperately needed to find out if Ada was real. He headed to the tapas bar as soon as he could and after scanning the room he saw Ryan, who was already drinking a Heineken.

"I ordered one for you buddy, don't worry," Ryan said, "What's going on? You didn't answer any of my other messages."

Ramon didn't know where to start. "I had the weirdest dream last night, Ry."

He proceeded to tell Ryan about Ada and how he had wandered into her dreamscape. How he had had an amazing time and couldn't stop thinking about her. And finally, how could he know if any of it was real?

"Could I have made it all up? Just my imagination? What do you think?"

Ryan stared at him for a moment. "That all sounds incredible, man. I mean, I have heard of people meeting actual people in their dreamscapes, so she *could* be real. What details did she mention, maybe we can google her?" Ryan laughed a bit as he said the last part.

They both took out their phones and started by typing Ada, Nottingham, UK into the search bar. Some Facebook profiles, Instagram accounts, and LinkedIn profiles came up, but there were a lot to go through.

"Who would have thought there would be so many Ada's," Ryan said. "What about her work? Did she mention anything? Did you happen to get a last name?"

Ramon looked up from his phone. "We didn't exactly do a formal meet with full names, Ry. She mentioned something about a publishing company she works at, but I don't know the name of it."

"Ok, let's try Ada, Nottingham, publishing house," Ryan suggested.

They tried that and got a couple of hits on LinkedIn, a couple with pictures and a couple without.

"Maybe I just made it all up," Ramon sighed. Having decided to give up for the time being, they finished their lunch and headed back to the office.

Around 3 pm Ryan came knocking on Ramon's office door. "Still thinking about her?"

Ramon tilted his head to the side and squinted his eyes at Ryan in irritation.

"What do you think, Ry? Not only is she consuming my thoughts, but I barely slept."

"Ok, ok, man, but I have an idea," Ryan said eagerly. "Download the dream! Have you tried that yet since you got the chip?"

Ramon sat up straight, his eyes wide, "I never thought about that. I haven't tried it yet. How do I do that, Ry?"

Ryan came around to Ramon's side of the desk and helped him log into his Dreamscape account. Inside Ramon's account were the options of Memories and Dreams. They clicked on Dreams, and a calendar came up to choose a date. Only some dates were showing in green, which represented the nights that he had connected to his chip. They clicked the previous night, October 1st, and saw two blue buttons. One said 'View' and the other said 'Download.'

"I don't want to download this on my work computer," Ramon said. "Let me log in on my phone." He proceeded through the same steps and hit the blue download button.

Now that he had the video he could watch it again to see if Ada had mentioned any other clues to help find out if she was real. Ryan wanted to watch it with him, but Ramon declined. His dreams were private. The last hour and a bit of work dragged on. He couldn't wait to get home and watch the video to see what information he could gather.

Ramon went to the download and pressed play while he was throwing together some left overs for dinner and poured himself a glass of wine. He watched the entirety of the dream multiple times, from his arrival at the cabin through his walk in the woods, seeing and meeting Ada, and then the abrupt wake-up. He took notes as the conversation went on with Ada, and took a screenshot of a moment when he had really focused on how beautiful her face was. It was strange to watch a video of your own experience, remembering what happened and watching it on replay.

He opened a search on his phone and used Google Lens, choosing the screenshot he took of Ada to upload. The search results appeared, and an old Facebook profile for Ada Carpenter with a picture came up. He clicked on it. It appeared she hadn't used it in a few years, but it was still there.

Just like me, he thought, and laughed. It exists, but isn't used.

He looked at what information was visible, and saw that she was from Nottingham as she had said. The picture was an older one, but it still looked like her.

"She's real!" he texted Ryan. "I found her!" He shared the profile with his friend.

"But what do I do now? She's not active on here anymore."

Twelve

It was almost 1 am, but Ada couldn't sleep. She'd been thinking about Ramon all day. "Why did my alarm have to go off at that time?" she kept saying to herself. She'd tried to go to bed early, but she'd been lying there awake, tossing and turning. Concentration at work had been nil all day. She'd even cancelled her regular evening at the Crown & Table with Frederic because she knew she wouldn't be able to hide her distraction. But if she was honest that wasn't the only reason. How could she go from such a fun and intellectually stimulating time with Ramon to the monotony of dinner at the pub with Frederic? She had discussed the dream with Kira all day long, and they decided that on Saturday they were going to join forces to see if he was real.

With sleep defeating her, she decided to check her social media and then her emails. There was a strange email from Facebook, alerting her to a friend request. That's odd, I don't even use Facebook anymore, she thought. Wondering if it was a scam, she decided not to click on anything in the email. Instead she opened the browser on her phone and went to log into Facebook.

"Password, password, password.... God, what would I have had?"

After three tries she got in and went to the notification for the friend request. *Ramon Díaz would like to add you as a friend.* Below the notification were the accept and decline buttons.

"Oh my god!" Ada said aloud. "He *is* real! And he found me!"

She wasn't sure if she was creeped out or flattered, but she was about to do the same thing tomorrow with Kira anyway, so she went with flattered. She hit the accept button, then texted Kira to let her know what had happened. Kira was likely out with other friends, so she hoped she'd respond.

Ding, ding, came the text from Kira. "Oooh Ada! Now you know! Are you going to say something? If he's from Toronto, then he should still be awake. Send him a message babe xo."

"Should I? It won't seem desperate?" Ada asked her. She wanted to come off as cool and nonchalant, not clingy.

"Babes, go for it! What have you got to lose? It's 2026, women can take charge. If you're interested, go for it."

Kira was right. Who was she to wait around for him to make the next move? They'd had a great time last night and might as well dive in and see what happened.

Ada went to his profile. Old posts, just like mine, she giggled to herself. She hit the message icon and stared at the screen. She could see that he was active on Facebook right now and wondered if he was thinking the same thing while staring at the message screen.

"Looks like you *are* real," she muttered to herself and decided to send him the same thought, with a winking emoji. *Received and read.* Oh shit, this is happening, she thought.

"I sure am! And so are you. Hope I didn't creep you out by adding you as a friend on here," Ramon replied.

"Not at all, but it's good to know that I'm not delusional and made you up lol," Ada joked.

"Shouldn't you be asleep? he asked. "It must be late there."

"You're right, it is, but I couldn't sleep. Too many things on my mind after last night." She questioned that last statement, and shook her head. Why does this feel like high school? she thought to herself. Typing... typing... oh man, what's he writing...

"Well, do you want to talk about it? I could try to go to bed early and we could meet up in your dream. I can't promise I'll fall asleep right now, but in an hour it shouldn't be a problem. Then you can have a head start on some shut-eye and I'll meet you there. If I can figure out how to get there again, that is. Any tricks?"

Who is this guy, Ada thought, that he wants to talk about things? This was all new for her. "Ok," she responded, "I'll try to fall asleep now and see you in there. Only trick I've heard of is to think about the person and they would be drawn to your dreamscape, but that doesn't really explain how you ended up there last night."

"Ok, sweet dreams and see you soon," he responded.

Ada finally fell asleep and accessed her chip to enter her dreamscape after levelling out her excitement. She sat in her cottage for a while and then wandered out by the fountain. Looking at it intensely, she closed her eyes and changed the water colour to a bright blue. *Snap.* She heard a twig break. She spun around quickly to scan the tree line. It's too early for Ramon, she thought. Step by step, she crept closer to the forest edge in the direction of the sound. She hadn't heard anything more than the one twig breaking as if under someone's foot, but she had that strange sensation again of being watched.

****

"Watch where you're stepping," Gustav sent telepathically to Andrei. "Slowly hide behind that tree, she's coming this way."

Both men crept quietly and slowly behind some larger trees, about five rows deep from the edge. Dammit, Andrei, Gustav thought to himself.

****

Ada stopped at the edge of the grove and started walking the perimeter, listening intently for any other sounds. She still couldn't shake the creepy feeling she was getting, the same one she'd had before. The only time she'd known for sure she was being watched was when Ramon had been there last night, yet she hadn't felt creeped out. Could someone else have wandered in here like he did? she thought.

"Hello," she shouted, "if someone is there, please come out."

"That was stupid," she scolded herself afterwards. "Would I have yelled that in a dark alley in real life? Come on, Ada."

There was no response, no noise except for the gurgling water of the fountain. Ada walked back towards it, on alert but trying to remain calm as she waited for Ramon.

****

"Time to go, Andrei," Gus sent out through his mind.

"I ruined it tonight," Andrei sent back. "Maybe one time it will be ok for me to talk to her. What do you think, Gus?"

"I don't know. It's a risk, and she could ask questions about how you got here. I'll think about it, but we are just watchers, remember, Andrei?"

Gus knew this day would come where Andrei couldn't just watch. He himself had wanted to talk to some of the people he had watched in the past, but never had. Safety was always first. They exited Ada's dreamscape and looked at the monitors to see who else they could watch tonight.

****

Ada sat on the bench thinking about Ramon, his green eyes, his smile. She looked down at herself and saw she was already wearing some black pants and a leopard print t-shirt.

"Can't always be in a dress," she laughed to herself.

"What's so funny?" she heard behind her, and turned around quickly.

"I never hear you coming!" She laughed again, but was thinking: he made it!

"You weren't here a little while ago, were you? And lurking in the shadows?" she asked.

"No, I just got here. I felt the pull, so you must have been thinking about me." He smiled and winked, showing his gorgeous perfect teeth. "Why, was someone here?"

"I heard a twig snap again and got that creepy feeling, but I wasn't sure if it was you in the forest or someone else. I'm a little nervous now that I know strangers can just come up on me here," Ada replied.

"It wasn't me, but we aren't strangers anymore, we're Facebook friends, remember?" They both laughed at that.

Time seemed to fly by. With no alarms to wake them on a Saturday morning, they kept talking. They laughed and decided to share a bench this time, seeming to inch closer and closer to each other as time went on.

"Eventually, I'll have to get up, you know. My mom and brother will be wondering why I'm sleeping so late," Ada said.

"Well, there's always tomorrow night, or rather to-night, I guess. Perhaps I could show you my dreamscape this time, if you're up for a walk in the woods," Ramon suggested.

"That might work. I'm supposed to go out with my friend Kira tonight, so it will be a late bedtime again. Then you won't have to go to bed so early," Ada replied.

"Sounds good to me. I'm having dinner at my parents with my friend Ryan, so I shouldn't be out too late. I guess just hang out here, and I'll think of you desper-ately in my cabin by the lake until you feel the pull to come to me," he joked.

"Oh, that shouldn't be too hard," she winked back at him.

They said their goodbyes and Ada woke up, realizing it was after 9am, and got out of bed. She spent the morn-ing with a smile on her face, thinking of Ramon and dismissing the twig-snapping before he arrived.

Ding, ding. A text from Frederic asking her to go to brunch at the pub.

"The pub," she thought dismally. "How about some-where else?" she replied to his message. "Somewhere fancy?"

"But the pub knows us, Ada," Frederic replied.

"So what if they know us, I'm tired of that place. I'll go to brunch if you can think of somewhere better than a pub." Ada wasn't having it anymore. Step up or step off, she thought.

They'd only been together about six months, but she was bored of the same old thing over and over again. "He probably doesn't know what to think right now," she laughed to herself.

Ding, ding, Kira texted. "Sooo, did you see him again?"

"Yes, and I'll tell you everything later xo," Ada replied with a big smiley face emoji.

Thirteen

Andrei was upset with Gustav for making him leave Ada's dreamscape. "She wouldn't have seen us, we could have stayed, Gus."

Gustav just shook his head. This kid was irresponsible sometimes.

"No Andrei, you were getting too close. We watch, observe people, that is all. You are getting too attached to this girl. If you talked to her you would make it known what we are doing."

"I wouldn't! She would just think I was there by accident," Andrei began, but Gustav cut him off.

"It's out of the question! You can leave, I don't need your help if you're going to behave in this manner." Gus had to put his foot down. He wasn't about to let some kid ruin the good thing that he had created.

He could see the message board blinking in his peripheral. *TheVoyeur* must have sent them a new communication. Gus went over to the monitors to check what it said. He knew it would be a chat and signed in with his screen name, *SilentIsTheNight*.

69

theVoyeur: New target - 3 million - Sunday
SilentIsTheNight: Details...
theVoyeur: London, UK or Nottingham, UK -
Arthur Millstone -sleepy time - no fuss -
age 56 - DOB 1970.02.25
SilentIsTheNight: Confirmed - staged?
theVoyeur: not necessary
theVoyeur has signed off

Gustav thought it was odd that *theVoyeur* didn't want a staged scene this time, like the last. He was concerned with the authorities connecting anything to the New York murders. He wouldn't need Charmaine this time, so the money was just for him and Andrei, if the kid could control himself. He always wondered about the targets, but thought it best to just do his job. London time was five hours ahead, so he had to calculate when the best timing would be to complete the job. He could log in at 9 pm and the target should be fast asleep, as it would be 2 am for him. First, what was needed was to familiarize himself with Arthur's dreamscape before he could make a plan of attack. He only had two nights to figure this out. It was 11 pm on Friday night now for Gustav, so 4 am in the UK. Gustav assumed this guy would still be asleep and he could get a glimpse around. Short timeline and prep means bigger pay day, he thought.

Gustav typed the parameters into his computer to find this Arthur Millstone. Unfortunately, he got a few hits with the name and area, so decided to narrow it down by the date of birth he was given. *Bingo!* Currently sleeping in London, but the information said he resided in Nottingham. That's why he gave me two cities, Gus thought.

Andrei walked back into the room after cooling off with some vodka and scrolling through social media. "We got a job?" he asked.

"We?" Gustav questioned. "Only if you can keep your cool. This is a short window and we need to start researching now. Are you in?"

"I'm cool, Gus, don't worry about me. This is work, not leisure. Tell me the details."

They went over the details together, and put on their headgear to enter Arthur's dreamscape. It was always tricky the first time, because they didn't know where they were going or what it would look like. To avoid being seen, they always tried to enter at the edge of the dream and work their way in. When they entered this time, they were on a cliff, on the outside of a huge mansion looking over the Aegean Sea. The water was crisp, the perfect light blue. They skulked around the outside of the mansion to see where they could gain access, and found a window on the main floor that was open, big enough for them to creep through. Once inside they used hand signals and telepathy to communicate with one another. They kept to the corners and listened intently for anyone moving around. There were some soft noises coming from a distance, so they knew they could get closer, but first they wanted to look around so they were familiar with the layout.

Time was short for them tonight, but if they knew what the floor plan was for tomorrow they would have time to create a better plan. Gustav turned to the left and Andrei to the right.

"Large living room and kitchen on this side, open concept, not a lot of hiding spaces, pantry and closets," Gustav sent to Andrei.

"Office, gym and guest room on this side, with closets, but the hallway will be hard to maneuver, stairs at the end of the hallway with a cupboard-like door beneath," Andrei reported back.

The noises they heard were coming from upstairs and they assumed that was where the bedrooms were. They snuck out onto the deck, which had an infinity pool overlooking the sea. Gustav pointed to the storage shed or pool house, not sure which it was, but it could provide cover for them. They slowly went out farther on the deck to see what they could of the upstairs. Three windows faced the sea, all dark except one. They kept to the shadows and watched for a while to see if Arthur would come to the window to enjoy his view.

"Pretty big house for one guy," Andrei sent to Gus.

"To each their own, it's his dreamscape," Gustav sent back. "He could have made a castle for all I care."

They needed to make some notes and left the dream-scape for that night. Arthur would have been up soon anyway. Once they were back in the abandoned house, they started drawing up plans from what they'd seen, almost like mock-up blueprints. It was almost 1 am when they finished and Gustav sent Andrei home so he could get some sleep.

"Tomorrow I'll do research on what he looks like, just so we know we're getting the right target, then we'll go back in around 9 pm to work out a plan for Sunday night," Gustav told Andrei before he left.

Andrei showed up around 4 pm on Saturday afternoon to help with the search if he could, but Gus had already found a picture of the target, so they didn't have much else to do. Gus sent him back out for some fast food, and after they'd eaten they went over the blueprints they had made of the first floor the night before.

"We can either enter off the deck by that shed or pool house, or through the guest room," Gustav suggested. The chances that a guest would be in the guest room were pretty slim.

"I think the guest room, in case he's out on the deck or by a window," Andrei replied.

"Good thinking," Gustav said. This kid did have some good ideas once in a while, he thought.

They had a plan. It was now 8:30 pm. "We should be okay to go now," Gustav said, so they sat down at the monitors, put on their headgear, and accessed Arthur's chip.

The guest room was blue, with a queen-size four-poster bed in it. The duvet was white and down-filled, and four pillows sat at the top of the bed. There was a bookshelf filled with different sized books, and a grey and black reading chair to one side. They quietly went to the door to listen for any movement on the first floor. This time they heard two voices coming from outside. "He must be outside with someone," Andrei sent to Gus's mind.

They exited the guest room and peered around the wall near the kitchen to see if they could see who was outside. Arthur was there with a younger man. Shit, thought Gus, he better not be here tomorrow night. He looked at Andrei and motioned him upstairs. "While they're outside, let's scope the upstairs," he sent to him.

They crept up the winding marble staircase to find six rooms: three facing the deck they'd seen the night before and three facing the opposite direction. Two rooms were lavish bedrooms and both appeared to be lived in. The four other rooms were for personal use. There was a room for arts and crafts, what looked like a yoga room, a library, and what Gus could only call a sex room, with toys and a swing in the middle of it. To each their own, Gus thought again.

He looked at Andrei. "It looks like this other guy, the young one, is here all the time too," he sent to him. "We need to figure out which room is Arthur's before they come in." Andrei nodded, and they split up to each take a room.

The room that Andrei searched had a lot of electronics in it and was a bit messy. The bed wasn't made, and clothes were strewn about. By the look of the clothes, they were likely for a younger man. The room Gustav was looking at was clean, the bed made, everything in order, but had strange eclectic ornamental masks hung on all the walls. He opened the closet and found it orderly, with suits and dress shirts all lined up. "I think I've got it," Gustav sent to Andrei. They met back in the hallway and decided to leave the dreamscape, make the blueprints of the second floor, and plan their attack.

Once they were out, Gustav set Andrei the task of the blueprints, while he decided to try and send a message to *theVoyeur* about the second person in the dreamscape.

SilentIsTheNight: Problem - 2nd occupant

He waited by the computer and hoped he would hear back that night. While he waited, he helped Andrei with the plan for the next day. It wasn't going to be an easy job; there were too many variables, so they had to come up with a few plans in case when they got there the first plan didn't pan out. If they'd had more time to watch Arthur, then they could learn his routine, but with only one and a half nights, it was going to be difficult. It was midnight before Gustav saw the indicator on the monitor saying he had a new message.

theVoyeur: Leave the 2nd - only the one must go.
SilentIsTheNight: Confirmed

Gustav was about to sign off when one last message came through

> *theVoyeur:* Send the deleted memory for an
> extra 1 million.
> *theVoyeur has signed off*

Gustav stared at the screen. This was the first time that *theVoyeur* had wanted proof. However, maybe it wasn't proof. Maybe he just wanted to watch.

Fourteen

Ada spent most of Saturday afternoon and evening with Kira. They talked about Ramon, they talked about Frederic, they talked about everything they had missed with each other throughout the week.

"We haven't had a proper catch-up in ages, Ada," Kira said. "You seem to get stuck in the everyday go-round of it."

"I know, my whole life is one big routine: sleep, work, home, repeat. Then for extra fun, the Crown & Table with Frederic and to top off the evening, Netflix," Ada said. "Where's the excitement?" She flopped down on Kira's bed, exasperated. "We should just get a flat together and finally move out, Kira."

"Excitement?" Kira questioned. "You have all the excitement in your dreamscape, hello? Ramon?"

"I know, but he's on the other side of the world, and even though we hang out together in the dreamscape, is that really anything real?" Ada asked. "I mean, we remember it, but it's not our actual human forms in there. We're in our beds, in separate countries. So how do I bring it to life, like *real* real life? Not to mention there's Frederic too."

Kira laughed at her dear friend. "You've met this guy twice in your dreams, and you're what? Planning a wedding? You have him on Messenger now, so ask for his number and then you can maybe video chat or text in *real* real life!"

Kira was still laughing, and Ada knew she had a point. What was stopping her from talking to him during the day? Why just the dreams?

Ding, ding. A text from Frederic. "Want to watch a movie tonight and order in?"

"His ears must have been burning," Kira said. "Are you ready for that excitement?"

"Kira, stop. We've been together for almost six months and I should just end it, well, I should have a while ago. I owe him that respect. Not like Ramon and I will ever be anything, but it did make me realize, even more, what I was missing with Frederic."

Kira agreed. "It's not like you were together a year or more and you just led him on because you knew you didn't want anything with him. You tested the waters with him and it's not working out. Life goes on. He's not offering you any opportunity for growth, so grow yourself. And you can explore what Ramon has to offer without any guilt. Even if you're just friends because of the distance, it's better to have no expectations of anything."

"Because we women do that so well, right, Kira?" They both laughed hysterically at the truth of it.

Ada texted Frederic back that she was with Kira that night, and suggested they talk tomorrow. His only reply was, "ok."

The weather was getting cooler now that it was October, and they both grabbed their jackets to head out and have some dinner in town. Kira drove them, and they stopped along Main Street for some shopping. Ada couldn't remember the last time they'd spent time like this together. They had known each other for years, but now that they were older and both had their own routines in life, it was harder to carve out the time for each other. They laughed and smiled as they shopped and reminisced about old times and inside jokes with each other.

Over their dinner at the new Italian restaurant in town, they each decided on one glass of wine and pasta, even though the menu had many different options to suit all their customers.

"Girl time and carb loading." Kira raised her glass of wine. "My kind of day!"

They clinked their glasses for the toast and resumed their girl talk about the men in their lives.

"So, Kira, did anything ever happen with John? That guy you met a couple of weeks ago at Susan's game night?"

"John? Oh, babes, he was like three men ago," Kira laughed. "I've been talking to Richard—he works at the cafe near my work—and I just happen to go in there when he's working and smile at him. So he asked me out... finally. We have a date tomorrow! Lunch!"

"I think you should start a chart for me so I can keep up," Ada laughed. "Seriously though, we need to keep in touch more. I know our lives are busy, but you're the best person in my life, Kira."

They smiled thoughtfully at each other and then their food arrived, smelling like heaven wrapped in cream sauce.

They continued to chat over their meal and Ada realized how much she missed having fun. She had gotten complacent in the routine of life, and the routine with Frederic, but she wanted so much more. She decided then and there that it was time to make a change in her life.

"I'm going to start looking for my own place," she said all of a sudden to Kira. "I think it's time to take hold of my life."

"Yes!" Kira said. "I'll get there at some point, but I'm enjoying the bills-free lifestyle of staying at home right now. I'm sure my parents will want me out at some point soon, but I'll save while I can. I think it's great that you're ready to move out, Ada. And move on!"

"It's time for a change, in so many ways," Ada said.

"Aww, babes, look at you grow, I love it!" Kira smiled. "I've always admired your drive and how you're not afraid to be yourself. Well, most of the time. You always played yourself down with Frederic, I'm sorry to say." Kira glanced up at Ada to see her reaction.

Ada was taken aback by the comment, but appreciated her friend's openness and honesty. Then it dawned on her. "You're absolutely right, Kira! I never saw it that way before, but you're right. Wow. I was meek and timid and felt like I had to walk on eggshells to not upset him by standing up for myself. I don't want to be that person. And I'm so lucky to have a friend like you who loves me for all my weirdness and honesty. Thank you, Kira."

Ada felt for the second time that night that she had been woken up about her life. She was vibrant, beautiful, funny, and smart, and could be brutally honest when she felt close to someone. And those that loved her for her, knew all that about her.

After they paid their bills, they walked arm in arm back to Kira's car. "I've had such a wonderful day with you, babes," Kira said. "I agree, we need to do this more often."

"Oh, me too," Ada said as they hugged before getting into Kira's 2023 Mini Cooper.

On the way to drop off Ada, Kira said, "So are you going to try and meet Ramon in his dreamscape this time?"

"That's the plan, but I'm not entirely sure how that will work out. Maybe I'll send him a message to see how we'll do this." Ada said as she opened the Messenger app on her phone.

"Hey, Ramon," she texted, "do you have an idea how I'll get to your dreamscape tonight? I've never left mine before."

Ping! "That was fast," she giggled as she opened the message.

"How about I come to yours and we see if we can take the path back through the forest to mine? That's how I got to yours," he had written.

"That sounds like a plan to me! See you there!" she wrote back with a smile emoji.

Kira and Ada smiled and sang to the music playing in the car from Kira's "Jamz" playlist. It was a mix of what they called old school and new music that Kira liked.

At Ada's house, Kira waited until Ada was inside the door before pulling away. Once inside, Ada said her hellos to her mom and brother, who were watching a movie on the sofa.

"No plans tonight, Davey?" she asked.

"They got cancelled," he replied as he stared at the TV screen.

She decided not to disturb them and went upstairs to her room. It was only 9 pm, and she calculated backwards. "Eight, seven, six, five, four. It's only 4 pm for Ramon, ugh."

Ping! That was the Messenger sound and she knew it had to be him.

"What time are you going to sleep tonight?" he asked.

Well, he doesn't know me too well, yet, she thought. "I will *attempt* to go to sleep around 11 pm, but I'm not the sort to sleep right away, so I'll read for a while first. I know that's still really early for you," she sent back.

Ping!

She opened the message. "Can you start to read at midnight? It is Saturday night after all," he had sent with a wink.

"Lol, I will take a bath and try to keep myself busy until midnight then," she replied.

Ping!

Ramon wrote, "I like your plan, enjoy your bath. Message me later if you're wanting some company."

"Thanks! I'll think about it," she replied with another wink emoji.

Ada lit some candles, filled the tub, and dropped in a bath bomb. She climbed in and sighed with delight as the heat of the water soaked her thoroughly and wrapped her in its soothing embrace. As she sat there in peace and quiet, her mind began to wander. She liked to lead with her heart and felt guilty for talking to another guy while she was in a relationship with Frederic. She had always believed in being truthful, and because she was entertaining the idea of another man, she felt terrible.

He doesn't deserve this, she thought. He's a good man, just not the one for me. I want so much more than he's willing to give.

She wondered how best to tell him, and whether or not she could wait until tomorrow. She knew how much she would hate it if a man was dating or talking to another woman while she was in a relationship with him.

She made the decision to video call Frederic after her bath and end it with him. Until then though, she would relax in the tranquillity of her long soak in the tub.

Once she was all dried off and in her comfy pajamas, she texted Frederic. "Are you free for a video call?"

"All done with Kira, I see," he texted back. "Give me 20 minutes and you can call."

"Ok," she replied.

That gave her twenty minutes to really figure out how this was going to go. She paced her room, going over the potential conversation in her head as the minutes ticked away. It was time. She pressed the video call button and waited for him to pick up. No answer. "Ok," she thought. She waited for him to ring her back, but ten more minutes went by and he didn't, so she tried him again. This time Frederic did pick up.

"Hey, Ada, sorry I missed you before."

"It's ok, I figured you must still be busy. Do you have some time to talk?" she asked.

"Are you okay? You sound a bit off," he replied.

"I'm okay, I just wanted to talk to you about something," she said.

She wasn't really sure how to continue, and she could feel herself pulling back already, walking on eggshells again. Twenty minutes ago, she had the whole thing planned out.

"Okay, what do you want to talk about?" Frederic asked, sounding annoyed.

There was a silence that felt like it went on for hours before Ada said, "I don't think we should continue dating. I'm not myself when we are together, and I want to be able to be who I really am." There, she had said it.

Frederic was peering through the video call at her with a perplexed look on his face. "You're not yourself with me? Okay, Ada, whatever you say. Well, it was fun while it lasted, I guess. Good luck with everything." That was the end of the call. She didn't have a chance to say anything else.

Ada felt aggrieved by how it had gone, but decided to move on. He wasn't her concern anymore. She also knew that Frederic shut down when it came to any sort of emotion, so having probably hurt him, his defence was to be rude. Ada texted Kira to let her know that it was done. It was 10:30 pm and she knew Kira would still be awake. *Ding, ding*, came the text from her.

"Great! Release him, babes! You are so much better off xo."

"I know, thanks for helping me remember how great I am xo," Ada replied.

"Of course!! You're amazing and don't let anyone let you forget that. Love you, my dear!" Kira replied.

Ada sat back on her bed and contemplated her life. She wondered why she was attracted to men like Frederic? Why she felt that she had to put their needs before her own? Where did this all stem from? Before she knew it, she was fast asleep earlier than she was supposed to be, with the weight of her thoughts sending her into a deep sleep and making her forget to access her chip.

****

Ramon walked in the direction of Ada's dreamscape to guide her back to his, but he seemed to keep walking and couldn't get there.

Odd, he thought, this was how I got here the last two times.

He turned around, went back to his cabin, and thought about Ada. He should have texted her before he went to bed, instead of wandering the woods. Back at his cabin, he sat in front of the fire, thinking about her, hoping she would appear like Ryan did before. Still, nothing happened, and Ada didn't come, so he decided to sit out on the dock for a while. He finally gave up as time kept passing by without her showing up. I should have texted her again to make sure we were meeting, he thought again, and left his dreamscape to wake up and send her a message.

Fifteen

Ada woke up on Sunday morning and saw some missed messages from Ramon.

I fell asleep and didn't go in my chip! she thought. He must think I bailed on him.

She opened the messages.

"Did you forget about me tonight?"

"I guess you fell asleep earlier, maybe we can arrange another time."

She responded to him, knowing that he would still be sleeping, "I'm so sorry, Ramon! I passed out and didn't access my chip. Yes, let's meet tonight if that works for you."

Then she got a little bold and sent another message with a wink emoji. "Or even maybe a video chat while we're awake."

Immediately, she closed the app before she wrote anything more embarrassing. She wasn't normally this forward, but she felt so comfortable with Ramon already and believed he was the type to not judge her, so she was becoming more confident in herself. The last thing she needed was another man in her life who criticized who she was and made her dim her light.

The day carried on like any normal Sunday: errands, helping her mum prep the Sunday dinner, cleaning her room. At around 3 pm Ada's phone rang with a strange jingle. She pulled it out of her pocket and saw that it was a video chat on the Messenger app she was using to talk to Ramon. She flushed a pink colour and froze on the spot, her heart pounding. She knew she couldn't answer right now because she was covered in flour from helping with the pie crust. So she declined the call and sent him a quick text. "Can I call you back in 30 mins? I'm just helping mum in the kitchen." She was the one who'd suggested the call, and she felt bad for declining the first one, as he was putting in an effort.

Ping!

"Of course!" Ramon responded. "Take your time and call me back when you're free."

He also left his phone number in case she wanted to use a different application.

Ada couldn't contain her smile. Shit, she thought, I barely know this guy and I'm smiling like a schoolgirl. She shook her head and made a simple reply to Ramon with her phone number and a thanks.

After she'd finished the pie she went upstairs to clean herself up and make herself presentable for a video call. She wasn't really sure why she was so nervous, but it was likely because this was real life now, while she was awake, not just a dream. She took a deep breath and called Ramon back through another messaging app with a video call option.

"Hey!" he answered. "Look at you, you're real." He had an enormous smile on his face, showing off its glistening brilliance.

Ada laughed. "Well, at least now I know for sure you're real too! Who knows, maybe you were altering your image in your dreamscape. You know, making yourself more handsome." They both laughed.

"Are you calling me handsome, Ada?" Ramon smiled sheepishly.

Ada was speechless. What had she just said? She sputtered out, "Well, I mean, of course you're handsome...."

Ramon laughed heartily. "Thank you, Ada. I didn't mean to put you on the spot like that, but it was amusing. Your face is so cute when you're feeling awkward."

Ada didn't know what to say, but she could feel her cheeks getting warm from blushing. It seemed he could already read her like a book. Time to change this line of discussion, she thought.

"I'm really sorry about last night, Ramon. After the fun and excitement with Kira all day, I completely passed out. Do you want to meet tonight to show me your dreamscape?"

"Of course we can tonight," Ramon smiled, "and don't worry about it, I understand completely. It was interesting on my part though, because I walked and walked and just never saw the trees change like they do when I get close to your dreamscape, so I figured you weren't in."

The video chat lasted for almost an hour, and Ada didn't know where the time went. They were the same people that they were in the dreams, laughing and joking with each other and not afraid to have serious conversations as well. She couldn't wait to tell Joel about all this on Monday at work. It was the type of dreamy love story he went crazy for. She knew that when Joel met his partner Arthur, it had been like a scene out of a cheesy romcom, but it was wonderful to hear about. Maybe this is *my* scene, Ada thought, but quickly dismissed it as being corny. Those things didn't happen, at least not to her. She heard her mother call her down for dinner and headed towards the smell of the roast.

****

Ramon couldn't stop smiling after the call ended with Ada. He couldn't stop thinking about how real she was, how authentic, kind, caring, and funny. She was also extremely beautiful and he began wondering if maybe they should meet in person, not in a dream, but in real life. He could fly to England, or maybe she would come to Canada. He felt like he was getting ahead of himself, so he decided to text Ryan and see what his thoughts were.

"Ry, remember that girl we looked up that I met in a dream? We're talking while we're awake and I'm smiling like an idiot, man. Should I pursue this?"

"What?" Ryan replied. "Dude, if she's got you smiling like that, then yes! I've never seen you like that before with a girl. Distance doesn't have to be an issue, especially when you can meet in your dreams. Go for it, and it will make your mother happy lol."

Ramon laughed at the message. "Yeah, then she can stop trying to set me up with someone. I could use a vacation sometime soon. Maybe England would be nice."

"Like I said, man, go for it. She sounds great, but just keep an open mind. Keep talking to her and get to know her before you fly out there, though."

Ryan had a point. This was butterflies in the stomach stage, and it had been a long time since he'd felt anything like that. "I'll keep a cool head, thanks, man. Just have to get to know her more."

Ramon continued on with his Sunday, and tried to contain his excitement about seeing Ada again in his dreams that night. He knew it would be a challenge when he saw her not to let his heart lead the way. "Keep it cool," he kept saying to himself. He would go to bed early so he could see her for a while before she had to get up for work, but with all the anxiety he was feeling, he knew it wouldn't be an easy thing to accomplish. He decided to go to the gym and burn off some of the extra energy and angst so he could relax before bed. This time he would message her before she went to bed so that they could coordinate. He would meet her in her dreamscape and they would walk back to his, because he still wasn't sure how the whole calling out to someone thing worked. After the gym, he thought, then I'll have a more level head to arrange it all.

Sixteen

It was 6 pm on Sunday evening in Detroit where Gustav and Andrei were having their dinner before finishing the plans for that evening's job. They had concocted the general idea, but needed to go over the specifics before going in. The blueprints had been completed for the first and second floors, and they planned to enter the guest room on the first floor again like the previous night. Tonight, though, would be different for them because of the second person in the dreamscape whom wasn't to be harmed. This wrinkle could potentially mess up everything if he wasn't asleep as well, which was why they were waiting until 9 pm to go in—2 am UK time. If the two men had work the next day, at that time of night, they should be winding down in their dreamscape.

Gustav was feeling anxious about the whole scenario. There hadn't been enough time to prep and learn the routines of the couple. They were basically going in blind and there were so many ways it could go wrong. He and Andrei had been planning all day for multiple outcomes, but the main point was not to be seen by the other party in the dreamscape. If that happened, it would all be over for them. He didn't think they would be easily caught, but it would get out that someone had entered and attempted to kill or had killed a person while they were in their chip. He didn't like this one bit, but he also didn't know how to say no to *theVoyeur*.

Gustav wasn't afraid to admit that he was scared of the guy. He had no idea what *theVoyeur* was capable of finding on the web, seeing as *he* had found Gustav and knew what he had been doing by spying on people. *TheVoyeur* had offered him money to utilize his skill for hacking the dreamscape system and his military background to kill. All he wanted to do was the spying. That's it. However, his guy somehow knew more than he should about Gus and where he lived and was exploiting it for his own gains. Why he wanted these people dead, Gus didn't know and might never know.

It was 8 pm and they had a few different plans ready, depending on the situation when they entered the dreamscape. The uncertainty of it made him seriously question calling it off. Time ticked away as they got everything ready. Andrei was just as nervous, but knew his part. Gustav also trusted that, if they had to adapt on the fly, Andrei would still be an asset to him. At one point, Gus had contemplated going in alone, but with the possibility of two people in the dreamscape, he needed a second person just in case. He really didn't want the second guy in the dreamscape to become collateral damage during this job. He already hated the killing part, so leaving the younger man alone was the one solace in the night's job.

Finally, it was time. They each put on their headgear and entered Arthur's dreamscape in the guest room on the main floor.

****

Ramon saw that it was 9 pm and crawled into bed. That was their agreed upon time for him to go to bed, and since Ada had stayed up a bit later, she should only have been sleeping for the last two hours. He had prepped with a meditation about thirty minutes earlier and was nice and relaxed, so when he turned off the bedside lamp, he fell asleep right away and entered his dreamscape. He was in his childhood cabin, where the fire was already blazing. Immediately he left and started to walk towards Ada's dreamscape through the forest path he had always taken. This time the trees did change, getting larger and larger as he walked. Eventually he saw the grove where she was sitting waiting for him. Ramon called out to her and she rushed over to the path where he was standing.

"So this is where you come in?" she asked with a smile. "Now I'll know how to get to you next time."

"Yes, it seems to be consistent when I come in. Let's get going, the walk feels like it takes forever," Ramon replied.

As they walked side by side through the dense forest, they chatted about what she would see in Ramon's dreamscape. They commented on the trees and how they were changing to smaller and different species, with more evergreens and firs, as they got closer to his cabin. When they arrived at the end of the pathway, which was scattered with stray pinecones and dried leaves, Ada could see a log cabin with smoke coming out of the chimney and a lake off to the left with a long dock. The sky was a permanent sunset as the colours caressed the ripples in the water.

"This is lovely, Ramon," Ada said. "The sunset is a nice touch."

"Yes, I changed that after you showed me how to make adjustments. As much as I love looking up at the stars, I needed more light. That night I mentioned, when I saw two people in a canoe out on the water, it was still bothering me."

They went up to the cabin and entered. It was toasty warm and it made Ada feel right at home. There were two chairs in front of the fireplace and she looked at them quizzically and then looked at Ramon.

"Nice for guests, but maybe something a little cozier for us?" she asked.

Ramon understood and closed his eyes like Ada had taught him, imagining a big comfy couch in front of the fireplace. When he opened them, there it was, with a red and black plaid blanket hung across the back.

"That's better," Ada smiled.

They sat on the couch right beside each other, their shoulders almost touching. Ada was smiling at Ramon and didn't know what to say. She was about to ask about his childhood here when he reached for her hand.

****

Gustav and Andrei sat patiently in the guest room, listening for movements in the house. They could hear pop music playing upstairs and assumed that to be the younger man. They also understood that, if they could hear that music, Arthur was likely not sleeping or resting in his own room on the second floor. There were loud thumps coming from upstairs and Gustav was hoping they weren't in the sex room. He and Andrei tried to pinpoint where the sounds were coming from and compared the location to the blueprints they had memorized.

"Sounds like it's the yoga room, but that's really aggressive yoga," Andrei sent to Gus.

"Maybe it's not just yoga. He could have added weights," Gustav replied.

That was the thing about dreamscapes; they could be changed in an instant. So even though they had blueprints, the couple could have remodelled the house tonight before they got there.

When they peered out of the door to view the hallway, everything seemed to have remained as it was before. They didn't see anyone within view and crept out towards the kitchen to see if they could find Arthur.

He wasn't in any of the rooms along the hallway, nor the kitchen or adjoining living area. Andrei motioned to Gustav that he would go towards the deck area. It was dark in the kitchen and there was a small fireplace burning outside.

From behind one of the supporting walls, near the entrance to the deck, that was just wide enough to conceal him, Andrei peered around the glass doorway for a better look outside. There, on the well-cushioned patio furniture, facing the fire, was Arthur, holding a glass of wine and a book.

"He's out there alone," Andrei sent telepathically to Gustav. "Side angle to get there, may be difficult to sneak up behind."

Gustav understood. He moved closer to the glass door to have a look around. First, they would have to exit through the door without being heard or seen in Arthur's peripheral. As Andrei and Gus were coming up with ways to get onto the deck, the loud music upstairs suddenly stopped playing and they couldn't hear anything anymore.

"Find somewhere to hide!" Gus sent to Andrei's mind, with an intense look to accompany it. They needed time still to figure this out, and couldn't risk the younger guy coming downstairs, or Arthur having heard the music stop and decide to come in. As they had seen the first time they entered, the hiding spaces in this part of the house were sparse. Gustav went around a corner near the pantry, and Andrei quickly moved into the kitchen and ducked behind the counter.

"Idiot, what are you doing?" Gus sent him.

"I don't know where to hide!" Andrei replied.

There was silence. No movement could be heard upstairs or out on the deck. Andrei was about to go for another look when they heard footsteps in the hallway. Meanwhile Gustav was ready to pull the plug and just exit the dreamscape.

"Time to go," he sent to Andrei.

"Not yet," Andrei replied.

He was still crouched down between the counter and island, remaining motionless while he listened for where the footsteps were going. Gus peered around the corner, hoping this guy didn't turn on any lights as he came into the room. "Move around the side ... now," he told Andrei.

Andrei heard the steps get closer and shuffled to the other side of the island as the young man went to the glass door.

"Babe, I'm all sweaty from my workout, want to come in?" the young man playfully called to Arthur out the door.

"I'm sure a good shower will do you wonders then, darling. I'm going to finish my wine and read some more before coming in. I'll meet you upstairs later," Arthur replied.

The glass door closed and the young man walked away, muttering under his breath, and went back upstairs.

"That was too close," Gus said.

They knew they had to act fast now. With Arthur being outside they would have to use the bag option they had come up with. Gustav pulled the kitchen garbage-sized bag out of his pocket, opened it inside so he didn't have to do it outside, and told Andrei to keep a lookout. He went to the glass door and opened it slightly to see if it caused Arthur to look up. Arthur was so engrossed in his book that he apparently didn't hear the door open or sense any motion coming his way. As far as he was concerned, Joel had gone back upstairs to shower.

Gus crept slowly and silently along the side of the house until he was directly behind Arthur. In one swift motion, he threw the plastic bag over Arthur's head and pulled it tight. Arthur dropped his book and flailed his arms, knocking his wine glass over to break on the deck.

Shit, Gustav thought, and hoped that the younger man was already in the shower.

"Andrei, listen for him coming back, the wine glass broke ..."

Arthur struggled to breath and tried to claw at the bag around his head. Gus quickly maintained his hold with one hand while detaining Arthur's hands with his other.

Arthur settled down as the life left him, but Gustav didn't want to let go until he was sure he was dead. He held onto the bag for another minute until he saw that Arthur wasn't moving. He removed the bag and went back inside to get Andrei. He could hear the shower still running upstairs and said to Andrei, "Let's get out of here."

They exited the dreamscape and looked at each other, breathing a sigh of relief. Gus knew that he had to delete the dream quickly so that the young man couldn't see anything if he found Arthur dead and woke up to download it. He remembered that he would get an extra million if he sent the dream to *theVoyeur*, so once they were out, he downloaded it before deleting it completely from Arthur's chip. Gus wasn't sure about sending it, though. The extra money would be nice, but then this creep of a guy would have proof of what they did and could potentially use it against him. He wanted to think about it before sending it to him, but he had to confirm the job was done. He logged in and sent a message:

SilentIsTheNight: Job complete.

Gustav waited for a reply. It was 11:30 pm and he had no idea what time zone this guy was in. Another thirty minutes went by before he saw the indication of a message waiting.

theVoyeur: Money will be sent shortly.
Did you get the portion of the dream too?
SilentIsTheNight: Yes, deleted and copied.
theVoyeur: Excellent
theVoyeur has signed off

Gustav assumed *theVoyeur* thought he would just send it, but he was going to wait and hold onto it for a bit. No point in putting himself in danger right away. He needed to work out terms with this guy first, but not tonight.

****

Ramon and Ada held hands and stared at the fire while they continued to talk. They seemed to gravitate closer together as time went on, and were shoulder to shoulder. Ada even rested her head on Ramon's shoulder for a few moments until she realized what she was doing. They laughed and joked, talked about work and family. Ramon shared with her stories of his trips to the cabin as a child and how he always felt it brought his family closer together. That was when he sometimes really bonded with his father. Ada told him that they didn't have family trips anywhere when she was growing up. She talked about her dad leaving them and how it had affected her mother, even after all these years.

"Do you want the grand tour?" Ramon asked her during a pause in conversation.

"You mean it's not just this one room?" Ada smiled as she replied.

"Let's go, silly," Ramon said as he stood up.

He put his hand out to help her up off the couch and she let him. They walked to the kitchen area, which still had old worn wooden cabinets and didn't appear to be modified at all. Ramon told her every detail he could remember and why he hadn't changed anything in here because of the memories of his mother and grandmother cooking in here and him helping them when he was old enough. They moved on to the study, which was off of the kitchen area. Ramon told Ada that even when they were up here to get away, his dad would still have to work sometimes and this was his father's cave.

Ada followed him upstairs as he showed her his bedroom with the bunkbeds as it had always been. He told her about his friend Ryan coming up sometimes to stay with him and how he would make him sleep on the top bunk because he felt confined so close to the ceiling.

As they went back down to sit by the fire, Ada knew she wanted more than holding hands. She wanted to be in Ramon's arms and feel them around her. She stopped suddenly before they got to the couch and he turned around to face her. She pulled him closer for a hug and they stood there in the warmth of the fireplace, holding each other while they swayed a bit to music that wasn't playing but seemed to be in their minds. She released him and they stared at each other and smiled. Ramon cupped his hand under her chin and leaned down to kiss her.

Seventeen

Monday morning came and went and Joel still hadn't been in to work. Ada wished she had his number so she could ask if he was all right. Even though they were work buddies, they had never socialized outside of work, so hadn't needed to exchange numbers. Eventually she went into the break room at the office and overheard some other editors talking.

"It's such a shame, he was so full of life."

"Joel must be devastated."

Ada knew this wasn't good.

"Sorry, are you talking about Joel?" she asked.

One editor, Marianne, said, "Yes, Ada, haven't you heard? Arthur, Joel's partner, passed away in his sleep last night. Poor Joel, he's just distraught."

"I ... I had no idea," Ada stammered. "Does anyone know how to contact him or where he lives?"

"I'm sure Gary has his information, they used to have drinks together," Marianne said.

"Thank you," Ada replied and went off to find Gary in marketing.

"Gary?" Ada said as she knocked on his open door, "Would you have Joel's contact information? I'd like to send my condolences."

Gary looked up from his desk and nodded silently. He could see her watery eyes and kept the interaction short. This event was a blow to the office as a whole. Everyone adored Joel and his upbeat attitude and couldn't imagine something like this happening. Gary handed Ada a piece of paper with Joel's number and an address.

"In case you want to send more flowers, that's his address. We sent some from the office. I'm sure he'd love to hear from you. You guys were close here."

"Thank you, Gary," Ada said. "For sure I'll send him some and give him a call."

She wasn't sure if Joel would pick up the phone, seeing as he didn't have her number, so she decided to text him first.

"Hi Joel, it's Ada. I just heard the terrible news, and I'm so sorry for your loss. How are you feeling? Can I stop by?"

She wasn't sure if that was too forward to send to someone who was grieving. Ada never knew what to say in these situations. Her heart always felt the pain for them, but her words always fumbled. She wished she could be one of those people who always knew the right thing to say.

Ding, ding. Joel had texted back.

"Thank you, Ada darling, can you bring some coffee with you?"

"Yes, of course, I'll get your favourite. I'll be there soon," she texted back.

From the address that Gary had given her, Joel wasn't too far away. She stopped first to get some flowers for him, and then popped into the cafe they both loved to get his favourite latte. She even asked for extra chocolate flakes on top.

After flagging down a taxi, it was a short ten minute drive to Joel's address. She could still see police vehicles in the area, and one was parked directly out front. Are they going to let me through? she thought. Why are there so many police cars here if he passed away in his sleep? She walked with purpose up to the front door and rang the bell. An officer of the Nottingham Police Department opened the door and looked at her. "I'm here to see Joel, he's expecting me," was all she could manage. The officer continued to eye her suspiciously, but moved out of the way to let her pass. Ada walked in through the front hallway and saw a living space off to the right, stairs to the left, and the opening of the kitchen down the hall towards the back of the house. She kept walking towards the kitchen, hoping he would be there.

"Joel?" she called out softly.

"In here, babes," Joel responded.

She could hear that his voice came from the direction of the kitchen.

Pouring a glass of white wine, Joel looked up at her as she entered the kitchen. His eyes were bloodshot and puffy from crying, and his face looked like it had aged ten years overnight. Ada put down the flowers and latte and rushed over to hug him. They embraced each other, and Joel broke down in tears again. Ada held him and rubbed his back until he stopped.

"Your latte with extra flakes," she said as she passed him the hot beverage and slid the wine glass away from him.

Even though they had never hung out after work, she felt an immense closeness to Joel. Like he was family.

"And those?" Joel asked as he pointed to the flowers she had put down.

"Those are for you. Point me to a vase, and I'll get them in water," Ada said.

Joel showed her where they kept the vases and she took care of the flowers while he sipped his latte. Ada didn't mind the silence. She was sure he'd been questioned by so many people already, and she just wanted to be there and present with him.

"Don't you want to know?" Joel asked.

Ada looked at him and smiled. "I figured if you wanted to talk about it, you would. You know I'm here to listen. So whenever you're ready."

Joel looked off into the distance and started to relay the events of the previous night. "You remember I had told you that we shared a dreamscape, so we really never got away from each other," he began, as his voice started to break. "We had an argument in our dreamscape last night. A small petty disagreement, so while we were still in our dreamscape, I did a workout while he was relaxing with some wine and a book on the deck. After my work-out, I wanted to make up and asked him if he was ready to come upstairs, but he insisted on reading some more and finishing his glass of wine. So I went to shower and wait for him. After a while, when he wasn't coming up, I went back down to the deck to see if he was still upset with me, and I saw him ... just sitting there ... eyes open, staring wildly, and his mouth open like he was screaming ... but he was dead."

Joel started to sob uncontrollably, and Ada went over to hold him. He composed himself and began saying, "I exited the dreamscape and tried to shake him awake in our bed, but he didn't move, so I called the police. They've been here since about 5am. They asked me to download his chip so they didn't have to get a court order and waste time, and I didn't mind doing it, but it was the strangest thing. There's a gap missing from when I asked him to come upstairs to when I found him."

Joel stopped, looking off in the distance, confused.

"What are you saying, Joel?" Ada asked. "Did he die that instant and there was nothing else?"

"No, the police don't think so, because his death would have been on there, and then the memory would have stopped. They think someone did something."

Ada was speechless, not entirely sure she had under-stood what Joel was saying. "So ... so they think that Arthur was ... murdered?"

"Yes," Joel said as he looked her full in the eyes. "They have to investigate more and do an autopsy, but they are classifying it as suspicious."

Ada was shocked. She still didn't understand how that was even possible, but all of a sudden she remembered Kira telling her about a couple in New York who had *died in their sleep* under suspicious circumstances. "Did the police mention anything about a connection with New York?" she asked.

Joel looked up at her again, squinting his eyes, confused. "No, what are you talking about?"

Ada pulled out her phone, looked up the article that Kira had sent to her back in August, and showed it to Joel. He read the article and looked at her. "Do you think the police know about this?" he asked.

"I would hope so," she said, "but with it being in another country they may not make the connection."

Joel got up immediately and went to the officer at the door. "Can you ask the detective chief inspector to come back? I have some more information." The officer nodded and went outside to call the DCI.

DCI Amir Karim arrived back at the house about an hour later and joined Ada and Joel in the kitchen. Ada explained about the news from New York in August and asked if they were aware of it.

"We did hear about it, and we are exploring all angles at this point, Miss Carpenter," DCI Karim advised. The generic answer, but at least they knew now that a possible link was being looked at.

"Is there anything else that you remember from the dreamscape that night?" DCI Karim asked Joel.

Joel thought about it as he replayed the dreamscape in his head from the previous night. "I don't think so. I mean, you have everything I saw and Arthur saw from the downloads."

"Anything out of place, furniture moved?" DCI Karim persisted.

"No, I didn't notice anything. I came downstairs after my workout, walked down the hallway, past the doors to the other rooms ..." Joel stopped.

"What is it, Joel?" DCI Karim asked.

"We normally always have all the doors to the rooms on the main floor of our dreamscape shut, but I remember the door to the guest room was open, just slightly. I didn't think anything of it at the time," Joel said.

DCI Karim started taking more notes. As he got up to leave again, he gave Joel his card in case he remembered anything else. He left saying that he would be in touch.

"Are you hungry? Should we order in and open some wine?" Ada asked Joel. He looked even more confused now than he had been when she first arrived. He was zoned out and she could see the wheels turning.

"Joel?" she tried again.

"Huh? Yes, food, order me some comfort food, babes, screw the diet. I'll open another bottle."

Ada ordered the food, and as she sat waiting, she couldn't help but wonder how safe the chip implants really were. All those times she'd felt that someone else was in her dreamscape …. What if it were true? She texted Ramon to tell him what was going on and that she wouldn't be in her dreamscape tonight because she was too freaked out about the whole situation.

Eighteen

DCI Amir Karim contacted Division 32 of the New York Police Department to find out who had worked on the case of the Adebayo deaths. He couldn't fathom a connection, but there were some missing pieces in his case and theirs. With the time difference he knew he might not get a reply from New York that day, so he carried on with his investigation. He rewatched the downloaded dreamscapes of Arthur and Joel, side by side, to see the whole story of the night. He felt like he had seen it a hundred times already but didn't want to miss anything, any slight detail that might give him a clue. Arthur's had been tampered with, that much had been obvious. The entire death was missing, as well as the lead up to it. Arthur was still there reading after Joel said he was going to take a shower. Then nothing. It was just blank until Joel's download showed him finding Arthur, 18 minutes and 36 seconds after he'd last seen him.

Out of the 18.36 minutes, Arthur's download showed he was still there for 3.42 minutes, so DCI Karim knew that the murder, if there was one, had happened within the almost 15 minutes that were missing. He decided to go back through Joel's movements and focus on the hallway leading to the stairs. Joel had mentioned to him earlier that he recalled the door being open to the guest room, which they always kept shut. Time to verify, Karim thought. He grabbed another cup of the horrid station coffee and sat down to watch Joel's movements throughout the night as he walked down the hallway. Each time he saw Joel on the screen walking down the main floor hallway he noted down the time and set the video in slow motion.

"Door closed, door closed, door closed, okay, that was about two and a half hours before the death of Arthur," DCI Karim muttered.

He kept watching, and at about one hour before Arthur's death, he noted, "Door closed, door closed, door closed, and he goes upstairs after the lover's spat."

So far, what Joel had told him was true; they did keep the doors closed on the main floor of the dreamscape. His phone rang and he paused the video. It was a number he didn't recognize.

"DCI Karim," he answered.

"Hi, DCI Karim, this is Detective Troy Anderson with the NYPD. I hear you were looking for those involved in the Adebayo murders?"

"Oh yes, thank you for getting back to me so quickly, detective. Have you classified them as murders then?" Karim asked.

"Well, it did appear like there was some foul play involved, so that is what we're still investigating. There are many moving pieces. What's your interest in it?" Detective Anderson replied.

"I seem to have something similar that happened last night on my hands, and I was reaching out to see if we could compare notes and determine if there's any sort of connection here. Would you be willing to share the case file with my team?" Karim asked.

"Well, shit, that does make it more interesting. I'll check with the captain and see if we can share notes. Let me just ask you this one thing, DCI Karim. When you downloaded the chip, was there stuff missing?"

This question from Detective Anderson stunned Karim. Maybe this wasn't a long shot after all. "Yes, the death itself was missing and the immediate lead up to it," he replied.

"Gotcha! Okay, let me talk to the captain and get back to you. It already sounds like you have something similar to what we've seen. Send me your email details so I can send a secure file once I get the okay," Anderson said.

"Thanks for your help, I'll send over my details now," Karim replied as they ended the call.

He sat at his desk, staring at the paused video. He knew something was up now and he needed more eyes on this case, but he wouldn't recruit help until he had the file from New York. Right now, he knew he had to keep watching the video, so he unpaused it and watched the next hour before Arthur's murder. He felt more confident in calling it a murder now that he had spoken to Detective Anderson.

Joel was up in his workout room doing no workout that DCI Karim had ever seen before. He was flailing his arms occasionally and tossing items around the room. A good way to ease the frustration after a spat, Karim thought. He watched this go on for about forty-five minutes until Joel was calmer. He exited his workout room and headed for the staircase leading down to the main floor. Here, DCI Karim slowed the video down so he could look at the doors again as Joel passed through the hallway.

From the direction that Joel was coming down the hallway towards the kitchen, he couldn't tell from his peripheral vision if the doors were open or closed. They all appeared to be closed. He knew that the guest room was the first door after the staircase in the hallway, so he rewound the video a few seconds and played it really slowly past that door again and again and again. Finally he paused it on the actual door. There was nothing definitive there, but he did see more shadows on the floor by that door than any of the others. It still wasn't clear.

Karim kept watching the video as Joel asked Arthur to come upstairs with him, got rejected, and then Joel's walk back down the hallway to go shower.

"Door closed, door closed, door open." He stopped, paused the video, and stared at the door. It was open just a crack, but it hadn't been all the other times Joel had been down that hallway. He took a screengrab of the video still and printed it. He then went back to the other times Joel had gone down the hallway where it clearly showed the door being closed and printed those as well for comparison.

The only other person who could have left the door open was Arthur, Karim thought. He went back through Arthur's footage for that hour after the spat to see if he had gone into that room at all. He queued up the video to the correct time and pressed play. After the lover's quarrel, Arthur had poured himself some wine in the kitchen, grabbed his book off the counter, and went right out to the deck to sit by the fire pit. Karim kept playing the video until Joel came back down. Arthur had only gotten up once to refill his glass in the kitchen about twenty minutes before their next encounter.

Karim sat back in his chair staring at the screen. He didn't go down the hallway, he didn't open the door, so who did? he thought. He was already working late, but he had gotten caught up in the videos. He noted down all the significant times in the two videos so that someone else with fresh eyes could watch them tomorrow. It was time to call it a night, but as he packed up his gear and headed for the elevators to take him to the parking garage, he couldn't help but wonder how it was all possible. Not being part of the Dreamcaster society, he had never thought of anyone being capable of something like this.

"Earth to Amir," he heard, and shook his head to clear his thoughts. DI Sandy Wilhelm was standing beside him, waiting for the elevator. "Long night?" she asked.

"Very, Sandy, and a very strange case. Hey, would you be willing to be my second pair of eyes on some video tomorrow?" Karim asked.

"For sure! Give me a ring when you're ready for me and I'll go over it," Sandy smiled at him.

They both took the elevator down to the parking garage and said their goodnights. Karim knew that Sandy had a keen eye for detail, so she would be the best person to have a look at the footage. They had worked together before and he was confident in her abilities. He never understood why she didn't want to move up to DCI. She had the talent for it, but just refused to do the exam.

Fortuitous meeting, he thought as he got into his car to drive home. First, he would stop for some takeaway, most of which he'd eat as he was driving before he even got home, a bad habit he couldn't seem to break. As he drove he hoped that by morning he would have an email from Detective Anderson with their case file attached. He thought it would be great if he could somehow get Anderson over here to help on this case too, but he knew that would be a long shot. Karim wanted the experience and knowledge that Anderson already had on this subject, but first he needed to see the file and determine if there was any sort of connection.

Then what, he thought. "What if there are more out there?

He didn't really want to involve Interpol, but he ought to do his due diligence and widen the search if he found there was a connection with New York.

"Bollocks," he said aloud, "this is going to be a big one, I can feel it."

Nineteen

It had been a few days since Ada had met Ramon in her dreamscape after the news about Arthur. Ramon understood and they had resorted to video calls late in the evenings for her, but she missed his touch and wanted to meet up with him again. They arranged to meet that night in her dreams. Her nerves took hold when she was about to go to bed, wondering how safe she really was, but DreamScape Ltd. hadn't put out any press releases regarding the New York murders or, for that matter, Arthur's. She assumed they were denying any responsibility and didn't want the bad press. Nothing had been in the papers about the link with regard to either murder, so unless you made the connection, which could just be a conspiracy, then you didn't wonder.

Ada tried to relax with a hot bath before bed so that she could easily access her chip when she fell asleep. As she crawled under the covers of her fluffy duvet she thought about Ramon and smiled, knowing she would see him soon when he went to bed.

Alone in her dreamscape, Ada did a thorough scan of the trees and surrounding area. She decided to wait for Ramon inside her cottage and sit by the fireplace. Although it was always a nice climate inside her dreamscape, she felt the added comfort of the fire as she waited. She thought of Ramon and the kiss they last shared together, his warm arms wrapped around her, his laugh when they talked, and his smile. She didn't recall ever reminiscing about these aspects of any other guy she had dated.

Are we dating? she thought. I mean, we talk every day, and we spend time together in our dreamscapes. Is that dating?

Ada wasn't sure what this relationship actually was now. She decided that she would ask him tonight, what they were. They had never been on an actual date, seeing as they weren't together *in person*, so she altered her cottage to set up a large movie screen and a big comfy sofa, with popcorn that stayed fresh, because it was a dream of course.

Date night! she thought and smiled to herself.

****

It was 9:30 pm and Ramon was excited to see Ada again, but he wasn't that tired. He knew that it was already 2:30 am for her and he needed to get to bed. The anxiousness of hanging out with her again kept him awake, so he decided to use the guided meditation that he first got when he had the chip implanted.

"Welcome to the DreamScape meditation for ease into sleep and deep connection to your dreams. Listen to the sound of the waves gently rolling onto the distant shore. Let the melodic overtones relax your body. Focus on your facial muscles, release the tension in your brows, take a deep breath and feel your jaw relax. Inhale deeply ... and exhale to release the tension in your neck ..."

Ramon was suddenly in his cabin, and immediately set off towards the forest path to meet Ada. He walked and walked until the trees got larger and larger, and then he saw the grove with the fountain in it. Normally that was where Ada would meet him, but as he walked through the grove, he couldn't see her at all. He began to wonder if she'd gotten too scared to enter again, but soon realized that this all wouldn't be here if she wasn't in her dreamscape. He walked the outskirts of the grove until he saw a stone pathway leading into the forest that wound its way around the trees to end at a cottage, so he took it.

Ramon knocked gently on the door to the cottage and waited until Ada opened it. What was merely seconds felt like minutes until Ada threw open the door, smiled up at him, and then rushed forward to hug him.

"I thought we could have a movie date night tonight," Ada said as she showed Ramon into her living space. "I'm not sure how this will work, but I'm thinking that if I've seen the movie already, it will play from my memory," Ada said.

"That sounds plausible, let's give it a try. You don't mind seeing it again then? And is that popcorn I smell?" Ramon asked.

"Yes! Fresh popcorn, comfy seats, and a big screen," she said, smiling. "And no, I don't mind seeing a movie again, as I think this is really the only way we can watch something unless we met in real life."

Ramon liked that idea, in real life. "Well, then, we'll have to put it on the list of things for when we meet in person." He smiled at her. "Am I coming to you or are you coming to me?"

Ada beamed at the thought of meeting in real life one day. "I think you'd mentioned something about vacation time that you had left," she suggested and laughed. She took this moment to ask her question. "Ramon, what are we? I know that's a weird question, but are we dating?"

Ramon took Ada into his arms and smiled down at her. "Yes, I would say we're dating. I've referred to you as my girlfriend to my friend Ryan, but I wasn't sure if you felt the same way."

"I would be happy to be your girlfriend." Ada smiled back at him as he leaned down for a long passionate kiss.

"Now that's out of the way and we're official," Ramon said, laughing, "I think it's time for popcorn and that comfy sofa you have there waiting for us."

Ada grabbed the two bags of popcorn, which were in movie-theatre-style bags and headed over to the sofa where Ramon was waiting for her. They sat close beside each other, and Ada leaned into him as they got comfortable.

"Okay, how do you feel about comedies? I have a few in mind that I could likely conjure up," Ada asked.

"Whatever you like, I'm here for the company," Ramon smiled.

Ada thought of a comedy movie she'd seen a few times, which would probably play from her memory, and it started to work. The film shone on the large canvas screen she had made and she snuggled in deeper to Ramon's side.

After the movie ended, Ramon asked her how she was feeling and how Joel was doing, a common thread of discussion the last few days in their video calls. He was genuinely concerned about her and her friend. He held her as she talked about her concerns, and they revisited the strange times they had each thought someone was in their dreamscape.

"I haven't seen anyone or felt anyone since that one time in the beginning when I thought I saw two people in a canoe on the lake," Ramon said.

But Ada had felt it more than once. "Twice I've heard a twig snap and it wasn't you, and a few other times I just had the sense of being watched. I know it sounds crazy, but if you could wander in here, then so could other people. Maybe they aren't dangerous and just wander back out, but what if they were?" Ada said.

"*What ifs* are your fears talking, Ada. I know you're on high alert right now with everything that has happened with Joel, but I don't think there's anything to worry about. Plus, I'm here with you now," Ramon said as he held her and kissed her forehead.

Ada looked up at him and, for that brief moment, there was nothing else in the world but his eyes. Her hands started to caress his biceps and chest. She could feel his muscles, not large, but not soft either. They kissed as they explored each other's bodies with their hands and Ada felt like a teenager making out in her parents' back room. She knew that they definitely needed to meet in person, and wondered if it would be any different in real life, or if they were both just exceptional kissers in their dreams.

Twenty

theVoyeur: It's been a week, where is the video?

Gustav saw the blinking message and knew what it was about. He had been avoiding the conversation with *theVoyeur* because he didn't want to willingly give evidence to this evil man. A man about whom he only knew that he wanted people dead and had the funds to pay for it to be done. How could he just give him evidence of the murder he had committed? It was a sure way to get himself sent to jail; if this man was willing to pay to kill people, he likely wouldn't shy away from turning in Gustav and Andrei to benefit himself. Gustav wasn't sure how he would get around this. One million dollars was a lot of money, but was it worth his freedom and safety?

Gustav walked over to the computers and opened the message. He was right. Now he had to think about how to respond, seeing as the system would show he was online.

SilentIsTheNight: What guarantees do I have that

this won't be used against me? I'd be handing over evidence.

theVoyeur: I'm paying you.

SilentIsTheNight: That's not a guarantee. I'd rather not send it.

theVoyeur: My honour is my guarantee.

SilentIsTheNight: I don't know you well enough to go with that.

theVoyeur: How can we make this even so I can have my video?

Gustav didn't like that, but figured it was the only option if *theVoyeur* was insistent. He also didn't want to piss this guy off, seeing as he could easily turn them in as well if he was displeased, or worse.

SilentIsTheNight: I'll think on it and get back to you.

theVoyeur: You have 2 weeks.

theVoyeur has signed off

Gustav sat back in his chair and stared at the ceiling. He closed his eyes and took a few deep breaths. He didn't want to get on the wrong side of this guy, but he wasn't sure how he could continue. He had Andrei searching Nottingham and UK news stories for the last week to see if there were any connections or assumptions about the chip, but so far he hadn't found anything. Just the news of Arthur's death and that it was suspicious, but nothing else.

"Hey, Gus! I've got dinner and some beers. Stop working and come get it while it's hot," Andrei shouted from the front door as he came in.

"I'll be right there," Gustav replied.

Maybe some food would help him think this through. The beer wouldn't, but it would take the edge off.

"Thanks for this, Andrei," Gus said, "it's much needed right now. *TheVoyeur* finally asked about the video."

Andrei looked up from his food. He didn't respond as his mouth was full, but Gustav knew what he was asking from his facial expression.

"I pushed him off, and he gave us two weeks to decide how to guarantee our safety of handing over evidence," Gustav replied.

"Do you have any ideas?" Andrei asked once he finished his mouthful. "I mean, how can we really guarantee this freak won't just use it against us?"

That was precisely the thing that Gustav had been wrestling with for the previous week. How he could willingly hand over his life, essentially.

"I'm not sure yet, Andrei," he responded, "but hopefully we can figure it out together. Let me know if you have any ideas, because I don't have any right now."

Andrei was nodding as he was eating, and Gus could see the wheels turning in his head.

"I will think about it, but we have two weeks, so we have to make sure it's really good. First thoughts: he sends us something incriminating about himself so we're equal and could use it against him," Andrei suggested.

"That's a good idea, Andrei, but we don't know anything about this guy, so how would we know that he's being honest and it's actually him?"

"Good point," Andrei replied. "Have we tried to find anything out about this guy before?"

Gustav had in the beginning, when he was first contacted by *theVoyeur*, but it wasn't a deep dive. "You know what; let's set our minds to that tonight. Maybe the two of us will do better digging than I was able to before," Gustav said.

After they finished their shawarma and fries, they took their beers into the front room to relax before diving into the system. They talked about the people they had been observing for fun and how Andrei was still fascinated by that girl, Ada.

"I think it's best to leave her be for the next little while. With all the news in Nottingham right now about the death, we don't want to make any mistakes," Gustav advised.

"I know, but it's been a week. Do you think she'd still be wary?" Andrei asked.

"Let's just sort this issue out with *theVoyeur* first and then you can go back into her dreamscape. For now, let's just watch other people in some different countries for now, okay?" he said to Andrei.

He could see the kid looked disappointed, but he knew that Andrei understood the need for safety. He couldn't help the poor guy having a little crush.

An hour or so later they went into the computer room and decided to start digging. They would start with the username *theVoyeur* and see where else it was logged. The dark web was vast and he could have different usernames for different sites, but they had to check it out. Andrei started hacking the system and found *theVoyeur* on a couple of snuff film sites, which made sense to them. He liked to watch, and he liked death. Maybe this was his only way of getting off. They also found him on some buying and trading sites that were for antiquities, and that made sense, seeing as the guy seemed to have a lot of money to throw around. Aside from those few sites, they couldn't find anything else where that username occurred, which led them to believe that he was quite tech savvy as well and hiding his tracks.

From there, they started to dig into what he was actually buying, trading, or watching. Gustav didn't want to watch the snuff films, so he left that bit to Andrei and hoped it didn't disturb the kid too much. Andrei wasn't really a kid, but compared to Gustav, he seemed so young, and that 's how he thought of him.

"Looks like this guy is into ancient Greek artifacts and Egyptian ones. A historian maybe?" Gustav said.

Andrei took a break from the death or attempted death he was watching to look at the artifacts. They looked them up to get a better picture of their appearance. It appeared that the Egyptian ones were from tombs in the Valley of the Kings that had been robbed decades ago and had been floating around the black market for years.

"Can we pinpoint anything? Maybe sales from him to museums?" Andrei suggested.

Gustav agreed, and they took an inventory of the artifacts they could find that were bought by *theVoyeur* so they could look them all up and work back to see if anything had surfaced in actual museums.

"This won't be done tonight, Andrei," Gustav said. "Did you find anything on your sites?"

Andrei looked at Gus skeptically. "Just that this guy is a sicko," he said. "He seems to pay for films where women are killed during sex. How this isn't known to be happening and in the news is beyond me. There's way too many of them. I guess he graduated from this to paying for murder to be done and now wanting to watch what he's paying to be done. His last purchase of a snuff film was about eight months ago, and we started working for him about six months ago."

Gustav was surprised at this information. "You're good, Andrei," he said. "I couldn't find that earlier. It does sound like he's escalated, but it also sounds like our best bet for finding more information is in these artifacts, because he's still active on those sites."

They decided to leave the snuff films alone for now, and work the next few days on figuring out what the artifacts were and investigating them. After this new information was discovered, they decided to take it easy for the rest of the night and watch some of their people they had been monitoring.

"How about the Rowlands? They just moved overseas to Germany, let's see how they're settling in," Andrei suggested.

Gustav knew the wife was a tall blonde with large breasts, and that the Rowlands would frequently walk around naked in their dreamscape. He had already taken Ada away from the kid, so he agreed to watch these two. "All right, Andrei, your choice tonight, set it up."

Twenty-One

It had been over a week and DCI Amir Karim hadn't heard back from Detective Anderson about the file. He called the number he'd received the original call from. "Detective Anderson," answered the person on the other end of the line.

"Hi, Detective Anderson, this is DCI Karim from Nottingham. Have you heard anything about approval for sending me that file?" he asked.

"Amir! So sorry, the captain has been a bit backlogged with some open cases," Anderson replied.

Karim was confused. "This isn't an open case anymore?" he asked.

The line was silent for a moment before Anderson responded, "I'm going to be honest with you here. As far as my department is concerned, they died in their sleep. Case closed. Which is why my captain doesn't see the urgency for sending the file over."

"So I'm not getting any assistance on the supposed connection then," Karim responded, a bit irritated.

"I would love to, and I agree with you. Believe me, I do!" Anderson said. "But I'm only one guy, and thinking that something fishy is going on when a case is deemed closed doesn't get me many likes around here, you understand, right?"

Karim understood all too well, "I get it, Troy. Is there anything you can give me?"

"Sit tight a bit longer," Anderson said, "and I'll see if I can feed you some information. Sorry I couldn't be of more help now."

They hung up the call, and Karim sat wondering how he could get the attention on this case that he needed. He didn't have a chip himself—he didn't like the idea of having technology in his brain—but he knew people in his immediate circle and family who had one. His brothers called him old for his way of thinking, but with this case now, he believed more and more that it was dangerous. Still, he needed some sort of connection before Interpol would even look into it. He knew he couldn't ask them to take a look into cases across 194 countries without any solid evidence. He was stuck. DI Wilhelm had confirmed his observations of the door being open on Joel's way back up the stairs, but that was all they had to confirm any sort of suspicious activity. His only option was to circle back to Joel and see if his mind was any clearer about that night. He knew the longer the time lapse after an incident the less clear a person's brain could become, but it was his only option at this point. He had already ruled Joel out as a suspect because of the video from his chip download from that night.

The next day he went to knock on Joel's door again. Joel answered the door in a bathrobe, holding a cup of tea. At least Karim hoped it was tea.

"Hi Joel, I was wondering if we could have another chat," he said.

"Uh, yeah, sure, come in, DCI Karim." Joel opened the door wider so that he could enter. They took their seats in the front sitting room. "Do you want some tea?" Joel offered.

"No, thank you, I'm fine," Karim said. "I was wondering if you'd had any more thoughts about that night. Anything else come to mind about the house in your dreamscape being off?"

Joel looked at him with his sad eyes. He had been crying. "The kitchen was dark, I didn't see anything. Just that door being open stands out. Sorry." Joel looked down at his tea mug and sighed.

Karim decided to prod a little further. "What about other times? Maybe in the days leading up to that night?" He didn't want to say death or murder, he knew he needed to be as gentle as he could be.

"Off the top of my head, no, nothing. But I'll think about it," Joel responded.

Karim knew that was his cue to exit. "Well, I don't want to take up too much of your time. Thank you for seeing me today, and if you can think of anything from the night before, or days before, just let me know. Maybe this person had been there before." He left another one of his cards and headed back to the office with nothing more for this case. He wondered if he knew anyone in other cities or countries that he could get in contact with to look for connections.

When he got back to the office, DI Wilhelm came up to him and said the deputy chief wanted to talk to him. This was never a good sign. "Thanks for the heads up, Sandy," he said.

He went to his desk and checked his messages before heading to the deputy chief's office. When he got up to head towards the elevators and up to the sixth floor, he saw Deputy Chief Superintendent Moore coming down the hallway.

"Deputy Chief," he said and nodded.

"Ah, DCI Karim, lucky running into you. I was hoping you could give me an update on the Arthur Millstone case. He was a figure in the community and we'd like to get this one closed off."

Karim knew what that meant. "Yes, sir, I can put some information together for you this afternoon and send it to you by the end of the day, if you like." He knew they wanted this one closed off as neatly as possible, just as the NYPD had done.

"Sounds great to me, thank you, DCI Karim," Deputy Chief Superintendent Moore said, and then continued his walk down the hallway towards the elevators.

Karim knew he was running out of time. How could he make them see that there was a connection to the chip? He headed to the breakroom to make some coffee. It tasted bad, but it would keep him alert enough to get the job done. He had four more hours, so he started assembling the case file and arranging the video stills that he had printed, along with the analysis by himself and DI Wilhelm. Now to work on his synopsis. How to be analytical and detached, yet pour his heart into it to get his suspicions and point across. He sat sipping his coffee, staring at the screen on his laptop, thinking.

With one hour to go before he had to get the file to the deputy chief, he called on Sandy for a review of what he had.

"Sure, let me have a look at it and see," she responded. She went through the file with him and they talked about all the pictures and notes. Then she read his synopsis and reread it.

"I don't really think there's too much more that you can add here, Amir. You have all the facts, you have your ideas and links, and even the video evidence that we validated."

He agreed with her, but he was still nervous. The case depended on this review. "Thank you, Sandy. I guess it's time to hand it off to the deputy chief," he said with a half-hearted smile.

"Best of luck, Amir," she said as she walked back to her desk.

Karim took the file including his synopsis up to the sixth floor to hand it off in person. He walked into the office area and saw the deputy chief's secretary sitting at her desk outside a closed door.

"Hi, I'm DCI Karim, here to see—"

"Yes, he's been expecting you," she cut him off. She picked up the phone on her desk and pressed a button. "DCI Karim is here to see you ... mm, yes, sir." She hung up the phone and looked back up at him. "You can go right in."

"Okay, thank you," he said and headed towards the solid oak door. He knocked before entering. "Hello, sir," he started, but was stopped there.

"Come in, come in, DCI Karim, and close the door behind you. Let's have a look at what you've got."

Twenty-Two

TheVoyeur sat comfortably on his mega yacht just off Port Hercule in Monaco, looking over his list of people who had betrayed him in business. The list was long, but not everyone would meet their final end. However, there was one group of individuals who were at the top. He wasn't one to get his hands dirty himself, and could hire anyone he wanted to get the job done, but right now his mind was on revenge.

At 59 years old, he had had his fill of luxury and success. As one of the top one percent in the world and income streaming in from his multiple businesses and technology investments, he could sit and enjoy the Monaco sunrise without a care in the world. He had no children to concern him, and no ex-wives, so all the money that he had made was his own, and most was tax-sheltered either in the Caymans or deep in the vaults of the Swiss banks. He also had multiple investments with private equity firms and real estate ventures across the world. Now he simply enjoyed spending time around the world where he could get away from everything and make his plans.

He had always been savvy in business deals, but one deal which had started in early 2022 and ended poorly in May 2024 had burned him and his reputation. Since then, he had been attempting to acquire new technology businesses and kept getting the door shut in his face. He was known around Silicon Valley as the "delayer." He rarely spent time at his home base in San Jose, California, where his six-million dollar gated home of 7024 square feet with its six bedrooms and seven bathrooms stood empty. He felt trapped there, but out here at sea on his 215-foot mega yacht, he felt freedom. "A million for every bedroom," he used to joke when he entertained potential clients at his luxury home.

That was a different time, and all he could do now was hide away and buy more properties to invest in, or spend his money on frivolous things like antiquities and murder for hire. He had tried to let it go over the last two years, but with every deal that had fallen through since that fateful day in May, his anger and resentment grew. Men and women who were his inferiors had outplayed him, outvoted him. His mind spun with his options. He wanted them to pay for the disgrace he had faced and the respect he had lost with the elite that he had spent a good portion of his life schmoozing and placating. He would show them the error of their ways, and what happened when you took short cuts.

****

Gustav and Andrei continued their deep dive into their benefactor's background over the course of nine days. He hadn't been in contact again, but they knew that their time was running out to find something on him.

"Aside from some fraudulent sales of counterfeit antiquities that it appears he had forged from the originals, we don't have much on him, Gus." Andrei was exhausted from the hours of digging into *theVoyeur*.

"I know, Andrei. He's covered his tracks well. There's limited visibility on the transactions and financials. It looks like he made his trades in cash. But wouldn't that suggest that a meeting took place?" Gustav knew he was grasping at straws, but he couldn't seem to find a wire transfer or any bank account details linked to *theVoyeur*. What bothered him the most was that he and Andrei were both very good at hacking, yet nothing could be found.

"What if we gave him the deleted part of the dreamscape and kept digging? There has to be something we aren't thinking about. We have to find out his real name somehow." Gustav was hitting a mental wall.

They decided to take a break and head out for some lunch. As they were driving in Gus's beat-up Volvo, Andrei had an idea. "For him to cover his tracks this well, he must have IT knowledge himself. Not everyone can scramble an IP address linked to a username, like he has."

This was their main area of frustration. Whenever they tried to decrypt his user profile, the IP address would change countries.

"It's like he's got some sort of VPN that is masking his identity," Andrei said. "A Virtual Private Network."

"If that's the case, then let's look for a pattern and see if we can figure out the algorithm for it. If we can hack the VPN, then we might be able to pinpoint where he is," Gustav replied.

After resting, eating, and some laughs, they decided to jump back online. Gustav could set up a network and gain access where he shouldn't be able to, but Andrei was the more gifted hacker of the pair. Andrei started to write some code to access the username again. This time the VPN showed London, UK. They took note and went in again. Monaco, New York, Kingston, San Jose, Toronto, Florence—it kept jumping around. They took note of them all and started to concentrate on each one to see if they could hack into them individually. One of them would have to be the main hub.

The hours ticked away and Andrei knew he wasn't going to be able to do it all tonight. He had made some headway in eliminating some cities, but the list kept growing.

"We have five days left. I think we call it for tonight, Gus, I'm tired."

"For sure, Andrei, let's call it a night. How about I go get some beers and we can just relax?" Gustav understood, the kid had spent his mental energy.

Andrei nodded his consent. He got up, went out for a cigarette, and refocused his eyes, as they were sore from staring at the monitor for hours. He seemed to forget to blink in his concentration.

As Gustav was pulling away from the house to get the beer, Andrei went back inside and sat in front of the computer monitors. It was almost 8 pm. They'd been going at it for twelve hours. He slid on his head piece and looked up Ada Carpenter to see if she was in her chip. "There she is," he said softly and went into her dream-scape. He stood in the forest for a few moments listening before he crept slowly towards the grove. The fountain was flowing in a bright unnatural purple colour that she had created. Andrei stood by one of the larger trees to conceal himself, partially in shadows, partially covered by vegetation. He couldn't see her anywhere. He walked slowly around the outer edge of the grove just inside the tree line to conceal himself. Still he couldn't see her. As he kept going, he came across a stone path that led into the forest, and he could see some lights in the distance. As much as he wanted to be able to just walk down the pathway, he knew he couldn't. He stayed in the bushes and trees and made his way in the direction of the lights. As he got closer, a small cottage came into view, with the lights on inside.

****

Sitting by the fireplace reading a novel, Ada was having a hard time concentrating. She couldn't wait to see Ramon again and remembered him being there with her. She got up to walk around the room, recalling everywhere they went. The smile on her face felt foolish, but she couldn't help it. She wanted to meet him in real life before her heart took hold and she fell in deeper without actually meeting while they were awake. Ramon was exactly how he looked in the dreamscape. She knew that because of all the video chats they'd been having. But in real life, it would be so different. Music, she thought, I feel like dancing. She created some speakers and a screen for her to choose some playlists. Soon she was dancing and twirling around the cottage, having fun in her joy.

****

Andrei could see movement in the window and wondered what she was doing in there. He wanted to go right up to the window and look in, but knew that Gus wouldn't like it. Moving closer to the house and crouching down in the bushes nearer the cottage, he could hear music coming from inside. Maybe she's not alone, he thought. Maybe she's having a party. He dismissed that thought because he had only ever seen her alone in her dreamscape.

He was desperate for a look at her, and crept a little closer to the side of the cottage where there were no windows. The music was louder here and he could hear her singing along. She sounds distracted, he thought as he peered around the corner towards the windows and door. Just as he was deciding to move closer, darkness came over him and he was jolted back to reality.

"What the hell are you doing?" Gustav yelled at him. "Safety! We agreed only to go in together. What were you thinking?"

Andrei sighed and looked at the ground. "I just needed to let off some steam and do something fun. It's been a long day."

"I get it, kid, but you could have waited until I came back. Don't do that again," Gus said. "Let me guess: you went in to see Ada?"

Andrei looked up abruptly and gave a small laugh. "How did you know? Yes, I went to see her. She was in her cottage listening to music."

Gustav stared at him, waiting for him to elaborate.

"I didn't go up to it. I just stood nearby, but I could hear the music and see her moving around inside. I stayed hidden," he said. He wasn't about to tell Gus how close he was to going up to a window and looking at her.

"Okay, but wait for me next time. This isn't a time to be reckless."

Andrei knew Gustav was right and he'd acted poorly. "I understand, I won't do it again," he said. They left the computer room to watch the hockey game and drink the night away.

Twenty-Three

Ada was surprised to see Joel back at work already. The management team had told him to take as much time as he needed, and although it had been two weeks, she was still surprised. He came into her office, sat in the brown leather chair across from her desk, and took off his sunglasses.

His eyes still looked raw and puffy, but he put a smile on his face. "Hey, darling, thank you for coming by over the last two weeks. Can I take you out for lunch today? I have a proposition for you."

Ada was happy to see him smile, but knew it was just a front for the office, a way of carrying on. "I'd love to, Joel. Swing by when you're ready to go," she said with warmth in her voice. She stood up and walked around her desk to where he was standing up to leave and hugged him.

Joel pulled away after a moment. "Don't make me cry, sweetie, but I appreciate it." He hugged her again quickly before heading to his own office with his sunglasses firmly in place.

Ada's heart felt heavy for him. She knew how much he had loved Arthur, but hadn't realized that Arthur had made him the executor of his estate and had left everything to him. They weren't married and Arthur didn't have any children, but Joel was still shocked when the lawyers contacted him. It had been a rough few days sorting out all the details.

Just before lunch Ada's phone *pinged* with a message from Ramon. "Good morning, beautiful xo." It was the same message he sent every morning when he woke up. She smiled at her phone and replied to him with a good morning and some hearts. She also told him that Joel was back in the office and they were heading out for lunch in a bit.

Ada knew she was getting swept away by her feelings for Ramon, but she couldn't help it. Everything was exciting and going so well with them. It seemed like they could talk about anything and the conversations were deep and meaningful, but also playful and fun a lot of the time. Kira couldn't get enough of the gossip when Ada gushed about Ramon. She was such a romantic at heart and interested in their story that she was constantly asking for details. Ada didn't mind, though. It was a nice feeling to have a close friend who supported her. She hadn't even told her family yet about Ramon. Still, they knew something was up because she was in her room a lot on video calls, or smiling at her phone in the kitchen. Her brother Davey had asked a few times if she was talking to a new guy, and she'd smiled and said

"Maybe." She wasn't sure they would understand the long distance aspect, and with them not knowing about her chip, how would she say they'd met? Online dating, she guessed.

Joel knocked on her door about half past twelve and she grabbed her long grey woolen jacket that tapered to just above her knees. They walked out into the rain. Joel opened his umbrella as they hurriedly dodged puddles to get to the Garden Bistro, their special spot. They found a table in the corner and, after they'd sat down, Joel reached across the table to hold Ada's hands.

"Honey, I really meant what I said this morning. You've been such an enormous source of love and support these last few weeks. Now I want to ask you something."

Ada wasn't sure where Joel was going with this request, but she'd grown closer to him during this time and loved him like he was family. It was terrible to think that Arthur's death had made them closer than just being work besties, but it had.

"Ok, Joel, go ahead," she replied.

The server came just then and they placed their orders before Joel could continue.

"I know you've been looking for a place to live and get out of your mother's, so I was wondering, now that I have all this empty space, if you would consider moving in with me?" He looked shy and unsure as he asked her, most likely fearful of her declining.

"Oh Joel! That would be amazing. I'd love to!" Ada smiled, filled with delight, and stood up to hug him.

Joel started to cry again. "Tears of joy, darling. Tears of joy," he said with a weak smile. "I may sell the place eventually because of the memories, but we'll see how it goes. Maybe we'll make new ones. And if I still have issues with it, we can sell and find a new place together. How does that sound?" he asked.

Ada understood completely. She had been with him in the house many times since Arthur had passed away and he would talk about their memories in whatever room they were in.

"Of course, Joel, we'll see how it goes. If you need to sell, then we'll find somewhere else, new."

They worked out the details of when she would be able to move in with him, and they joked about how her mother was going to take it. They talked about Ramon and work and all the other gossip that was going on in their lives and at the office. The rain had stopped by the time they headed back to the office so there was no need to rush.

Back in her office, Ada texted Kira the news. "Babes! You'll never guess what just happened. Joel asked me to move in with him! Now to tell my mother and Davey that I'm moving out ... eeek!"

She then messaged Ramon something similar. She knew it was going to be a difficult conversation that night at home, so she was looking for advice. She already had Joel's input. He had heard many stories over their lunches about Ada's drama at home with her mother, so he offered the advice of saying she was just going to move in for a bit to help him with his grief. Then as time went on her mother would be used to it and Ada could make the full move later.

She knew that Ramon would be at work and in meetings most likely, so she understood she wouldn't hear back from him right away. However, she definitely knew that Kira would be available because she worked in an office as well and had her phone by her side all day.

Without fail, *ding, ding* came her reply.

"Oooh! That's exciting! It will be so great for you to be there to support him!" Kira began. "Your mother won't like it to start with. She had a hard enough time when your brother, Craig moved out. But you're 24 years old, babe—she can't expect you to stay forever. Let her know why you're moving in with Joel and that it's still in the city, so you won't be far. That should help."

Ada agreed. "You're right, it's not like I'm moving to London like Craig. I'll be a 15 to 20 minute drive away." Ada was already feeling more confident about the conversation. She was doing what was best for her and she had to stick by that belief.

Later in the day she heard the *ping* of a message from Ramon. "You've got this!" he said. "I know you've mentioned the strain of your relationship with your mom, but I also know that you love her dearly. Just remember you're not doing this to hurt her, but to help Joel and yourself. Good luck, darling! xo."

Ada swelled with emotion. She couldn't believe how caring and supportive he was. It was new for her to date a man like this.

"Thank you, babe, xoxo," she replied.

Filled with confidence, Ada left the office to head home and talk to her mother about her plans. She knew that, when she started to help her mother with dinner, she could talk to her while they worked together, and hoped that it would ease the conversation.

When she arrived home, she could hear her mother in the kitchen chopping vegetables, and went in to offer a hand.

"It's okay, sweetie, I'm almost done. Would you like some tea?" her mother offered.

"Sure, that sounds great. I'll put the kettle on. Would you like one, too?" she asked.

"Yes, make enough for us both, love."

Ada filled the kettle, took out a couple of mugs from the cupboard and put a tea bag in the china teapot from her grandmother they still used. Once the tea was made, Ada set the steaming mugs on the kitchen table and waited for her mother to sit down. Here goes, she thought.

"Mum, remember I told you about my friend Joel and how his partner died a couple of weeks ago?"

"Yes, dear, you've been spending a lot of time with him while he grieves," her mother replied.

Ada took a deep breath and went for it. "Well, Joel has asked me to move in now that he's alone and having a hard time. So I thought it was a good idea. To help him and for me to have my own space as well."

There was a long pause as they both sipped their tea. She could see her mother's mind working it over.

"He lives over by your work, more in the centre of town, yes?" her mother asked.

"That's right, mum. We can walk to work or take a short bus ride together. And it's only about 20 minutes from here. So I was thinking I could pack some things and head over to stay with him starting next weekend."

There was another long pause as they sat at the table, neither one making direct eye contact but staring at their mugs of tea.

"If you think it's best, dear, then you should do it. It will probably help him a lot, too."

Ada couldn't believe it. "I'm so glad you agree, mum. I was worried you'd be upset because it was so fast."

Her mother looked up at her for the first time and said, "I know I can't have you here forever, Ada, but I do enjoy the time we have together. So I hope you'll still come for dinner when you can."

Ada was touched. It was rare for her mother to open up. She stood up and hugged her mother. "I will, mum. I'll still be close by."

Twenty-Four

Having still not found the location of *theVoyeur*, Gustav and Andrei decided to send the deleted portion of Arthur's dreamscape from when he was murdered and to keep investigating their employer. They didn't have a choice.

"I'll make contact with him a bit later today and send the file," Gustav said.

Andrei agreed as he continued his search for more information on who this creep was. The tracks of his IP seemed to be originating from all over the world. They knew he couldn't be in every one of those spots, but they were hoping that one might lead to more information or a home base for him.

After they ate their dinner, Gustav logged into the encrypted network and sent the file.

SilentIsTheNight: File transfer on its way. Send payment.

He knew he should have waited for the payment first, but this was how the guy operated. It was hours before they saw the flashing light indicating that he had responded. They stopped their investigations into him and read the message.

> *theVoyeur*: Couldn't find any dirt on me
> I suppose. Much appreciated.
> Payment has been sent.

Gustav didn't even want to respond to that, but it made him uneasy that they were leaving a trail behind them in their search.

"Andrei, let's start erasing our footsteps in this. I don't know if he knows how much we're digging, but I don't want to anger this psychopath."

Even though they were the ones who had carried out the killing, they were still terrified of *theVoyeur* and his power. Andrei began erasing all previous searches that they'd saved and took paper notes instead. Gustav checked his Cayman Island account and saw the one million dollars deposited a few moments before via secure wire transfer.

He stared at the screen, wheels turning in his mind. "Follow the money," he said aloud.

Andrei looked up at him. "What money? We tried that with the sales of the artifacts."

"No, no, our money!" Gustav said, smiling. "There must be a way to see where our deposits come from.

Who's paying them into our account. It may very well be a legitimate business that he's using, but it may give us a better start."

Gustav was so desperate to know something, anything, about this guy that he was willing to go this route. He knew very well that he couldn't offer this information up to authorities because he'd lose all his money, but for his personal knowledge and a place to start, he was willing to go there.

"Gus, I think you're forgetting that he set up the account for us. Well, for you, and it's a numbered account. As in, no names, for him or us. Only the bank manager would know his identity. Plus, I already tried that route when we were digging before. Sorry."

Andrei was a smart kid, and Gustav was feeling defeated now. He thought he'd had a brilliant idea, but it was just his old ways getting the better of him.

"You know, back when I was doing contract work for agencies, they always paid in cash. Then I could sprinkle it around in my accounts so that it didn't set off any alarms with the government. Now I have this numbered account and, poof, money appears— millions of dollars —and it doesn't feel safe to me."

Andrei understood. "It's okay, old man, I've got the security side of things. You just keep your mind sharp for the master plans, okay?"

He knew that Gus was frustrated and didn't like it when times changed, but he was excellent at his job and had set up their whole system for going into people's chips. Gustav was letting the search for *theVoyeur* distract him.

"How about we take a break for a few days, Gus? Clear the mind, maybe get away?"

Gustav sat silently for a while after Andrei made his proposal. He wanted answers, but he also knew that his mind was clouded with anger and it was no way to work efficiently.

"Okay, Andrei. Let's take some time off away from the monitoring, the searching. If you want to take a vacation, you should. I'll stay here and watch the equipment."

"Can't we hire someone to watch the place and then you can have a break too, Gus? I know you. If I leave, then you'll still be here and tempted to keep digging."

The kid was right and Gustav knew it. Although he had this house on an abandoned street where his operation was set up out of the way of prying eyes, he also had a cabin out in Colorado where he could go for a break. The fresh air and solitude would do him some good.

"Let me look into a surveillance team to watch the place and we'll each go away for a week. I'll go to my cabin in Colorado near Sentinel Peak. Where are you going to go?"

Andrei was already looking at flight prices. "I bought a small place in Mexico, in Puerto Vallarta, that looks onto the beach. Some sun will do me good now that the weather's getting cold."

Both of them booked flights to leave on the following Monday. Gustav was packing when he wondered about any incoming messages from *theVoyeur*. He didn't want to piss this guy off by having him think his messages were being ignored.

He called to Andrei. "Hey, kid, is there a way to monitor any incoming messages from the server while I'm away? What if he makes a request?"

"Gus, the whole point of a vacation is to shut off. But I get that you're freaked out by this guy. Let me see tomorrow when I come over if we can connect anything to your laptop."

"Ok, thanks, kid. See you tomorrow."

Gus wondered if he should send a message to *theVoyeur* saying he would be unavailable, but wanted to see if Andrei could work something out first. If it wasn't going to be secure, then he couldn't do it. Time off, he thought, I have all the time in the world already. He shook his head at letting Andrei convince him to do this.

The following day when Andrei was sitting at the computers, trying to see if they could transfer any data from the untraceable server to Gus's laptop, a message came in.

"Hey Gus," Andrei shouted, "it's blinking. Hope this doesn't mean we have to cancel our plans." Gustav came into the room and opened the message.

> *theVoyeur:* I've put an extra $500,000 in your account for good faith and excellent skills. The video is superb.

"This guy is a psycho!" Andrei shouted. "Gus, we need to distance ourselves from him. The money is great, but we can't be associated with him."

Gustav was just as concerned as Andrei was.

"I know, but we have to hang on a bit longer to find out something. Stop trying to transfer the data, I'm going to let him know we won't be available instead. Set the expectation that we aren't at his beck and call."

> *SilentIsTheNight*: Appreciated. Letting you know we won't be available until the 15th, taking time off.
> *theVoyeur*: Well deserved.
> *theVoyeur has signed off*

Now that it was settled, they shut down the servers and locked the room with a padlock. Gustav had hired an old friend from the business, who was going to stay in the house while they were gone, to keep an eye on things. The guy had said this was his vacation from his family and he didn't mind at all. Not to mention the $10,000 he was going to get upon Gustav's return. Andrei left to finish his packing and said goodbye to Gustav and that he would see him next week. Gustav's flight was in four hours and he was ready to go. He opened a beer while he waited for his old pal to arrive in about an hour.

Twenty-Five

Ada moved in with Joel in the middle of November. The weather was grey and chilly, but not as cold as Ramon had said it was in Toronto. Davey and her mother helped with all her bags and a few boxes, as she wasn't bringing any furniture with her.

"You have way too many clothes, Ada," her brother said as he hefted bag after bag of clothing out of the car.

It only took one trip to bring everything over because Kira lent them her car while she was working, so they had two vehicles to jam everything into, plus themselves. Kira was planning to come by after work for the dinner they were all having together.

"Welcome!" Joel said at the door as he went out to help unload the cars. "Let's get this all inside before it rains," he added.

Ada and her mother unpacked everything from the bags and boxes that were now in her new room, hung up her clothes, and put other items away in the long wooden dresser.

"This is a nice room," her mother said. "It looks like they renovated it."

"Yes, last year," Ada mentioned. "They redid the upstairs and the bathrooms."

The bed was a queen size with a full down duvet and multiple decorative pillows in a range of colours. The walls were a very pale grey with white trim to match the white doors.

"It's bigger than my room at home," Ada said.

Davey was helping Joel prepare the dinner, though "helping" was a generous term. He was chopping vegetables into large chunks when Joel said, "It's not firewood, Davey. We'll need bite-size pieces for our mouths."

Davey laughed. He knew he was no good in the kitchen, but now that Ada had moved out he would have to learn so he could help his mum with dinner.

"I'll have to come over for lessons," he answered Joel as he halved or quartered the pieces he had already cut.

"My mother would be appalled," Joel joked. "This is her Sunday stew recipe. My brother and I used to help her make it on Sunday afternoons and then it would be ready for dinner later."

Joel smiled at the memory. It had been a few months since he had been down to Plymouth to visit his mum, but he would make it a point to go and see her soon.

"I hear a lot of laughing coming from down here," Ada said as she was coming down the stairs.

She and her mother joined them in the kitchen and asked if they could help with anything, but Joel just poured them each a glass of Prosecco and told them to sit down and relax. The sitting room was open to the kitchen, so they could still chat while Davey and Joel prepared the ingredients for the stew on the kitchen island. Once Joel had everything in the large red stewing pot on the stovetop, he poured himself and Davey a glass of Prosecco each as well and joined the ladies in the sitting area.

Ada's phone kept *pinging* with messages from Ramon, likely checking in on how the move was going. Since she hadn't told her mum or Davey about him yet, she wasn't answering them. Joel looked at her, giving her a knowing side eye every time it *pinged.*

"Aren't you going to answer those messages, Ada?" he said with a broad smile on his face.

Davey and her mother looked at Ada and then at each other, not knowing the context.

"Are we missing something?" Davey asked.

Ada could feel her face flushing, and she didn't know if she could hide it because her face would start to turn red. She sighed deeply, trying to figure out how to start because all three of them were staring at her now.

"I've been talking to someone for a couple of months. His name is Ramon, but we haven't met in person yet."

Davey jumped right in to tease his sister. "Oooh, Ada has a boyfriend. Why haven't you mentioned anything, dear sister?" he said coyly, "I guess that's why you've spent so much time in your room lately, huh?"

Feeling the embarrassment rising, Ada swallowed her pride. "Yes, we've been video chatting because we haven't met in person. I wanted to keep it quiet until we met," she said.

Throughout this exchange with Davey and Joel teasing her, her mother sat silently, not really reacting. Ada figured she'd hear something about it later, but knew that her mum had been jaded after their father left and wasn't very supportive in this area of her life. She opened the messages, responded to Ramon about how the move had gone, and let him know about the plans for the evening with Kira and her family.

"Excellent! Enjoy the family and friends time in your new home, sweetie xo," Ramon responded.

The laughs and jokes continued on as Joel kept getting up to watch the stew and stir it every so often. The aroma was hearty and Ada couldn't wait to try it; two glasses of Prosecco would go to her head soon if she didn't eat something.

Kira knocked on the door at about half-past five and was greeted with hugs all around. She had two more bottles of Prosecco with her for a kind of house warming, and Joel put them in the fridge to cool. Ada set the table for the five of them and her mother started to slice some pieces off the French stick that Joel had bought.

Once they were all seated, Joel stood up to give a toast. "Thank you to all of you for your help today and bringing Ada here to stay with me. I know it was sudden, but it will be a great help to have her here during this time. And thank you to Davey for helping me cook and to Kira for the extra bottles for later." He winked at her. "To good friends and new family," he said as he raised his glass in the air.

"Good friends and new family!" they all said before sipping their drinks.

After dinner, Davey and their mother decided it was time to go. They gave Ada long hugs, thanked Joel for a lovely time, and hoped to see him again soon.

"You're welcome here any time!" Joel said. "We're like family now, but dinner is at your place next time," he added, smiling.

As they waved goodbye Joel said, "Well, that went better than you expected," and gave Ada a little nudge as he walked back to the kitchen.

Kira opened another bottle while they cleaned up from dinner. "Now that the adults have left, it's time for some fun!" she said.

"Kira, darling, you're spending the night. No way are you driving home after we finish these bottles," Joel said as he took the car keys away from her.

Drinking, cleaning and laughing, Ada couldn't believe that this was her new home. She knew there would be hard days and a routine eventually, but being here with Joel and Kira was some of the best fun she had had in months.

"Well, I guess I don't have to worry about you two liking each other," Ada said to them. "First time meeting and you're already besties and getting me in trouble."

"Me and my girls!" Joel shouted and raised his glass in a toast.

Ada messaged Ramon around midnight, letting him know that she wouldn't be in her dreamscape that night. She sent him a video of the shenanigans they were getting into and the ridiculous dancing that was happening. Ramon sent back messages of him laughing and asking them for dance requests. He asked if they could have a video call the next day, which would be a Saturday, so he could have the grand tour of her new place with Joel.

"Stop smiling at your phone and start dancing, lady!" Joel shouted over the music. Ada said goodnight to Ramon and put her phone down to join in the fun with her two favourite people.

Twenty-Six

TheVoyeur sat in his yacht looking over his list of names, sipping some Glenfiddich reserve from 1995. He hadn't seen the media attention he wanted to on Arthur's death and decided to step it up a notch this time. He knew his *agents* were on vacation, so he had time to decide who was next. Archibald Newbury in San Jose, California was a particular pain in his side, being a large investor and competitor over the last few years. And the she-wolf of corporate holdings, Estella Crain, the CEO of Varcity Telecom, who had voted him out on multiple occasions during negotiations. He wondered if he could make a splash with two in one night. He sent his message, even though they wouldn't get it until their return.

> *theVoyeur:* Hope you enjoyed your time off.
> *theVoyeur:* I have a job, 5.5 million.

He left it at that until they returned. With a smile on his face, he finished his scotch and asked for his favourite stewardess to join him in his private room. The women he hired on his yacht were always power and money hungry, willing to do whatever they could to gain his favour. He knew the type and preferred them. No independent women on his yacht, just pretty and simple ones to look at and join him in the hot tub when necessary.

****

On returning home from the mountains, Gustav booted up the servers again and paid his old pal the ten grand for keeping an eye on the place while he was away. They shared a drink before saying their goodbyes and Gustav sat down in front of the monitors to make sure everything was in working order. As he logged in, he saw the blinking light indicating that he had a message. He read the note from *theVoyeur* and sent a text to Andrei for him to come by when he got back.

SilentIsTheNight: Target? Details?

He waited for a reply, but not knowing where this guy was in the world, he didn't know if he would be awake right now. It was already 7 pm and he was tired from travelling and all the commotion at the airport, so he decided that it could wait and went back into the sitting room to watch the hockey game.

He fell asleep in his large threadbare armchair and awoke around 3 am. He shut off the TV and stumbled, in his half-awake state, towards the stairs to go to bed. As he passed the server room, he saw the indicator blinking, but couldn't be bothered with it and headed up the stairs. He tossed and turned for the rest of the night while continuously waking and thinking about the blinking light. By 7 am he decided it wasn't worth trying to sleep anymore and got up to make some coffee and see what the bastard had said.

With his steaming cup of coffee in hand, he sat down in front of the monitors and logged in to see the message, or messages as it seemed to be.

> *theVoyeur:* Archibald Newbury, San Jose, CA, 64, Pelland Estates.
> *theVoyeur:* Estella Crain, Vancouver, BC, 57, Varcity Telecom.
> *theVoyeur:* Same time, double shot, one clean, one dirty.

Gustav wasn't fully awake yet and was trying to understand what the messages meant. He decided to text Andrei again. "You back yet? We have a job."

It wasn't long before he got a reply. "Donuts? I'll grab some on the way. I got back late and need strong coffee."

"Donuts and coffee sound great," Gustav replied. Even though he had his coffee in his hand, it was crap compared to where he knew that Andrei went.

When Andrei arrived bearing gifts of sustenance in the form of donuts and coffee, Gustav immediately brought him into the room to show him the messages.

"Two people in one night?" Andrei asked.

"That's what it sounds like, but not just the same night. At the same time. So we would have to each go in alone."

"Shit, okay. How much time do we have to scope?"

"I still need to negotiate,"

> *SilentIsTheNight*: When? We need time.
> *theVoyeur*: 5 days enough time?
> *SilentIsTheNight*: Should be.
> *theVoyeur*: Advise when complete.
> Bonus for video.
> *theVoyeur has signed off.*

It was Monday morning and they had until Friday night, so they jumped right in to find the two individuals. With two people to research and learn their schedules, they weren't going to have much time to continue their investigation into the *man* himself.

"Let's see if we can get the surveillance done in a few nights so we can still look into him. We need to find out something because he wants more videos. This time I think we disguise ourselves in masks for a bit of protection," Gustav said.

"Yes!" Andrei agreed. "I'll look into Estella and you look into this Archibald guy."

Estella Crain had been the youngest female CEO in history—at 32 years old—and had grown her company and capital through savvy investments in other technologies. She had a seat on multiple boards and was a well-known spokeswoman for female entrepreneurs. She had short blonde hair and always pictured wearing a bland power suit.

Archibald Newbury wasn't known for much aside from his business deals. He didn't own anything in particular, but a portion of multiple companies, mostly in the private financial and technology sectors. From the photo, they could see that he was partially bald and very stocky, about 5 foot 7 and 250 lbs.

"He's got his chubby little fingers in a lot of pies," Gustav joked.

Once they had descriptions and pictures, they went into the dreamscape system and looked to identify their chips. With both targets being three hours behind them, they had to stay up late to make sure that both of them would be asleep. They found Archibald's first and decided they would scope it together for safety.

It was 2 am and they figured they would try. Surprisingly, his dreamscape was a small beach shack with a thatch roof made of palm leaves right on the water's edge. There wasn't much cover for them, but they started in the small trees and tall grasses surrounding the beach. They could see him sunbathing in an orange striped lounge chair with a table beside him where he had a cocktail with a small paper umbrella in it. They couldn't see anyone else; the beach was completely empty. It was just him and the waves lapping at the shore. They watched for quite some time from the grasses, but he didn't move, so they decided to leave and try again the next night.

They searched for Estella's dreamscape next and found it after weeding out others with a similar name. They entered her dreamscape at the very edges and found themselves in a Tuscan villa overlooking fields of sunflowers. The building was old and surrounded by gardens, with a gazebo made of marble at the back of the garden. They crept to the surrounding wall and moved to the gate to see if she was around. The sun was in a permanent state of setting and the shadows it cast was enough for them to creep just inside the garden area and into the shadows.

They made their way towards the villa and started to peer carefully into the windows, looking for a point of egress. Estella was in the kitchen cooking, so they moved to the opposite side of the villa to find an entrance. There were only two entrances, one at the front and one at the back, but they could see some open windows on the second floor. With a good layout of the outside, and a starting point for another night to enter her dreamscape, they decided to back out as it was almost 5 am for them.

Gustav let Andrei stay the night. They agreed that for this week they would have to alter their sleep schedule to stay up later, and that Andrei should bring some clothes over to spend the week. Both exhausted, they went to bed. It was a good thing that the windows were boarded up so that they could get some extra sleep after the sun rose. There was a lot of planning that needed to be done for these two targets and both dreamscapes seemed a bit difficult at the moment. The surveillance would have to continue, but before they could go in, due to the time difference, they would have time to investigate *theVoyeur* a bit more during the day.

Twenty-Seven

After a week of living with Joel, Ada had fallen into a new routine with him. They cooked together and respected each other's alone time. She felt it freeing to be out of her mother's house, though she found that she missed having her and Davey around to just say hi to. Her mother had called earlier in the week to see how she was settling in. They talked for almost an hour on the phone, which struck Ada as odd, because even at home they didn't sit down and talk for that long.

Maybe this will bring us closer together, Ada thought.

Joel was enjoying the constant girl talk. They were no longer limited to their lunch breaks for gossip, and they would sit up late some nights just talking about life, Arthur, and Ramon. Joel was still grieving and loved having Ada there to talk through his moments of pain and sadness. He would dig into Ada's love life with Ramon and how it was working out with the distance, and she would always reply that it was hard, but she hoped they could meet soon in person.

Ada took a few video calls while Joel was in the room and they laughed together for awhile before Ada excused herself to her room to continue the call in private. With the adjustment of living with Joel, she had only met Ramon in her dreamscape once the last week and a half and missed him.

It was a dreary Wednesday, around noon, when Ada received a message from Ramon. *Ping.* "Tonight, sweetie?"

She couldn't help but smile and replied, "Yes! It's been too long. Your dreamscape or mine? Thanks for brightening my day."

"Yours, of course. You have a talent for creating things so easily and I haven't acquired that yet, at least not on your level," he texted back.

"I'll build something fun before you get there," she responded.

They said their goodbyes for the present until they would meet later. Ramon was going for dinner at his parents after work, but would be home with enough time to go to bed early to meet her. Ada wished for the hours to fly by so that she could go to sleep, but she also wanted the work day to end so that she and Joel could have their special dinner tonight. They had agreed on ordering out once a week, and seeing as they hadn't done their weekly shop yet, tonight was going to be the night. Ada was paying some money to Joel to live there, but only enough to cover some bills as Arthur's estate had paid off the house, so they treated themselves, in Arthur's memory, with a takeaway.

After work, they made their way home, discussing each other's cravings for food that night. Joel won with desiring a nice curry. As they waited for their food to arrive, Ada opened a bottle of white wine and poured out two glasses.

As she handed Joel his glass, she said, "Joel, would it be okay if Ramon came to visit? I mean, would it be okay if he stayed with us while he was here?"

Joel smiled devilishly at her and said, "Of course, my sweet, he is welcome here. It will give me a good chance to suss out his character. I will only have the best sort of man for my Ada."

They clinked their glasses and Ada told him about the surprise she was going to give Ramon tonight. Without having actual dates, she liked for them to have fun in some sort of way in their dreams without it always being sitting and talking and sex.

"Do you find the sex the same as in real life or different?" Joel asked, and then continued, "I found it much the same, but sometimes quite heightened in our dreamscape. Like our senses were more alive."

Ada giggled. She really hadn't thought about it. "Well, I haven't been with Ramon in real life, so I'm not sure. But in comparison to Frederic in real life..." Here she paused and scrunched up her face as if she was thinking, "Ramon is way better!"

They laughed together as the doorbell rang, letting them know their food had arrived. As they were setting out the food, Ada asked, "What if he's not as good in real life?"

Joel looked at her as he was splitting up the naan bread. "Honey, I don't think you need to worry about that. Frederic wasn't in touch with his emotional side, and that affects how you make love and how present you are. So far, from what you've told me, Ramon is very present."

Ada topped up their wine as they sat down to eat. They toasted to Arthur and thanked him for his kindness and generosity.

After dinner was over they watched some cheesy reality TV on Joel's streaming service. He had watched it with Arthur and Ada didn't mind keeping up the tradition. Tonight's episode was about how the rich women couldn't seem to make all the food for a hosting party and regretted thinking they could do it without caterers. It was an utter disaster and Ada couldn't look away from all the mess that happened. Joel hugged her after the show was done and again told her how much he appreciated her being there. He had been doing that a lot lately, and she knew it would slow down and stop over time, but she always told him how much she appreciated being there with him too. After they said their goodnights, Ada was ready to start making her surprise for Ramon as she drifted off into her dreamscape.

****

After two and a half days of digging into *theVoyeur* during the day and surveillance of the new targets at night, Andrei was ready for a break.

"Can we go in and just watch someone for a bit, Gus? My brain is getting tired."

Gustav was feeling it too, and he still wasn't sure how to attack Archibald Newbury. He seemed to always be on the beach in his chair.

"Sure, kid, we can take a break. I'm guessing you want to check in on that Ada girl?" he said with a smirk and a wink. "It's probably been a while for you."

Andrei looked at him and blushed. "What do you mean?"

Gustav laughed at the poor guy. "I know you like her, kid. You always want to go into her dreamscape when we have a chance. And you did go in alone that one time. What is it about her that has you so interested?"

Andrei looked away and sighed. "I don't know, it's just something. She's beautiful for sure—her long brown hair, the way she dresses, her creativity with her dreamscape. It's not like the others who just create luxury homes for an alternate lifestyle. She has this little stone cottage and a grove in the middle of the trees and seems happy to just be there."

Gustav nodded silently and smiled. "You sound like a heartsick pup, but let's go see what she's up to."

They logged into their dreamscape system and accessed Ada's chip. It was 8:13 pm in Detroit, so it would be 1:13 am in the UK. She was asleep, so they entered her chip in their usual spot, just beyond the grove on the opposite side of the cottage. Ada couldn't be seen from where they were; she wasn't in the grove or by the fountain, so Andrei waved to Gustav to follow him around the grove towards the stone trail entrance that led to the cottage. They crept through the trees and shrubbery until they saw the stone pathway and stopped just to the side of it to peer into the forest where the cottage stood. There were no lights on in the windows, nor smoke coming out of the chimney.

"I wonder where she is?" Andrei sent telepathically to Gus, with a confused look on his face.

Over to their right they heard some noise coming from deeper in the forest that sounded like branches snapping loudly, so they ventured into the trees and headed along the left side of the cottage to have a look. They peered around the corner and saw Ada about 300 metres away, standing amongst the trees with her eyes closed. Then the loud snapping of branches came again and they moved their gaze up to the treetops.

"See? This is what I mean. She's incredible!" Andrei sent to his partner's mind.

Gustav had to admit that this was impressive. She was creating plankboard bridges between the trees that spanned quite a large area. All the rope barriers along the bridges were lit up with lights that led to a platform she was making to overlook the grove. On the platform were two chairs and a table with a bottle of wine on it. She added more decorative lights hanging from the branches and smiled when she looked up at her creation. Andrei and Gustav were amazed, but stayed where they were to watch from a distance.

Ada had moved from their view and was entering the grove to put some final touches on her sky-high perch, or so they assumed. They moved to the opposite side of the cottage to make sure the coast was clear before trying to get any closer to where she was now.

"Let's go to the other side of the bridges and watch from that side of the forest. I feel too exposed around the cottage area," Gustav said to Andrei's mind.

Slowly and silently, they crept to the far side of the forest, being careful not to step on any fallen branches from Ada's creation. Once they were to the far right of the cottage and bridges and closer to the grove, they hunkered down behind some bushes to see what she was doing next.

At first they couldn't see her and Andrei wanted to move closer, but Gus stopped him and cautioned him to wait where they were nicely hidden. Ada was walking around the fountain and seemed to be thinking, by the look on her face. She suddenly stopped, stared at the fountain for a moment, and closed her eyes again. The fountain changed before their eyes, adding two more tiers to its height so that it was closer to the platform she had made.

She had opened her eyes and was staring at the fountain when she then looked to the opposite side of the grove and waved her hands joyously above her head.

Andrei saw a man entering from a pathway. He'd noted the pathway before, but hadn't known what it was for. He watched as Ada ran up to this man and hugged him and they kissed. His heart sank.

Gustav could see the look on the kid's face and knew this wasn't good. "Let's go, Andrei."

But Andrei wouldn't budge. He was staring at Ada as she walked the man towards the stone pathway. Gustav decided to exit and pull Andrei out after him. He needed the kid to have a clear head for surveillance later that night.

****

"Look what I made!" Ada said as she pointed up to the treetop bridges. She led Ramon to the pulley system at the far end that would take them up there.

He stopped on the pathway, looked up, smiled, and then began to clap his hands. "This is the best surprise, but I don't think I ever mentioned that I'm afraid of heights," he said as he grimaced.

Ada stopped short. "Oh, shit, I didn't even think of that. It's okay, we don't have to go up there."

Ramon laughed uncontrollably and then kissed her on the forehead. "I was just teasing, sweetie. You should have seen your face! Now, how do we get up to our treehouse?"

She gently smacked him on the arm and they laughed. Then they climbed into a wooden box and pulled on the ropes to help them ascend. It took longer than expected, but once at the top they secured the box so they could get down safely again afterwards. As Ada did so, Ramon leaned over to her and whispered, "Maybe a slide for the way down?"

Ada turned around and smiled. "Remind me when we're done."

They walked hand in hand through the eight different bridges that she had made until they reached the platform.

"Would you care for a drink, my dear sir?" Ada jested.

They sat in the chairs looking over the four-tier fountain that had pink water flowing in it and toasted each other with a clink of their glasses.

Twenty-Eight

Andrei sat startled as he was pulled out of Ada's dreamscape so quickly.

"I'm sorry, Andrei," Gustav said softly. "It was best we left then. We need to rest up before tonight, too. Are you okay?"

The kid sat there with a dismayed look on his face and answered in a depressed tone. "Yeah ... I get it. I'll be fine."

"Hmm ... okay, kid. I'm going to have a nap before we eat and have to get back into the surveillance. Wake me up in an hour, okay?"

Seeing Andrei nod his head in assent, eyes cast down, Gustav decided to leave the room to head upstairs to bed. Andrei sat staring at the floor, then his shoes, and his eyes traced the red swoosh on the side of them. He listened carefully to the house, to Gustav's footfalls on the floor above as he got ready for his nap, to the wind howling outside the windows as it began to snow again. Absentmindedly he kept staring into nothing. His mind was swirling with the thoughts of what he had seen: Ada hugging and kissing a man.

He listened for Gustav's soft snoring before he went back into Ada's dreamscape. He knew he shouldn't go in by himself, but he needed to see more and determine who this guy was. He put on the head gear and entered the woods he'd been so rudely whipped out of. He could hear them laughing, but didn't know where they were. He looked around and then up towards the platform to see them having a drink at the table she had created. He took the binoculars from his pack to get a closer look at the guy. As he focused in on Ada, he stopped on her smile and the way the dimples in her cheeks showed when she laughed. She was so beautiful he couldn't understand why she was with this guy. He moved over to him and looked at his face, slightly tanned looking, his dark hair, his big smile with perfect teeth. It was like he was out of a magazine.

This must be a fake image he has of himself for the dreamscape, Andrei thought.

As he kept looking at the man, he had a sense of familiarity, as if he'd seen him before. He couldn't place it, but he thought he knew him. He stared a bit longer to memorize his features and tried to listen for a name as they talked. He put down the binoculars and closed his eyes to listen carefully.

"Now that I'm living away from home and have more space, it would be lovely if you could come and visit," Ada said.

"I'm all in, Ada darling. Do you know when the best time would be? I'll have to see about getting time off work," the man replied.

"Oh, Ramon, anytime, I can work it out on my end. You just check with your work and let me know," Ada said with excitement.

That was enough. Andrei now knew the man's name and could research from there. He exited the dream-scape and went into the living room to relax until he had to wake Gustav up in 25 minutes. So many things were going through his head. Who was *theVoyeur*? Who was this Ramon guy? Not to mention the surveillance for the job in three nights' time.

He and Gustav were getting nowhere in their research, just dead ends with every search they created. The two new targets were difficult for them to do on their own, each of them completing the job at the same time. And now, he had to find some spare time to search out Ada's companion, and to look into her too. She had mentioned her move and another man's name, Joel.

Thirty-seven minutes later he heard Gustav coming down the stairs. "You didn't wake me up!" he said when he got to the bottom and headed into the living room.

Andrei looked up at him. "So you got an extra 10 minutes or so, no big deal. What should we eat before we do some research? We still have another three hours before we can go in."

It was just before 11 pm when they got in the car to drive around and see what was open. The roads were empty and a bit snow covered, so they drove slowly until they reached Jimmy's Diner, open 24 hrs. They pulled into the parking lot and went in to sit down at a booth. The waitress came over to them in her blue apron and asked if they wanted some decaf coffee.

"No decaf, sweetheart, we need to stay awake. Two regular coffees and two burgers with fries," Gustav said.

They ate in silence. Gustav could tell the kid was still torn up about that girl, but he would save the pep talk for later. Pie was ordered afterwards with more coffee to drag out the time. He didn't want to do more research right now. They'd been going at it hard for the last couple of days and needed some more time away from the monitors.

It was almost 1 am when they arrived back at Gustav's place, with the snow getting worse outside and the roads icier. They sat in front of the computers and checked the time. It was 10:03 pm on the west coast.

"Okay, Andrei, we have to still be vigilant tonight to check their routines. I know you're feeling hurt by what you saw today with that girl, but you need to shake it off. We have a lot of money on the line to do these jobs right and we're going in alone on Friday."

He really needed Andrei to be present for this job. Any mistake could ruin the whole thing. As a rule, the kid was good at his work and Gustav relied on him.

"I get it, Gus. I'm here. And her name is Ada," Andrei replied with a slight squint in his eye. "Let's focus and see if either of the targets are asleep already."

Gus agreed with him and they checked both Archibald's and Estella's chips. He watched Andrei and noticed that the depressed schoolboy look had faded and he appeared focused. He had to give it to the kid. He knew how to brush it off, even if only for the time being.

"Estella is asleep already, I guess she wanted her beauty sleep," Andrei said.

"Right, let's check her out first and see what she's up to tonight," Gus replied.

They entered as they had the night before into the gardens by the back door where there was plenty of shadow from the setting sun. The previous times when they'd been in her dreamscape surveilling she had been cooking, or reading in the garden at the front, but tonight they couldn't see her anywhere. They peered in the windows, but she didn't appear to be on the main floor. The previous night they'd had the chance to quickly get a floorplan of the inside of the villa while she was reading in the garden, so they knew where to look for her. Gustav told Andrei to enter the house, and as he did so they noticed another door just beside the back door they were entering.

"I didn't see this yesterday," he said, and Andrei nodded in agreement. Gustav opened the door slowly so as not to make a sound and found a dark stairway leading down.

"Wine cellar?" he questioned.

He took out his flashlight and started down the stairs as Andrei followed and closed the door behind them.

As the flashlights shone around the small dark room, they could see walls lined with bottles.

"This might be a good place to enter next time," Andrei suggested, and Gustav agreed.

They stayed in the wine cellar to listen to the sounds of the villa. They could hear some noise, and knowing she wasn't on the main floor, it had to be coming from upstairs.

"Okay, so she's not consistent in what she does every night," Gustav said. "She's been in three different places on three different nights. Let's see where she is tomorrow and go from there. We'll come in a bit later tomorrow and see if she settles into one spot."

They stayed a while longer to see if she would settle, but she was still moving around a lot. Not hearing any voices, they knew she wasn't with anyone, and assumed she was alone like the other nights.

By the time they exited Estella's dreamscape it was 2:48 am for them, so they checked Archibald's chip and saw that he was sleeping. Again they entered to the rear of the beach where they could hide in the tall grasses that were encroaching on the sand. There he was, as still as a statue again, sitting in his orange striped beach chair with a drink beside him.

"This guy is just enjoying his retirement early," Gustav said to Andrei. "Just watching the water and drinking the night away."

Only once had they seen him get up to stretch his legs, but he was as still as ever right now, so they crept to the back of his shack for a better angle. They still hadn't decided who was going to kill whom, but Archibald seemed like an easier target, aside from the vast open space. They stayed watching and waiting for him to do something, but the only changes were the colours of the paper umbrellas in his drinks.

It was almost 5 am when they exited Archibald's dreamscape and decided to head to bed, weary, as they had been over the last few days. Andrei wasn't one to nap, but he thought tomorrow he might have to. They shared a quick beer together before heading up to bed and starting it all again when they arose.

Before they parted ways at the top of the stairs, Gustav turned to Andrei and said, "Thanks for convincing me to have the vacation. I don't think I would have been up for this if we hadn't had a break."

Andrei smiled. "I wish I was still on the beach drinking my own fruity drinks instead of just watching another guy do it," he said, and laughed before he headed to his room.

Twenty-Nine

The next day was much the same as the rest of the week had been for Gustav and Andrei—sleeping until early afternoon, researching *theVoyeur* and coming up empty, and prepping for the last night of surveillance on the two targets. That was the plan, at least. However, during the research portion of the late afternoon, Andrei had an idea about how they were looking for information.

"Why are we looking at his past dealings? We know he's a psycho, that much is clear, but we can't find any proof or links to who he is in real life," Andrei said.

"You're not telling me anything I don't already know, kid," Gustav replied in a frustrated tone.

"I know, I know, but hear me out," Andrei said. "Why don't we look at what he's doing now? You never wanted to know why names were given to us, but why don't we look into the names and see what they tell us? Maybe it will bring us closer to him, if he has some sort of link to them to want them dead."

Gustav stared at Andrei for a moment, and then a moment longer. "Shit, kid! Okay, let's plan for all that next week, after this job is done. I don't want any distractions before this double hit tomorrow."

They both agreed to put it off, and started going over the blueprints they had created for both Archibald's and Estella's dreamscapes to work out the plans of attack.

"Masks this time, so we aren't on video. I don't want to give that fucker anything more with my face in it. Do you know if Charmaine is in place in San Jose?" Gustav asked.

Andrei nodded. "She's all ready to go. *He* wanted one dirty, so she'll stage the place to look like some rich dude got robbed and murdered. Happens all the time, right?"

Gustav glanced at him sideways. "Not as often as you seem to think."

They worked out who was going to go where, with Gustav taking Archibald because of the wide open spaces. Gustav knew how to be stealthy in order to sneak up behind him, while Andrei would take Estella, entering through the wine cellar.

With a plan more or less sorted out for the next night and only one night left of surveillance, Gustav went off to have his nap around 7 pm.

"Be sure to wake me no later than 8:15, and don't forget this time. I don't know how you can stay awake the whole day and into the night. Hmph, youth," Gustav muttered as he headed up the stairs.

Andrei sat in the living room for a few minutes, listening for Gustav to fall asleep and start his snoring. Once he heard the soft growls of the old man, he went back to the monitors. He set the alarm on his watch for 8 pm so he wouldn't stay too long spying on Ada, but he had to see if she was active in her chip, and she was. It would be just after 12 am for her, so he put on his head gear and entered her dreamscape at the edge of the grove.

At first he looked around and couldn't see her anywhere, so he headed around the tree line towards where he knew her cottage was. He saw smoke coming from the chimney and lights on in the windows, so he figured she was inside and hoped that Ramon guy wasn't with her. He crept through the trees, slowly approaching the cottage, stopped fifty metres or so from the front, and took out his binoculars. He peered through the lenses to get a better look at the windows and watch for any movement like Gustav had taught him, but didn't see any movement. He decided to scan the forest area to see if she was around and not actually in the cottage, but he couldn't find her anywhere. Putting the binoculars away in his pack, he moved closer to the porch that spread across the front of the stone facade.

He listened for music playing or any sort of noise, but could hear nothing. Wanting to see her, desperately, he climbed the steps and crouched beneath one of the windows. Again, he listened intently for any sounds but heard nothing. He moved to the side of the window so that he could peer in from the edge. The cottage seemed empty. Just a kitchen and stairway were visible from where he was standing; the fireplace must have been on the other wall that he couldn't see, he thought. He crouched down again, moved to the other side of the window, and stood up to glance inside. There he saw her —sitting on an oversized plush red chair, reading a book. He couldn't look away, and stood outside her window watching her sit there in peace, alone.

****

Ada was reading, or rereading, one of her favourite books, *Great Expectations* by Charles Dickens. An old read, but still a classic in her eyes. She knew she wouldn't be seeing Ramon that night and was still on a high from the previous night, so she enjoyed the peace and quiet of her book and the crackling fire. She often wondered if people thought she was odd because she enjoyed solitude, but then remembered that it didn't matter what other people thought. She loved being her own person and doing the things that she enjoyed despite others. As she was about to end volume one, she started to get that weird sensation she had felt before in her dreamscape. Inside the cottage she felt safe, but she wouldn't hear any twigs snapping to alert her to anyone.

Not even having reached chapter two of volume two, Ada couldn't shake the feeling that she wasn't alone. She never felt this uneasiness when it was Ramon who was entering her dreamscape, or most of the time when she was alone, so she lowered the book and slowly glanced around the room. In her peripheral vision she saw a slight movement to her left and quickly turned her head in time to see the shocked face of a man staring in her window. They both paused for a moment. Then Ada stood up quickly, grabbed a chunk of wood that was yet to be thrown in the fire, and rushed towards the door.

The face was gone from the window and she opened the door quickly to startle him if he was still on the porch. Brandishing the chunk of wood in the air, ready to strike, she looked from side to side and couldn't see anyone. She then heard the snapping of fallen branches and bushes rustling. Looking out towards the grove, she saw the man fleeing from the cottage and then disappearing entirely.

With her heart rate accelerating, she woke herself up and sat breathing heavily in her bed. She didn't want to wake Joel, and she knew that Ramon was out with friends, so she didn't want to bother him either, at least not right then. She took some deep breaths to calm herself, picked up her headphones, and put on some piano jazz music to calm herself further. She also grabbed her phone and made a note of everything that she remembered about the face she'd seen. Shaggy brown hair about ear length, straight pointed nose, eyes ... brown? She wasn't sure. Small thin lips, black sweater, long green pants, tall, slim build.

****

Andrei exited Ada's dreamscape in a panic. He had never been seen before and realized he'd been careless. Even in his panic, he was also quite impressed by her grabbing that log by the fire and trying to chase him away with it. He closed down her profile and went back into the living room, where his watch alarm went off about ten minutes later. He went upstairs to wake Gustav up and knocked loudly on the old man's door.

"Huh, yeah ... yeah, I'm up," he heard Gus say behind the door.

Going back downstairs, he headed right for the kitchen to grab a beer from the fridge to calm his nerves. Seeing it was empty, he went for the half-full vodka bottle on the counter instead. He took a swig right from the bottle and tasted the bitterness of it, then listened to see if Gus was coming downstairs before he took a second swig.

Thirty

Ada didn't get much sleep for the rest of the night. She was glad that it was Friday, so she just had to make it through that day. She needed to talk to Joel and decided to tell him as they were having breakfast. She sat down at the table and he put a steaming cup of tea in front of her before going back to the skillet with the eggs in it.

"It's Friday, sweetie! Why are you looking so glum? Did something happen with Ramon last night?" he asked as he looked at her staring into her mug of tea, oblivious of anything around her.

Ada looked up at him and started to tell him about what had happened.

"No, nothing with Ramon, we didn't meet up last night. I was enjoying some relaxing time in my dreamscape, and then I saw a man staring at me through the window of my cottage."

Joel almost dropped the skillet as he was dishing out the eggs onto the plates.

"What do you mean a man was staring at you? Are you sure? Could you have imagined it?"

Ada got up to take the plates from him and placed them on the table. "It was definitely a man, a man I haven't seen before. I wrote down his description when I woke up. I didn't get much sleep after that. I know it's possible for people to come into your dreamscape because Ramon wandered in somehow, but this guy ... he was just watching me! It really creeped me out."

Joel waited for her to continue because he could tell that she was still thinking about things.

"I was sitting there just fine, and then I got this bad feeling and a chill ran down my back. I've felt it before, but it was never when Ramon entered my dreamscape. Maybe, all those times I felt it and heard a twig snap or a bush rustle in the forest, this guy was watching me."

Joel gave her a long hug and reminded her that they had to get ready for work, so they cleared the dishes away and went upstairs.

On the way to work Joel finally spoke. "I have a few ideas, and don't get mad at me; I understand you were freaked out by this, but what if it was just someone who wandered in? Could be. Or, it could be someone who's been watching you and you caught them. Either way, I think you should talk to DCI Karim. I can give him a call to meet us this evening if he's free."

"Why DCI Karim? He doesn't police people's dreamscapes, Joel."

Joel's face turned serious as they stopped at a crosswalk and he turned to her. "Because if someone can just come into your dreamscape and watch you like that, then it's very possible that someone wandered in and murdered Arthur, and DCI Karim needs to know that."

The work day moved slowly for Ada, with her lack of sleep and her thoughts consuming her. She messaged Ramon to tell him what had happened and that she and Joel were going to try and meet the detective that night. By noon, she heard back from him as he was getting ready for work. "Ada, darling, I'm so sorry I wasn't there with you last night. I think it's a good idea for you guys to let the detective know, and please call me afterwards. For the time being, can I suggest that you only go into your chip if we're to meet up?"

Ada smiled at his concern and agreed. She didn't want to be alone in there. "But because of the time difference, I'm alone in there for a few hours before you arrive," she sent back to him.

Ping, a message came right back. "Right, so we'll have to figure something out. Maybe setting an alarm to wake up and then enter the chip partway through the night, or we don't meet for a while and you stay out of your chip. I don't like these options, but it's all I have right now. I'm going to see when I can get time off to come over there."

Ada didn't like the options either, but did like the last statement. "Please see if you can come soon! I'll try to think of other options, too," she sent back to him.

A little past 2 pm Joel came flying into her office. "I have an idea! And DCI Karim will meet us at home at 5:30 pm this evening."

"Okay, what's your idea?" she asked.

"Have you logged into your chip before to download anything?"

Ada knew where he was going with this. "I've been in a few times, but I like this idea. Let's get this guy's face from my chip."

Joel stood just behind Ada's shoulder while she logged into her chip and flipped through the reel of the previous night.

"There!" she exclaimed when she saw him in the window.

They took a screenshot of that image and sent it to print.

"You said you chased him, so keep going and see if there are any more shots," Joel said.

As they watched the next few moments, she heard Joel gasp and breathe more heavily as he saw the event unfold.

"You're out of your mind for chasing him, sweetie, but wow, you looked like you meant business with that log in your hand," he said.

They took a few shots of the man running away through the forest, and then decided to download the whole reel of last night onto her phone to show the detective.

With the printouts in hand, Ada kept staring at the man's face in the window. She had been right in her description: brown shaggy hair, thin lips, and long straight nose. Deciding that she couldn't be distracted anymore, she shoved the papers into her carryall and got back to work. Most of the office staff were packed up and ready to leave at 4:45, as was the case every Friday. Basically no work was done after 4:30. Joel had on his jacket and carryall and sat in one of Ada's chairs while he waited for her to get ready to leave.

"You know, I think you're the only one, including management, who doesn't want to leave early on a Friday," he said to her and laughed.

"I just hate leaving things incomplete for Monday and, with my mind all over the place today, I didn't get much done," she said. "There, all done." She closed her laptop and put it in her bag. "Let's go," she told Joel as she put on her jacket.

As they rounded the corner of their street, they saw that DCI Amir Karim had beat them there. He was leaning on his car having a cigarette and spotted them coming up the street. He dropped his smoke and ground it out with his boot as he crossed the street to meet them at the door.

"Hi Joel, Ada, nice to see you again. I know I'm early, I hope that's okay," he said to them.

Joel shook his outstretched hand and said, "Of course, come in and we'll sit down to chat. Would you like tea?"

"Thank you, that would be nice," DCI Karim answered. With the tea having been served all around, they took their seats in the living room, Joel and Ada on the sofa facing DCI Karim on the opposite side in a reading chair.

"So," DCI Karim began, "what did you want to share with me?"

Ada took a deep breath and started to describe the events of the previous night in her dreamscape. She showed him the printouts from the reel and then loaded the video on her phone and let him watch it.

DCI Karim watched the video four times as he sat there silently.

Joel finally spoke up. "We were thinking that if someone could be in Ada's dreamscape, then maybe this is proof that someone could have come into Arthur's to murder him."

DCI Karim looked up from the video and handed the phone back to Ada. "Can you email that to me? My address is on the bottom of my card. I'll look into this and see what I can find out. Have you ever seen anyone else in your dreamscape before, Ada?"

She looked at Joel and then at the detective. "Yes, actually. I met my now boyfriend that way. He wandered into my dreamscape a couple of months ago through a pathway in the forest. I've followed the pathway as well to get to his dreamscape, it's like they're connected. But no one else other than him."

DCI Karim took notes and asked for her boyfriend's details so that he could talk with him as well.

"I've felt watched before, and heard twigs snap in the forest of my dreamscape, but never saw anyone," Ada said. "You can confirm with Ramon, because he was watched early on as well. He has a lake in his dreamscape and saw two people in a canoe on the water one time."

Having concluded the interview with them, DCI Karim got up to leave and assured them he would look into the matter. "Thank you, this may be a missing piece that we need," he said as he shook their hands.

Joel closed the front door and Ada sat down on the stairs. "I hope that helps him, but he seemed unsure about what to make of it," she said.

"Let's give him some time and follow up with him in a week to see what he has to say. How about we see if Kira is available to come for dinner and have some fun tonight to get your mind off this?" Joel offered.

"Yes, I'll give her a quick call and ask her to come over and then I have to call Ramon to update him on what happened," she said.

Half an hour later, Ada came back into the living room. "Kira will be here in twenty minutes, and Ramon didn't answer. He must be in a meeting," she said as Joel poured her a glass of wine.

Ping! Came the tone of a message from Ramon. "Speak of the devil," she said as she opened the message.

"Just popped to the bathroom from a client lunch meeting. I hope it all went well, and if it's ok with you, I will be arriving on Monday ;) Meet me at the train station at 2:25 pm?"

Ada couldn't believe it. "He's coming to visit on Monday!"

Joel smiled and put his arms around her. "See, everything is working out. Now I get to see if he's worthy of you!"

Thirty-One

The day had come for Gustav and Andrei. It was Friday and they frantically made their last minute plans for the two jobs they had to do that night. Gustav was still nervous about Andrei completing the job on his own. He was a smart kid, but didn't always use all of his brain. They had confirmed the plan of Gustav targeting Archibald and Andrei going after Estella. They needed to be in and completed the job in about the same amount of time so that to the authorities the deaths would have taken place at a similar time and couldn't be linked. Charmaine was ready and had been watching Archibald's place the past two days. She would stage a crime scene and rob what she could from him. She knew that he set his alarm at night and had acquired a decoding device to source the password for a silent entry once he was asleep.

The plan was to stay up until 4 am so that it would be 1 am for the targets, who should be asleep by that time. From their surveillance all week, it didn't appear that these two were very social. When they looked at their credit card details, neither one had dinners or hotels on a regular basis to suggest an active social life. Andrei was going to take a rope and a knife with him into the dreamscape. Each item depended on him being silent and getting close.

Now they waited. Gustav went over the plans for Andrei's attack four times before the kid spoke up. "I've got it! I know what I'm doing, Gus. I'm going to stay in the wine cellar until I know where she is by listening to her move about. Once I know she's not on the main floor of the villa, then I'll enter the kitchen area to see if I can hear her upstairs or see her through the windows if she's outside. I've done this with you before, just trust me," he sighed at the end.

"I know you've done it before, kid, but I've always been there with you, and it's easier with two sets of eyes. I just worry about you. Let's get some rest, it's going to be a late one tonight."

Gustav headed upstairs to have a nap and Andrei stayed in the living room watching TV. He hadn't had time to go back and delete the video from Ada's chip. He'd been so stunned that it slipped his mind completely and then Gus woke up and they started work all over again. Once he heard the gentle grumbling snores from upstairs, he went back to hack the database for access to Ada's chip.

He found the folders and looked for the previous night's date. When he clicked on the folder to open it, it was blank. She must have downloaded the file already, shit! he thought. He knew he shouldn't have looked, because now he was agitated and upset that he had let this slip. He had to stay focused for that night, but he couldn't help beat himself up for his mistake. He wondered what she would be doing with the file. Would she take it to the police? No, it was just a dream. Maybe she'd deleted it. So many thoughts were swirling through his head, so he decided to head out into the snow for a walk to clear his mind.

At 1 am they both sat down at the monitors again in the hopes that the two targets went to bed early on a Friday night. They had the chips of both targets up on the screens to watch when they were accessed, but couldn't see anything yet. Andrei had bought some coffee and doughnuts while he was out, not the good stuff because of the late hour, but something strong enough to keep them going on caffeine and sugar.

"Why don't you nap?" Gustav asked him.

"I've never been one to nap. Just keep going on adrenaline for jobs. Maybe when I get to be your age, I'll need one," he laughed.

It was almost two in the morning when they saw that Archibald had accessed his chip. "One down and one to go," Gustav said.

Throughout the week, both the targets had accessed their chips by this time, so they decided to check Estella's credit cards for recent transactions. She had made a charge for $263.78 on her card for a swanky restaurant called Le Petit Chef that had expanded from France a few years back.

"Of course she goes out tonight of all nights," Andrei said.

It was after 3 am when they finally saw Estella access her chip, so they decided to wait a bit longer to make sure that she was fully in her slumber.

"Remember to create a watch with a timer on it when you enter her dreamscape. Set it for thirty minutes, and I'll do the same, then we should have the jobs completed at roughly the same time. We have twenty-five minutes to make our approaches and five minutes to do the deed," Gustav instructed.

"Got it," Andrei replied.

At 3:45 am they decided to put their headgear on and enter the chips, which meant that they would be done around 4:15 in the morning.

"Good luck, kid," Gustav said.

"You too, Gus," he replied, and they pressed the button on their respective computers to enter the dreamscapes.

Gustav hunkered down in the tall grasses about a hundred metres from where Archibald was sitting in his orange striped beach chair, sipping a pink drink with a blue paper umbrella in it. He knew he would be quick, so he settled where he was as time ticked away on his watch.

Andrei entered Estella's dreamscape in the wine cellar, which was pitch black and damp. He turned on his flashlight for a moment to orient himself to the room and where the staircase was to lead him up to the kitchen.

He could hear her on the main floor moving around, sounding like she was in the kitchen area.

Shit, he thought, she needs to move away from here.

He stayed in the corner silently listening to her when he heard her speaking. He tried to listen for a second voice but couldn't hear anyone, and thought maybe she was talking or singing to herself. He wondered how he would alert Gustav to anything if he couldn't do this job because of a second person being there. Instead of thinking of failure, he stayed put and listened some more.

Thirteen minutes had passed on Andrei's watch and Estella was still in the kitchen moving around. He started to think of alternates to the plan like a blitz attack, storming out of the cellar door and attacking her. He knew Gustav wouldn't like that, but it would get the job done. Just as he was contemplating another scenario, the light to the cellar staircase came on and he panicked. He tried to squeeze himself in between two of the wine racks off to one corner of the room so that he couldn't be seen as she came down the stairs.

Estella was humming to herself as she turned on the second light for the cellar room. If she turned around, she would see him. His heart was pounding in his chest and he tried to keep his breathing smooth so as not to give himself away. She was perusing the racks looking for a certain bottle and getting closer to where Andrei was trying to hide. He had his mask on to cover his face, but had nowhere else to go. As he shifted slightly against the rack, his bag dropped and thumped onto the floor.

Estella turned around quickly, startled, and spotted Andrei in the corner. He had to act fast. His rope and knife were in the bag on the floor and he could see that she was about to make a run for the stairs. He grabbed what was closest to him, a bottle of wine, and threw it at her. The bottle hit her on the right shoulder and caught her off-guard, which gave him enough time to lunge at her. He pushed her against the racks, which shook enough to have a few bottles break at his feet.

He reached for her throat to strangle her, but she was tough and kept trying to get out of his grasp. She kneed him in the groin, but that only loosened his grip on her neck as he still had his full body pressed against her from the waist down. He doubled over, but stayed applying pressure so that she couldn't get away. He saw a broken bottle at his feet and grabbed for it quickly because he could feel her moving loose. With one swift action, he stabbed her in the chest with the broken bottle and her eyes went wide as she slumped to the floor.

He had to tell Gustav to do his target sooner, so he quickly exited Estella's dreamscape and entered Archibald's. He slowly moved closer to Gustav and sent him a message telepathically that he was there. Startled and alarmed, Gustav knew it was bad news.

"You have to do it now, Gus. I had a complication and had to go early," Andrei sent him.

Son of a bitch, Gustav thought. He moved slowly through the sand and, as he got closer to Archibald, he quickened his pace while treading lightly. Laying a hand on either side of Archibald's head, he broke his neck with one swift motion.

"Out!" Gustav said and they exited the dreamscape. "What the hell happened?" he demanded.

Andrei recalled the full two minutes of what had happened. "It was all so fast. I had to make a decision before she had time to exit the dreamscape on her own from being frightened. Either way she'll be dead in her sleep, and they just won't know how."

Gustav paced the room. He hated it when things didn't go as planned, but he had to admit, the kid was right. If she had exited and startled herself awake, that would have been worse.

"Okay, they were pretty close in time, a few minutes apart. Text Charmaine and give her the go-ahead to work Archie's place over and I'll go in to delete the scenes."

Gustav went into Archibald's dreamscape to download and delete the scene of his murder. He saved it in an encrypted file and then moved onto Estella's dreamscape to watch what had happened and then download and delete it. He opened the files for the night. They were empty. His heart started to beat faster and he could feel the warmth of anger and confusion flood over him.

"Andrei!" he yelled for the kid to get back in the room.

Andrei entered the room again, looking confused as to why he was being called for so aggressively.

"Are you sure she was dead when you exited?" Gustav asked.

"What? Of course she was, I stabbed her in the heart with a broken bottle and she fell to the floor," Andrei answered.

"Just because she was on the floor doesn't mean she was dead! The file isn't here, Andrei! She's already down-loaded it!"

Thirty-Two

DCI Karim was enjoying his Saturday off. It was rare that he had a weekend all to himself without having to follow up on any casework. After a day of errands and a nice long hike in the woods, he sat down to watch the news. He almost dropped his mug of tea when he read the news scrolling across the bottom of the screen: *Breaking News: Estella Crain, CEO of Varcity Telecom in Vancouver, BC alleges an attempted murder on her life while in her dreamscape.*

He waited for the story to come back around after all the other bits of news had scrolled across the bottom in case he had read it wrong, but there it was again. *"Attempted murder... dreamscape."* He couldn't believe it. He grabbed his tablet and looked up the story online. There were many reports, mostly in Canada and the United States, mentioning the story and quoting from "inside sources" about what had happened. Crain had been in her dreamscape when she was attacked in her wine cellar and left for dead. However, she wasn't and had exited her dreamscape to download the dream.

This is it! he thought. He finally had something more concrete to link his case to.

On his way to the department, he called Detective Anderson.

"DCI Karim, how can I help you on this glorious Saturday?" Troy Anderson said.

"Heya, Troy, I'm guessing you've seen the news about that CEO woman in Canada that says she was attacked in her dreamscape?"

"Yes, sir, my friend Amir, I'm preparing documents at this very moment to link the Adebayo murders to it. I'm guessing you're going to do the same with the Millstone case?" Anderson asked.

"I sure am! I'm still not sure if the chief will go for it, but I'm going to try. I'll see about sending my files to you as well, if you can do the same? Then we'll have more evidence," Karim said.

"Okay, I'll try, but I know my superiors don't want to be opening closed files. This is my last chance at it, and if they don't see any connection, then I'm out of it," Anderson said.

"I understand, it's a long shot, but we have to try," Karim replied before they said their goodbyes.

Karim headed up to the file room to grab the case folder as it had been stored away after Deputy Chief Inspector Moore deemed it closed. This was it, his last chance to figure it all out. It was already dark outside by the time he reached the department, but he couldn't wait until the next day to get to work. His mind was abuzz with information and links that he had to start writing down, so he took out his notepad and started with the names he knew of. *Arthur Millstone, Brian and Amara Adebayo, Estella Crain.* Then he remembered the video that Joel's friend had sent him earlier that week of the creepy guy staring at her through a window in her dreamscape. He looked up her name and added *Ada Carpenter* to the list.

The next thing he did was search for the detectives who were handling the case in Canada so that he could get in contact with them for more accurate information on the details. With Ada's video, maybe they could compare notes. He called the Vancouver Police Department and found out that the two detectives on Ms. Crain's case were Detective Julia Schmidt and Detective Chris Hill. He asked for their numbers and, knowing that they would be in the thick of it at the moment, also asked for an email address for each of them so he could send them the video if needed. He tried both of their mobile numbers and left a message for each of them explaining who he was and a bit about the case he had. He also mentioned the video he'd received from another source.

Knowing they wouldn't get back to him right away, he opened a search in the internal database for any deaths that had happened while a person was sleeping. Aside from some elderly people, he couldn't find anything unusual. He texted Detective Anderson to carry out the same search to see if anything came up for him. Without further connections and details he knew he couldn't complete his report that night, so he turned off the desk lamp, shut down his computer, and put on his jacket to leave.

As he was leaving the building he sent one last text to Sandy. "How do you feel about coming in on a Sunday, Wilhelm?" He wasn't even sure anyone would get back to him by then, but he'd go in and take another look at the case anyway.

****

Joel had been going on about the news out of Vancouver all day, and Ada was getting tired of hearing about it. She was caught up with Ramon arriving in a couple of days and making sure everything was going to go smoothly when he arrived. She opened a beer for Joel and one for herself, then walked into his path of pacing the kitchen to hand it to him.

"Let's call DCI Karim on Monday," she said reassuringly. "Let him have the weekend to look into things and then we can ask if he has any news. It's too soon right now, and I'm sure he'll reach out to you as well. He has my video and if they need it they'll use it."

Joel took the beer from her and put it on the marble counter. He stared at her with hope and worry in his big green eyes. "You're right, Ada. Let's watch a movie to get my mind off this for today. And we have to do a shop tomorrow for food. Do you know what Ramon likes to eat?"

"We'll figure it out tomorrow. Right now, let's sit down and try to relax or you won't sleep tonight," she replied.

They opted for a romcom to lighten the mood and then another after that, as they weren't prepared for sleeping yet with all the excitement of the day. Joel eventually fell asleep on the sofa during the second movie, and Ada put the faux fur throw over him and turned off the lights and television before heading upstairs to bed. She messaged Ramon to meet her in her dreamscape that night so that she could fill him in, although he likely already knew about the news, seeing as he lived in Canada. He had said he would be busy prepping at work all day Saturday for his vacation time and wanted to make sure that all his cases were taken care of.

Ping! She received a message back from him. "I know why you want to meet, and of course we can. I just got home and am exhausted, so I'll head to bed soon. Can you stay awake another hour or so? I don't want you in there on your own."

She smiled at his concern, and got even more excited at the thought of finally meeting in person. She replied, "Yes, we stayed up late and I can wait another hour. See you soon xo."

She lay in her queen-sized bed, all curled up under the down-filled duvet, imagining Ramon beside her. Only two more sleeps until he would be here and sleeping next to her. She smiled to herself and laid her hand on the opposite side of the bed where he would be, and closed her eyes for a few moments. Before she knew it, she was in her dreamscape inside her cottage on her oversized red chair.

"Dammit!" She knew she had fallen asleep and Ramon wouldn't be here for a while yet. She stood up and looked around her cottage for a weapon to protect herself, but remembered that she could create anything that she wanted, so she imagined a guard dog. A large German shepherd appeared and sat down by her side.

"You will be named Luna, and you must alert me to anyone coming, with a growl or a bark."

Then she created a knife in a holster that wrapped around her thigh. She was ready, so she and Luna went back over to the fire to wait for Ramon.

After a while, Luna began to growl in a deep tone, so Ada stood up and went to the window to peer out from the side. Luna continued her low growl until she heard footsteps on the front deck and gave a few loud barks that startled Ada. She looked towards the door area of the deck and saw Ramon freeze where he was.

"He's okay, Luna. Shhh, Ramon is a good guy," she said to the dog while she opened the door.

"Is it safe to come in?" Ramon asked her.

"Yes, she's okay, her name is Luna. Just come in slowly so she can get to know you. I needed to do something, I fell asleep too early."

Ramon approached the door slowly and held out his hand to Luna for her to smell him. After the introductions were done, Luna went back over to the fire to lie down.

"I see you prepared with more than just a new pet," he said as he looked at the knife attached to her thigh.

Ada laughed. "A girl's gotta do what a girl's gotta do," she said and then removed the holster from her leg. "I have you here now, so I'm good. Where are your weapons, may I ask?"

Ramon laughed and said he didn't have any, but he would use her as a shield if he needed to, and they both laughed until they relaxed on the sofa to talk about the news.

Thirty-Three

Andrei and Gustav had been watching the news all day on Saturday, flipping from one channel to the next and looking at the different articles online. So far not much had been said about leads that the detectives had, but they knew it wouldn't be long before more information became available.

Charmaine had left San Jose early that morning after mutilating Archibald's body. Gustav had given her the directive immediately after his kill to make it look bad so that the two crimes wouldn't be connected. She had cut demonic symbols into his chest and removed his fingers, leaving a stump with thumbs only on both hands. She also cut off his remaining hair and sprinkled it around the bed sheets. After that was done she smashed every mirror and picture in the house and stole what she could that looked to have value. She was wearing a bio suit to make sure her DNA wasn't going to be found anywhere in the house, but her last act was to make the scene even more gruesome. She took the needle out of her case and started to drain Archibald's body of two pints of blood. Once she had that, she walked around the house and splashed the blood on the walls in small quantities, dribbling the last little bit up the stairs. None of it would make sense to a crime scene investigator, aside from someone having a sick mind.

Gustav could see the indicator blinking on the computers that they had a message from *theVoyeur* and he knew it wasn't going to be good news. *TheVoyeur* would have been checking for the news of the two deaths he had paid for, and would have mainly seen the breaking news around the world about a woman who was almost killed in her dreamscape. Gustav would have to answer him soon, but he wasn't ready for it yet. He knew that they had to find a way out of this, and soon.

He asked Andrei again, for what felt like the hundredth time, "You're positive that you had your mask on?"

Andrei sighed loudly. "Yes! I had my mask on, I'm 1000% sure that I did."

"Okay, then I don't see how they can link it back to you ... or me," Gustav replied.

Andrei had had enough of the news and decided to be more productive. He went to the computers and saw the blinking light, but didn't want to see the messages either, so he accessed the dark web and stared at the screen, hoping that inspiration would come to him. He needed a way to prove himself, and he figured the only way to do that was to find something on *theVoyeur* for their own protection. He spun around in his chair, staring at the ceiling and the wall stains around the windows that seemed to get larger every winter from leaks in the brickwork and frame. Facing the computer again and placing his hands on the keyboard, he started to type in some names: Brian Adebayo; Amara Adebayo; Flora Esposito; Carmine Esposito; Arthur Millstone; Estella Crain; Archibald Newbury. These were all their targets from *theVoyeur*. Gustav had a rule about not looking into why the man wanted these people dead, but Andrei thought it was about time to do so.

From his first attempt at listing all the names, he couldn't find anything that included them all. Maybe they're just random people who've wronged him, he thought. Not seeing an immediate connection, he left the computers to see if Gustav wanted anything to eat. He knew he had to think about this some more, but how he was going to do it was the difficult part.

"I'm going to grab some pizza, do you want the usual, Gus?" he asked as he was putting on his brown leather jacket and gloves.

"Sounds good, kid, get some cheesy sticks this time, too. Bad news makes me want more food."

Andrei agreed, got the keys to the beat up Volvo, and headed out to get the food for them. While he drove, he had the names of the people they had killed going through his head. He was wondering if searching by city would make a difference, or just one or two people at a time. Doubt started to circle into his thoughts These people were worldwide; how could they have something in common? Realizing he'd already missed one stop sign, he decided to focus on the drive until he was back at the house; he was thankful for it being an abandoned neighbourhood so that no one saw him or was in danger of his driving.

After they finished eating, Gustav decided to check the messages from *theVoyeur*. "Are you ready for this, kid?"

Andrei wasn't sure what to expect, but sat down with him to see how much shit they were in. They saw twelve messages spanning the time period from around 5 am until the latest one around fifty minutes ago. They had both gone to bed to try and sleep for a bit right after it had happened, but in their own panic, neither one was able to, and just sat, waiting for the news to break.

> *theVoyeur:* No confirmation of a job well done tonight, gentlemen?
> *theVoyeur:* Where is my confirmation?
> *theVoyeur:* Hellllooooo? Did all go as planned?
> *theVoyeur:* YOU IDIOTS!!!!!!

They could tell when he had found out the news about Estella, but they didn't expect these messages and the seemingly chaotic frame of mind he was in.

> *theVoyeur:* You will not be paid for your failure! She didn't die! FOOLS!!!
> *theVoyeur:* I'll pay you for Archibald, dear fellows, his death was exceedingly enjoyable

to hear about, or just the scene of it. Bravo.
theVoyeur: I know you're frightened right now,
and rightly so, but we can work this out.
Perhaps a little more incentive?
theVoyeur: Still not answering me!
You cannot make me disappear!!
I know things, remember?!
theVoyeur: I'll send that Arthur video to the
police, anonymously.
theVoyeur: Answer me, dammit!
Kill her today and all will be forgiven.
theVoyeur: I was upset, I wouldn't send the
video of you. Let's figure this out together,
just answer me.
theVoyeur: Do another job for free in the next
three days and all will be forgiven.
I can protect you.

Gustav and Andrei read all the messages and then sat
back and looked at each other in disbelief. They were
speechless. They'd known he was a psycho, but now he
was also a complete lunatic. Gustav started typing.

> *SilentIsTheNight:* We thought she was dead,
> she made it seem so. We didn't plan for this
> to happen. We were as shocked as you are.

They could see he wasn't online at the moment, so
they waited to see if he would respond. They sat at the

computers for nearly half an hour and then decided to see what new information there was about Estella Crain's story. Every half hour Gustav looked for the blinking light on the computer to indicate that *he* had responded, but nothing had happened. With the sleep schedule that they had kept all week to surveil the targets, and no sleep the previous night, they were both exhausted by 9 pm and decided to head upstairs to bed.

"What if he writes back?" Andrei asked when they shut off the television.

"He'll just have to wait again. I'm sure he knows where we live, at least what part of the country, and that we'll be sleeping. And I don't really care if he goes on another rant. Tomorrow we'll look into him again and find our own evidence to save our asses, if we have to," Gustav said as he stood up to head to the stairs.

Andrei didn't want to tell him of his plans yet, so he just nodded his head and followed him up. They parted ways to go to their rooms to get a good night's rest before the chaos they knew would greet them in the morning from the *theVoyeur*.

Thirty-Four

Ada and Joel had done their Sunday errands and picked up everything they needed for three people instead of just two for the next week. Joel seemed more excited than Ada while they were shopping, asking if Ramon would like this or that, and she felt bad because she didn't really know the answer to those questions. Talking to someone on video or calls, and in dreams, doesn't mean you know what they like to eat or how they take their food. She knew this would be a learning experience for her. The only thing she knew was what his favourite food was, and she was planning to make it for him on Monday. She would have most of the day to prepare and make any mistakes she needed to before he got there.

She and Joel grabbed a chicken to roast in the oven, corn tortillas, green tomatoes, cilantro, and a green chili. They found some sliced Havarti cheese and picked up some cream, as well as the onions and garlic. Ada had found a recipe online for green enchiladas and was going to attempt it without Joel's help, seeing as he was usually the chef between the two of them.

Ramon's flight was at 7:45 pm from Toronto, and she knew that he would still be packing and sorting out last-minute things for his case files. She wanted the time to go by faster, but it only seemed to make it go by slower.

Joel noticed her being anxious. "Honey, why don't we go out to the pub to take your mind off things? Staring at the clock and your phone aren't going to make him get here any faster. He'll be here tomorrow. One more sleep!"

Ada agreed and asked if they should invite Kira as well. Joel smiled and said, "Of course! The more the merrier!"

She messaged Kira and told her where they were headed to, the Bell and Tower, just down the road from Joel's place, adding that she was welcome to spend the night if she didn't want to drive home.

Ding, ding. Ada's phone rang back immediately. "Count me in!!! I'll be there in 30 xo," Kira had replied.

They all ordered their dinner, which arrived by the time they were ordering their second round of drinks. Ada was at the bar buying the round of beers when she saw the TV behind the bar showing the news out of Vancouver. No more information seemed to have been provided to the public, but the story was still hot and running non-stop. She brought the first two pints back to the table just as the food was being served and went back for hers on the bar counter. Just as she was grabbing the pint, out of the corner of her eye she saw "Breaking News" flash in big letters on the screen.

She paused for a moment and turned to the television while Joel called for her to come and sit down.

"Just a moment," she shouted back to him as she tried to read the closed captions of what the reporter was saying.

There was something about a man, and a video downloaded from the dream. The police were toying with the idea of getting the public's help to see if anyone knew the man, but sources weren't revealing the video or any pictures from it just yet.

Ada immediately went back to the table and told Joel what she'd read on the screen. "That might be a good idea for DCI Karim too. Maybe he can release the still of the man who came into my dream?"

"Now who's being impatient? Weren't you the one who told me to wait until Monday, which is tomorrow, you know, so that DCI Karim could have a nice weekend?" Joel replied.

"I know, I know, but when you do talk to him tomorrow, just throw that idea in there, too," Ada said.

"Of course, darling. If these cases are connected then he'll want to do that, too," Joel said reassuringly.

"Okay, enough of that," Kira piped up. "Let's eat before it gets cold and enjoy tonight! Some of us have to work tomorrow." Kira winked and nudged Ada's elbow as she rubbed it in that Ada was off for the week.

****

Ramon was packing his toiletries, the last thing needed to go in his case, when he got a call from his dad.

"Hola, hijo! Como estás? Are you ready to go meet this mystery girl we know nothing about?" Carlos greeted his son when Ramon answered the phone.

"Bien, Papá, gracias. I love how you bring the Spanish out when you want to know something. It's always a giveaway. I've told you about Ada. You're just worried because you've never met her, but I promise we'll video call you and Mamá so you can meet her that way."

"You know what your mother is like with technology, Ramon, but I'll try to get her to sit down for it. Just let us know when to expect the call, okay, hijo?"

Ramon laughed at the thought of his mother on the video call, "Sí, Papá, I'll let you know. Let me meet her in person first and spend some time together and then I'll set up a time."

"Bien, bien. So do you have all your work sorted out for your leave? I don't want to hear from Caldwell that you let things slide."

Ramon sighed. "Of course, everything is settled. I have all my cases handed over to other lawyers and I've contacted my clients to let them know that I will be off. I've even agreed to take a few client meetings while I'm away and they know how to contact me if it's an emergency."

Carlos was satisfied with his son's diligence and work ethic, so they ended the call with well wishes for a safe flight and Ramon promising to contact them when he landed. He had four more hours before he had to be at the airport and knew this was the one downfall of being a planner. "All packed and ready and nowhere to go, yet," he said out loud. He had been packing for a week just to make sure he didn't forget anything, but now he was ready too early. He decided to see if Ryan was available for some lunch before he had to head out to Pearson Airport.

"You free for a quick lunch before I leave?" he texted him.

"For you, man, of course. Meet you at Amsterdam Brewhouse, Queens Quay West in 20 minutes for a send off," Ryan replied.

Ramon was seated at a table by the windows when he saw Ryan walk in and waved him over.

"What, no drinks already?" Ryan said as he sat down.

"I was waiting for you, there are too many choices here," Ramon answered.

They flagged down a server who was dressed all in black with a small red apron around her waist. "What can I get you two?" she asked.

"I'll have a Boneshaker," Ryan said, and Ramon said, "I'll have an Amsterdam blonde, please. Can we get some menus as well?"

"Of course, I'll be right back," she replied.

Three drinks in and their bellies full from the burgers they'd ordered, Ramon and Ryan headed back to Ramon's condo to wait out the remaining hour until the taxi arrived to take him to the airport.

"Make sure to let me know how it's going, and I'll keep you up to date with the work crap," Ryan said.

"Of course. I'll make sure to write a whole romance novel to you about my time with her .... C'mon, man," Ramon laughed. "I'll message you when I can."

They said their goodbyes in the lobby as Ryan's Uber showed up and Ramon waited with his suitcase and carry-on luggage for his airport taxi.

Once at the airport, Ramon checked in and made it through the long lines for security with still almost two hours to spare before boarding. He found a seat near the gate and filled a bottle with water for the flight before he messaged Ada to let her know he was almost on his way.

"At the airport now, sweetheart. I'll see you tomorrow!"

****

Ping! went Ada's phone. They were just returning home from the pub when she saw the message from Ramon.

"Can't wait! Have a safe flight babe xo," she messaged back.

Kira had gone home because she had to work in the morning and Joel was ready for bed after a few too many pints, so he headed straight upstairs. Ada was too excited to sleep, so she stayed up for a bit longer to stream a show on the TV. She made herself a nice hot cup of chamomile tea and curled up into a blanket while she imagined the meeting with Ramon the next day.

Thirty-Five

DCI Amir Karim didn't hear back from Detectives Julia Schmidt and Chris Hill until Sunday around 7 pm. The time difference for them was eight hours, but he was still going over notes with Sandy when they called. He put the call on speakerphone so that Sandy wouldn't miss any information either. The call was brief; they'd just wanted to touch base and hoped to share information. Their first plans of action were to share the videos with each other and the case files to be looked over. DCI Karim agreed right away and said he could send them later that night for them, and they agreed to do the same before their shift ended. He also mentioned Detective Troy Anderson with the NYPD and his case, wondering if they'd like to bring him in as well. Schmidt and Hill didn't seem overly impressed with the idea of a connection to the Adebayo deaths, but were willing to hear him out.

They all agreed to go over the shared case files on Monday before reconvening for a conference call that would be set up for Tuesday at 5 pm for DCI Karim, noon for Detective Anderson, and 9 am for Detectives Schmidt and Hill. They asked Karim to get Anderson involved and to send the file if he could. They would share theirs with him when they received it. Karim explained the issue that Anderson faced with his captain not wanting to reopen the case, but assured them that he would try his best to get them all the information.

After the call was over, Karim called Anderson, who answered on the second ring.

"Hey, buddy, working on a Sunday, too?"

"Sorry to bother you again on the weekend, Troy, but I heard back from the detectives in Vancouver. We're going to have a conference call on Tuesday to discuss the cases. If you're able to share your file with them, then they will send you theirs. I can send you mine as well if you can send yours here? Then we have a day to go over them before the call to work out any similarities, if there are any."

Karim waited for Anderson to stop mmhmming before continuing, "So do you think you'll be able to get access to the file again?"

Anderson sighed. "The brass here really don't want to open it again."

Karim replied, "But with the connection in Vancou-ver ...."

Anderson cut him off. "I know, and they know. Nevertheless, they don't want to be reopening high profile cases like this. I tried yesterday after you called. I also looked into other deaths during sleep, like you asked, but didn't find anything out of the ordinary."

"Shit, neither did I," Karim said.

"The issue is that I can only really search in New York, but the US of A is more than just me here. Without cause, I can't just rope in the FBI to look country wide on this. I need more, Amir. If you can find some connections, then maybe I can take that to them to reopen the case," Anderson finished.

Karim felt defeated after the call ended and sent a text to Detective Schmidt that Anderson was out for the time being. He had Sandy set up the electronic file to send to them, and forwarded the video that Ada had sent him as well.

"It's late, Sandy. Let's get out of here once this is sent off and we'll start going over their files in the morning," Karim said with a yawn.

He had spent most of his weekend off at the office, but it had been worth it. They were heading out to their cars when Karim got a text back from Schmidt saying, "No worries, I've sent the files now. And here's the link for the downloaded video of the incident, in case you want to get started tonight. You can skip to the one hour and three- minute mark."

"Sandy!" Karim shouted across the car park. "Come and see this!"

Sandy jogged back to where Karim was rooted in the same place she had left him.

Karim waved her closer. "I have the video," he said as they stood side by side, and he pressed the link.

It opened to Estella's view of her Tuscan villa, with textured plaster and stone walls and an exposed beam ceiling. She appeared to be in the kitchen area of the villa, looking around at the sage green cabinets with white marble counters along one wall and an enormous wooden island in the middle with bar-height chairs on one side. She then walked over to two wooden doors on the opposite wall that appeared to be a walk-in pantry.

"Let's fast forward, did she give a timestamp?" Sandy asked.

"Sorry, I've never seen anything like this before. I think she said just after the one-hour mark," Karim replied.

He dragged the indicator along the bottom until it said one hour and they watched from there.

Estella was muttering to herself while preparing a meal when she went to the wine rack at the end of the cabinets. She mustn't have found what she was looking for because she turned towards another wooden door beside what looked like a door to the yard. She opened the door and turned on a light to descend the stairs to a large wine cellar. She was perusing the shelves looking for something specific when a noise startled her.

Karim and Sandy saw her turn to her left and see a man in the corner with a balaclava covering his face, wearing a black sweater and black trousers. He threw a bottle of wine at her, and she moved slightly to avoid it, but it still hit her on the right side around her shoulder.

She seemed to be off balance when he lunged at her and pinned her to the wine rack as she started to scream. He had his hands around her throat as she struggled to free herself. She jerked suddenly, and they couldn't tell what happened as the man doubled over, but seemed to hold her where she was. Then Estella jolted and gasped loudly, seeing the broken bottle in the man's hand, and as she looked down at herself, she could see blood spreading from a wound in her chest. She slumped down onto the floor and remained still, then closed her eyes. The video had turned black, but they could hear the shuffling feet of the man and the breaking of glass underfoot as he moved around. Then all was quiet and Estella opened her eyes to see that she was alone in the cellar.

At that point, the video ended, which was when she must have woken herself up to exit the dreamscape and download the content. Karim and Sandy were silent as they stared at the blank screen.

"That would have terrified me," Sandy said.

Karim could only nod his head in agreement. "I'll see you tomorrow, Sandy. Let's look at this with fresh eyes tomorrow," he finally managed to say.

"Oh, as if I'm going to be able to sleep now," she said as she walked back to her car.

Karim wasn't sure how he managed to get home safely because he didn't remember the drive. His thoughts were consumed with the video he had just watched. He knew that he would have to compare stills of the man from this video to Ada's video the next day, and he would have Sandy go over the file from the Vancouver detectives because she was great at analyzing material and finding connections.

Karim went right to the fridge to open a beer and took it into the sitting room, where he sat in silence staring at the wall in front of him, trying to digest the scenes from the video. Seeing an attempt on someone's life through their own eyes was terrifying. He could feel the fear and adrenaline as if it were happening to himself. Somehow, he knew he had to calm his nervous system down; otherwise, like Sandy, he wasn't going to get any sleep that night either. He decided to turn on the television to find something light and airy to watch, and as he was flipping through he came across the Great British Baking Show in its twenty-third season. He stopped there to listen to the witty banter and try to forget the horrifying scene he had witnessed.

****

It was Sunday evening and Gustav was getting concerned that they hadn't had a reply from *theVoyeur* since his initial rants.

"Should we send another message?" Andrei asked. "Maybe he missed the ones you sent yesterday."

"He seems a little unhinged, kid. I think we should just leave him alone for now. He'll see the message and respond eventually. Were you able to find anything more from the searches you mentioned about the names?"

Andrei had told Gus earlier on Sunday about his theory for the victim names, but so far hadn't found anything connecting them. "I'm almost thinking we'll have to look at them one by one at this rate," Andrei replied.

Gustav got the thinking look on his face; all scrunched up as if the wheels turning in his head caused pain. "Okay, let's split the list and dive into each one," he said.

They'd been commissioned to eliminate seven victims, four of whom were one-half of a married couple. Gustav took Brian and Amara Adebayo to look into, as well as Carmine and Flora Esposito, while Andrei had the three singles: Arthur Millstone, Archibald Newbury, and Estella Crain. They decided to look at where each one had got the majority of their wealth, thinking perhaps they were involved in something on the black market, just like *theVoyeur*. Diving into financials was Gustav's least favourite thing to do, but Andrei brought in two beers and they began their digging.

Thirty-Six

Ada woke up early, even though she had the week off and didn't need to get ready for work. She could hear Joel getting ready and, knowing that today was the day, couldn't contain her excitement. She practically bounced down the stairs to greet him with a "Gooood morning!" as she beamed a smile at him.

"Someone is extremely chipper this morning .... I wonder why that could be?" Joel said sarcastically with a side grin.

Ada blushed, and Joel continued with his sarcasm. "Should I not come home after work? I suppose I'll need to find somewhere else to stay for the week, seeing as this will be the loooove nest, ugh."

They both laughed. Ada knew that Joel was just as excited to meet Ramon as she was. They had spoken on a few video chats since Ada had been living there. Joel was playing the big brother and wanted to approve of him.

"No matter how the enchiladas taste tonight, please say they're good, Joel. I'm not a master of the kitchen like you are, and I've never made anything like this before," Ada said.

"Oh, honey, don't you worry. They'll taste great. You've been helping me a lot, so just follow the recipe, and if you have any questions, call me at the office. What time is his train arriving at the station?" Joel asked.

Ada took a deep breath to gain her culinary confidence and said, "You're right, I'll be fine. And his train should be arriving at Nottingham Station for 2:25 this afternoon. I'll be able to get the green sauce done and the chicken roasted so it has time to cool before I have to pull it all apart. The rest ... maybe he can help me with."

Joel headed for work and Ada was left wandering the house, making sure that everything was perfect. She didn't want to shower until she had made the sauce in case she made a mess of it. After tidying the common rooms and her own room, Ada laid all the ingredients out on the marble island top for the sauce.

"Okay, I have eight green tomatoes, a bunch of cilantro, an onion, garlic, one green chili, salt, and pepper," she said to herself.

It took her a few minutes to locate which cupboard the blender was hidden in, but she eventually found it. Having washed everything and chopped them into smaller pieces, she followed the instructions to blend them together in smaller batches, adding some water when needed to thin it out.

Once the sauce was ready and in a large bowl, she covered it in plastic wrap and put it in the fridge for later. She took out a roasting pan, and began to coat the chicken in olive oil, salt, and pepper. Having prepped the chicken fully, she placed it in the pan while she waited for the oven to preheat. She glanced at the clock on her phone and saw that it was already 10:42 and she hadn't even had a cup of tea yet. While waiting for the oven to heat up, she boiled the kettle so that she had an excuse to sit and relax for a bit once the chicken was in the oven. She could feel her excitement building and knew that Ramon's flight would be landing any minute.

As she sat down on the sofa with her tea, her phone *pinged*. It was a message from Ramon, saying that he had landed safely and would see her soon.

She messaged back, "I can't wait! See you at 2:25 xoxo."

She could feel her cheeks hurting from the size of her smile. After finishing her tea, she waited for the oven timer to ding while doing the dishes that she had used for the meal prep. At the forty-minute mark the chicken wasn't done, as expected, so she basted it in the juices and added twenty more minutes to the timer.

They'd bought a larger chicken so that she could use some that night and have leftovers for another night. Once it was done and golden brown, she left it on the stovetop to cool and headed upstairs to get ready for the day. This wouldn't be a regular day and she knew her shower would take longer, with all manner of feminine preparedness for what might or might not happen. Out of the shower, she stood in front of her closet and just stared at her clothes. She'd had an outfit all picked out and now it didn't suit her mood, so she tried on all sorts of items for that first impression look. Finally, she settled on some black leather pants, a tunic length red and white off the shoulder sweater, and some high boots, with her three quarter length grey wool jacket that she would leave open at the front.

It was just after noon, and she was ready. *Ping!* went her phone. It was Ramon to let her know that he was on the train.

She responded, "2 hours to go!"

What was she going to do for two hours? The chicken had cooled enough to be separated into what she needed for tonight and what they would use later, so she put that all in the fridge. Then she made another cup of tea while she willed the time to go by faster, and by 1:30 she decided to head to Nottingham Station and hang around there until Ramon's train arrived.

She could see from the display boards that his train was on time and should be arriving in five minutes. She stood in the greeting area watching the doors that led from the platforms. She decided to text him that she was by the news stand just inside the greeting area when she saw the number of people exiting into the station and was afraid she would miss him. She scanned every male face that came through the doors and still hadn't seen him when her phone *pinged* with a message from him. "I see you." Her heart all aflutter, she looked up and all around and felt silly for not recognizing him, but couldn't see anyone looking at her that was him.

Finally, she saw a man waving at her from the seating area. He wore a large grin showing off his dazzling white smile, and she smiled back. It was Ramon. She ran over to him, he stood up, and they hugged in real life for the first time. They embraced for what seemed like ages when Ramon finally pulled away from her and leaned down to kiss her. Ada felt like the earth beneath her feet had fallen away with that first kiss and all her worries of how the week was going to go melted away.

"How did you sneak past me?" she was finally able to ask once her senses came back to her.

Ramon smiled and laughed as he said, "I saw you looking so intently at the doors that I went and found another way around, and came in here to sit down. I watched you scan the crowds and was trying to surprise you."

"Oh, I see, you watched me looking like a fool waiting in great anticipation for you." She swatted his arm gently.

Ramon picked up his bags and they headed to the exit to get a taxi. "You didn't look like a fool," he said, "but it gave me a moment to calm my own nerves."

Ada was continually surprised by Ramon's willingness to express himself and smiled to herself, thinking, wow, who is this guy?

Once back at Joel's house, Ada helped Ramon settle in and unpack. He hadn't gotten much sleep on the plane so they decided that a lazy afternoon on the sofa was just what they needed. Ada texted Joel to let him know that they were back at the house and they would see him later.

"I know it's early," Ada began, "but how about some Prosecco to celebrate us being here together?"

Ramon smiled. "I adore you, Ada. Let me help you with that, and maybe some snacks too."

As Ramon opened the fridge to get the bottle off the shelf, he noticed the bowl of green sauce. As he closed the door he asked, "Is that green sauce in the fridge?"

Ada flushed bright red. "Oh no! That was supposed to be a surprise," she said.

"You weren't making my favourite tonight, were you?" Ramon asked as he grabbed her by the waist and kissed her.

Ada smiled. "Of course I was. Now whether it tastes as good as what your parents' chef makes is another story."

Joel arrived home with more bottles of wine to celebrate, and decided to leave Ada to make the enchiladas while he got to know Ramon. Ada carefully did a quick fry of the corn tortillas and then assembled the enchiladas from the chicken she had shredded an hour earlier with Ramon's help. Once they were in the oven with the cream and cheese all ready to cook, she joined the guys in the sitting room where they were laughing as if they had already known each other for years.

"So, darlings, was it love at first sight?" Joel coyly asked them, and Ada blushed again as she remembered that kiss at the station.

"No answers, just blushing faces. Oh boy, the pair of you are smitten," Joel continued.

Eventually, Ada was saved by the oven timer chiming. She decided to warm up some of the leftover green sauce for them to add to their plates while she turned on the broiler to crisp up the cheese on top.

Ada served up three plates and put the extra sauce on the table for them to use. She hadn't tried the dish herself and had never had enchiladas before, so she didn't have a basis of comparison.

Joel and Ramon looked at her. "Well, go on, try it," she said.

They all cut into their food and Joel was the first to remark, "It's actually really good, honey."

Then she watched Ramon's face as he took his first bite and saw that a slight smile was spreading across his lips. "Ada, this is amazing," Ramon finally said. "Thank you for making this for me, you're really the best."

Thirty-Seven

By Monday afternoon, Andrei and Gustav had searched the wealth and financials of all seven victims. Most had their vast income from investments in large companies they owned shares in or from selling their own companies. The amount of money among them all was in the billions of dollars. Andrei found that Arthur Millstone's money had mostly come from a fashion line that he had started when he was young and then, according to news articles, had sold the brand off for £147 million when he got tired of trends and the fashion industry. From there he started investing in real estate and buying into companies to become a majority shareholder. One of the companies in which he had held eight percent of its shares was DreamScape Ltd.

Once they found out that Arthur had been a board member for DreamScape Ltd., they started to look more closely at the other victims to see if they had ties as well. One by one, they searched for a link to DreamScape Ltd. and found that all the victims had been recent board members, with the most recent addition in May of 2024 of Estella Crain, holding 12 percent of the company's shares. Among all seven victims, they had held 48 percent of the company, with the CEO, Walter Dumas, holding the remaining 52 percent to control the company.

"Is this him?" Andrei asked. "Could the CEO dude be *theVoyeur* and is weeding out his board members instead of buying them out?"

Gustav sighed. He didn't know much about corporate holdings. "I don't know, kid. It's possible. Why don't you dig into him a bit further? But at least we have a connection now to work off and I'll keep looking at the others."

Gustav let Andrei get to work while he dug into the Espositos to see how they'd got involved in DreamScape Ltd. Flora had come from money; her family went back generations as part of the Italian nobility prior to its dissolution in 1946, but they retained their wealth and societal rank. Carmine had been listed as a businessman only, yet he seemed to bring in a lot of money compared to what his job would suggest. "Hmph ... Mafia, I bet," Gustav muttered before moving onto their stake in DreamScape Ltd. The Espositos had invested when DreamScape Ltd. was only an idea and later owned 10 percent of the company shares between the two of them, which allotted them both a board seat. However, Gustav discovered that Carmine was at first a sole investor and Flora later bought into the company at five percent in January 2024. Gustav searched back prior to 2022 and found that Carmine had invested in other companies that Walter Dumas had intended to start but had never came to fruition. He took down a note—*revenge, black-mail, money owed?*—wondering if Carmine had pressured Walter for money he was owed from the other failed ventures, which maybe had got him killed.

Brian Adebayo appeared to be the only one of the Adebayos who had invested in and was a board member of DreamScape Ltd.. Gustav found that Amara Adebayo was more of a trophy wife than a co-business owner with him in any of his ventures. Brian, however, had made his money selling real estate. Ten years after he got his licence, he had become the top agent for the wealthy to call on when they wanted to purchase a new home or a vacation home. His commissions were what had made him his money. Even if he had only sold a few homes a year, he would have been well off, but he always wanted more. Selling over ten homes above the million dollar mark every year and raising his commissions had made him a millionaire. Gustav looked at his net worth for the previous year, which showed that Brian Adebayo had made $3.7 million and was sought after by his clients for his skill in finding the perfect home for them. Brian hadn't bought into any other companies aside from DreamScape Ltd., where he owned eight percent of the shares and held a board seat. Gustav made another note—*only six had seats on the board, Amara collateral damage?*—This got him thinking about why Amara had been eliminated in the first place.

He decided to move onto Archibald Newbury, his most recent kill, the one that had gone unplanned due to Andrei's error with Estella. Archie was an investor and Gustav couldn't really see any actual work that he had done to gain his money, but he didn't need to know where it all came from, just the outcome. Archie was involved in two trust companies that helped people get mortgages and a few technology companies, including DreamScape Ltd. and another one that sounded familiar to Gustav. He cross referenced the name Varcity Telecom and a picture of Estella Crain came up.

"Well, shit," he said aloud.

Andrei stopped his own research and asked, "What? What did you find?"

"I'm not quite sure yet, but this Archie fella was invested in DreamScape Ltd. and in Estella's company, Varcity Telecom. I'll have to look deeper," Gustav replied.

Archie was an investor and 10 percent shareholder in DreamScape Ltd. as well as owning five percent of the shares in Varcity Telecom. He was a board member only of DreamScape Ltd., but appeared to have connections with Estella for other matters. Gustav dug into their personal lives and the Varcity business, which resulted in numerous emails between the two of them discussing board decisions and other corporate deals that seemed to be going on behind the scenes for years. Estella seemed to lean on Archie's guidance, and there were multiple emails about someone they referred to as CTG and how she needed to get him off the board of Varcity.

To Gustav, it seemed that Archie knew of this person as well because there was nothing good mentioned about CTG. In fact, they sounded like a couple of high school girls writing to each other about another girl they disliked in the class. There were, however, a few lines in some emails that stood out as he scanned them: "*CTG is a bully, always voting against when everyone else agrees. It's like he does it on purpose to delay.*"

And "*... of all the childish things CTG could do, it would be this. Voting out my cousin and buying her shares up to control more of MY company, now he has 15%!*"

Estella seemed angry from what Gustav was reading. This CTG person was trying to control the board meetings and buy people out, which plagued her company. He decided to do a search for the initials CTG in the emails so only the relevant ones came up between the two of them, as the ones he was seeing were from October of 2023. But just as he placed his search, he saw the light blinking on the control panel, indicating that *theVoyeur* had sent them a message.

"Shit, Andrei, here we go."

> *theVoyeur:* I need the video of Archibald's death to complete your payment.
> *theVoyeur:* Then you're going to fly to Vancouver and do whatever you have to do to end that bitch.

Gustav and Andrei looked at each other after reading this.

"Do we really send him more videos?" Andrei asked.

Gustav wasn't sure, but he had been wearing a mask this time. He knew that, if both the Arthur murder and the one of Archibald were compared, the authorities could see that it was him from his body, with or without the mask. However, he also knew that they only had Andrei on video so far, and he and Andrei were not the same body type. He decided to reply.

> *SilentIsTheNight:* I'll send the last video for an extra $1 million.
> *theVoyeur:* Done. Sending the money now, in good faith.
> *SilentIsTheNight:* We don't do live murder, so you'll have to find another way.
> *theVoyeur:* You will if you don't want your face and video sent to the police. I will pay all expenses and pay you $2 million to get it done properly.

Gustav had given this lifestyle up long ago and didn't want to get back into it. In a dream, where it wasn't real, and there was no blood to wash off, it was different. It was clean and easy.

"I knew this would come back to bite us in the ass as blackmail," he said.

Andrei wasn't saying a word, just watching it all unfold. Gustav was thinking and staring at the screen as his eyes narrowed, and Andrei knew he was pissed.

> *SilentIsTheNight:* Be careful who you try to blackmail. Make it $3 million and this is our last transaction. Contract terminated.
> *theVoyeur:* I knew you'd come to your senses. I'll give you time to sort it all out, but I want it done in the next 8 days.
> *SilentIsTheNight:* Payment first, and then we'll start to plan.
> *theVoyeur:* I'll send $2 million now, and the other $1 million when she's dead.
> Now send me the video and we're done.
> *SilentIsTheNight:* Sending now.
> *theVoyeur:* Appreciated.
> *theVoyeur has signed off.*

"Umm, Gus?" Andrei was confused and could see how angry Gustav was. Gustav sent the video of Archibald's murder and stormed out of the room.

Thirty-Eight

It was 5 pm Tuesday evening in Nottingham and DCI
Amir Karim and DI Sandy Wilhelm were ready for their
conference call with Detectives Julia Schmidt and Chris
Hill in Vancouver. They had poured over the case file
the detectives had sent via email the day before and
had both come to the same conclusion that these cases
were certainly connected. The similarity in build of the
attempted murderer and the guy in Ada's video who was
watching her had been analyzed for height and body
structure, and they were a 93 percent match. Karim had
begged for a rush analysis from the forensic technology
team, and as he was a senior member of the department,
they had granted him the favour for his meeting the
following day. He knew the Vancouver team had likely
done the same thing, but that was okay; he just wanted
the proof for himself.

Earlier in the day, he had received a voicemail from
Joel wondering if there were any connections to Arthur's
case, but as he couldn't tell him anything yet, he delayed
calling him back. He and Sandy were seated in one of the

250

open task force case rooms on the third floor, typically used at the beginning of a case for displaying all the evidence to the team. Today, it had whiteboards covered with the pictures and descriptions of the three cases that he knew about. The New York murder of the Adebayos had minimal coverage because Anderson couldn't send the file, but Karim had been able to get a few bits of information out of him the day before and printed pictures of Brian and Amara off the internet to place at the top of their column of evidence. He was ready.

They dialed the conference line and were immediately let into the call. Having the call on speakerphone in the centre of the table, Karim introduced Sandy to the team.

"Good morning to you! This is DCI Amir Karim with the Nottingham Police, and I have my associate, DI Sandy Wilhelm, joining the case with me."

"Hello Sandy and Amir," Schmidt began. "This is Detective Julia Schmidt with the Vancouver Police, and I have my partner Detective Chris Hill with me."

"Hello," Chris chimed in, "we understand that Detective Troy Anderson isn't able to join us today, is that correct?"

Karim knew that this looked bad. "That's correct. His department wants to leave this case closed, but he was able to share a few details with me, mostly things that are public knowledge. It did help us, though, as we didn't have to go through news articles looking for the information."

252 ~ H.M NEWSOME

With the formalities done with, they decided to dive into the Millstone case first and work through any comparisons to the Vancouver and New York cases. They knew that Arthur's body had been found by Joel in the dreamscape, and that that portion of the dream had been deleted before the investigators could view it. This brought them to the Adebayo case in New York. Anderson had provided the information about how the couple was found dead in their beds, and the fact that, when his team had gone to download their dreamscape, there was a portion missing at the end.

"That aligns to what we have," Schmidt stated. "Estella had an attempt on her life in her dreamscape. We were lucky enough that she was able to download it for us before anyone else could access it."

From there they discussed the video from Estella's dreamscape and the masked man seen in the wine cellar. Karim had been right that the Vancouver team had done their own body scale analysis and compared it to the video and screenshot from Ada's video. It had also matched at a 93 percent likelihood of being the same man.

"If we run with this," Karim said, "then we can use the face from Ada's video of the man watching her through the window as the suspect that you and I are looking for."

Detective Hill agreed with that approach, but said they would need their captain's approval before leaking a suspect to the press. Karim had the same hindrance, and they agreed to get their department heads on board before taking that step and coordinating the release together.

With a suspect in mind, they discussed further steps and speculated that this likely didn't impact just their three jurisdictions.

"I have a connection with Interpol who works with our department," Sandy offered, "and once we have the go ahead to release the suspect's information, and our captains agree to the link, we can have my contact do a search throughout Europe."

Consensus was reached that they needed to expand their search to other regions, but Schmidt and Hill could only involve the RCMP to search Canada.

"We need to get Troy involved and send the information to the FBI to search the United States," Karim said.

He wasn't sure if that was going to be possible, but hoped that, with these connections established, the NYPD would reopen the case and involve the FBI.

Sandy piped up again at this point. "If my contact in the Swiss Interpol office finds any connections in Europe, she can involve the Interpol offices in Canada and the United States. It might take a bit longer, so I'm not sure if you want to wait for her to get involved or if you want to involve the RCMP and FBI right away."

"I think we need to get at least the RCMP involved right away," Hill said, "because they can work with the Interpol team here if any other connections are established. Without knowing about the cooperation of the

NYPD at this point, it might be better to get Interpol in the US involved if we can."

They had their action plan. First was approval by department heads for release of the suspect's image. Then Sandy was to involve her friend Inspector Dorina Keller, an agent with the Swiss Interpol office, and Karim was to contact Anderson to get the NYPD to reopen the case. The call ended after almost two hours of discussions. Karim decided to go immediately to Deputy Chief Moore to tell him about the connections they'd established and the suspect. He left Sandy with the evidence and the key to lock the room when she was done.

At some point before the photo was released, he would have to go and see Joel and Ada and let them know what was happening. He didn't want them to see this guy's face on the news without any warning. He and the Vancouver team had run the man's face through their systems and hadn't come up with any matches.

Discovering whether this was either a single individual who was hacking into people's dreamscapes, or a team, was an angle they were still working on. The idea of him being a hacker seemed the only plausible explanation for the suspect to be able to access their chips without them knowing it. And the sophistication of deleting the events meant that he was able to be in and out within seconds. Karim felt uneasy for anyone who'd had a chip implanted, and grateful that he had never decided to do it. He had argued that the public should know about the danger with implanted chips, but Schmidt, Hill, and even Sandy all disagreed because it would cause a mass panic. Karim understood that in the end.

Deputy Chief Moore wasn't available right away, so Karim decided to call Anderson and talk him through the evidence. Sandy was still compiling her email to Agent Keller when he came back into the room and called Anderson from the speakerphone in the middle of the table.

"Troy, it's DCI Karim, how are you?"

"Hey, Amir! How was the meeting?"

They discussed the outcome of the meeting and how they were going to need the backing of the NYPD.

"Can you put this in an email and send it to me, buddy? Then I can take it right to the captain to try and get the case reopened. I think the proof you have between the two cases and the links to the Adebayo case should be enough."

Anderson was positive this approach would work this time, and if his captain still wanted to retain his closure numbers, he was going to take it to the commissioner himself. So Karim and Sandy sat at the long wooden table for another two hours and went through their evidence to send the same email to Detective Anderson and Agent Keller in the hopes of securing their involvement.

It was almost midnight by the time they finished. Karim left a message for the deputy chief that he needed a meeting the next day to discuss the case. They locked the door to the task force room and left their evidence on the boards to head home for the night.

"Thanks for your help on this, Sandy," Karim said. "How about a drink to celebrate?"

Sandy was beat from a long day, but agreed to go for one drink. They needed to wind down, so she followed him to the Crown and Anchor for a pint.

Thirty-Nine

After a night cooling off from the exchange between himself and *theVoyeur*, Gustav started fresh on Tuesday morning, going through the results of his search for CTG in the emails between Estella and Archie. There were more emails in October 2023, but they just appeared to show the displeasure of this person being on the board. However, when Gustav got to December 2023, he saw more emails about CTG, with Archie being the initiator.

"He's doing the same thing here too. Always against in the votes and has been working with GV on side deals to get his decisions passed through. But GV is not interested in them all and at the last meeting threatened to buy him out. I'll let you know if it happens, but that would give us an even number of board members. You should look at investing if we need a seventh person."

Gustav wasn't fully aware of the dealings in a corporation, but he was guessing that this CTG guy was trying to gain more control. He moved onto emails in January 2024 from Archie to Estella.

"He did it. He bought out Gregor and holds 12% now. WD isn't pleased and all meetings are suspended until we can get another member. Do you have the money available?"

He assumed that "WD" was Walter Dumas, the CEO of DreamScape Ltd. He had a newfound interest in this Gregor person. Guessing that the "GV" from the previous email was him, that would mean he was Gregor V, which would turn up a lot of results. So, Gustav narrowed the search to the DreamScape Ltd. lists they had from 2023. There he found Gregor Valinski, who had owned five percent shares in the company before CTG bought him out. From the address and birthdate information he took from the company logs of shareholders, he found Gregor relatively quickly. "Deceased," Gustav muttered.

By the end of January 2024, Gustav saw that Flora had been added to the board by purchasing one percent of the shares each from Arthur, Brian, and Archibald, and then two percent from her husband Carmine, giving herself a total share of five percent. Archie's email described the scene when the announcement came.

"He lost it! He had been trying to do deals with all of us to buy us out and get the board members down to five people instead of adding another person, but we got him good! CE's wife bought some shares from the rest of us and is now sitting in the meetings. He threw a chair! Almost broke a window, can you imagine? A chair flying out of a thirty story window like that? We have to find a

way to get him off this board and yours. Any luck on those finances yet?"

These emails were painting a picture for Gustav. He was now almost positive that this power hungry and deranged person, CTG, was *theVoyeur.*

"Andrei!" he called out, as the kid was taking a rest on the couch in the living room.

As Andrei walked in, Gustav said with a big smile on his face, "I think I've got him! Look here at what I've found. I bet this CTG guy is him!"

Andrei read the emails that Gus had set aside and came to the same conclusion.

"But did they get him off the board? Or is he just killing people off to take their shares? I don't get it, Gus."

"Let's keep looking, but I bet you this is him," Gustav said as he pulled up Estella's emails.

"I have my board pooling resources to vote him off my board by dividing shares like you did to get another person. By bringing in this extra person to the board with all kinds of corporate recommendations, it will leave us with an even number, so we will have to take a vote and eliminate a member. I even gave some of my shares to get this person onboard."

From what they could see, by early March 2024, Estella had managed to get CTG voted off her board with the backing of the other members. After her email to Archie about the success, he had responded, describing the outrage CTG was showing at DreamScape Ltd. He asked if he could share the plan that she had used with Walter

Dumas to see about getting CTG off this board too, and said he would put her name forward for the position. The exchanges became more frequent in the month leading up to Estella's appointment at DreamScape Ltd. May 1st, 2024, which put the board at eight members, so a vote was to take place.

"We did it, Stell! He's out, and did you see how pissed he was when you showed up for the vote? Oh, I wish I could have taken a picture when he saw you walk in and sit down at the table to be introduced. It was priceless! Celebratory drinks are in order before you head back to Vancouver. This was a great success. We all voted against him and he looked like he wanted to flip the boardroom table. Walter was smart to have security on hand to escort him out. He's a loose cannon that one. See you tomorrow!"

Gustav knew this man had to be the one he was looking for. He searched the early shareholder logs from 2022 to 2024 to find names starting with the letter C and came up with dozens of results, but most were smaller shareholders not included in the board meetings. Looking for the highest percentage of shares held by these names, he found César Thiago Gomes.

"Ok kid, let's start digging. I think this is him."

They both started working on background information for Gomes, Andrei focusing on the financial background and Gustav the personal.

Andrei found that César Thiago Gomes had a net worth of $632 million. He was a savvy businessman when it came to investing his money in companies and stowed most of it away in offshore bank accounts to protect it from taxes. He was known for his antiquities and lavish lifestyle, but hadn't been part of the Silicon Valley community for the last two years, and purportedly had been living on a massive yacht that roamed between the Mediterranean and Tyrrhenian seas.

Gustav discovered that Gomes had never been married or had any children, but was known for throwing exquisite parties at his mansion in San Jose prior to him being voted out of DreamScape Ltd., where he had since become a pariah and seemed to have exiled himself. He was 56 years old, of Brazilian descent, and, from the photo they found of him, he seemed to have maintained his physique and didn't have a speck of grey hair in his luscious, perfectly coiffed, dark brown hair. He was tanned in the photos, which appeared to be taken on his yacht, and shirtless, showing his muscular yet tall and slender frame. The picture that Gustav printed was of Gomes standing on his yacht wearing white shorts, no shirt, and some deck shoes that had a blue stripe down the middle.

"We've got him, Andrei," Gustav said.

Now he just had to figure out how to put this information together and get it to the authorities without implicating himself or Andrei. He had already decided not to kill Estella, but to let Gomes think that he was going to do it when instead he was going to contact the police. Gustav just wasn't sure how to do that yet, but he knew he still had some time to figure it out. Half of the money for the hit had already arrived in his account, and it was time for him and Andrei to make a game plan on how to extricate themselves from this situation.

"Let's call it a night, kid. Go get us some food and I'm going to print off a few more pieces of evidence to beef up our case against him."

"Sounds good, Gus. I'll be back soon," Andrei replied.

Gustav printed the pertinent emails and shareholder logs to prove how he'd made the connections, and went back into the dark web to find the few transactions made by *theVoyeur* in the black market antiquity deals. He knew that the more information he had, the better chance the authorities had of catching him, unless Gustav could find him first.

Forty

Ada was lying in bed on Wednesday morning while Ramon was in the shower, reminiscing about the last two nights of passion that she'd shared with him. His kisses all over her body, his tender touch as they made love. She could still feel his hands on her body and smiled to herself. She ran her left hand over her body with her eyes closed, imagining it was his.

"Can I join this party?" Ramon asked as he walked back into the room with his towel on and startled Ada.

"I think you're overdressed for this party," she replied coyly.

He removed his towel and climbed under the duvet to meet her naked body with his as they entangled themselves in each other's arms and kisses again.

After spending most of the morning in bed enjoying each other, they decided to head out for lunch and some touring around Nottingham. Ada showed him where she worked and decided to show him some of the oldest and most interesting pubs in the city. She loved the unique atmosphere that each one held. Her favourite was Ye

Olde Trip to Jerusalem that was cut into the rockface of the hill under Nottingham Castle. The walls and ceilings inside a portion of the pub were carved into the hill and were so uneven and protruding in some areas that Ramon couldn't stand upright at the bar height table without bending his back and neck.

Their last stop before heading back to the house to get dinner started for Joel was a quick tour of Wollaton Hall, an Elizabethan mansion set on five hundred acres of beautifully sculpted land.

"This is all so different from Toronto," Ramon said. "Everything seems to hold so much history and character, whereas Toronto isn't that old, and the architecture is new skyscrapers."

Ada understood his amazement, because even though she'd grown up here, she still enjoyed finding out new things about the history of her city.

"Well, I'll have to come to Toronto and see for myself," she said as she leaned up to kiss him on the cheek.

Joel and Kira would both be there for dinner tonight, so they stopped to grab a few bottles of wine on the way home, and then started chopping vegetables together while some R&B played in the background. Ada was taking the marinated pork out of the fridge when she turned around and saw Ramon holding a wooden spoon up to his mouth and serenading her, lip-syncing the lyrics to the song that was playing. She almost dropped the tray while she smiled and laughed. This is what I've always dreamed of, she thought as he grabbed her waist to pull her closer.

Kira arrived first and started to interrogate Ramon about his intentions, so Ada handed her a glass of wine and quietly whispered, "Easy, babes, let's not scare him away."

Joel arrived home shortly afterwards and said, "I could get used to this, coming home to the smell of food cooking and a glass of wine waiting for me. Ramon, you should come more often!"

As they chatted and sat down for a dinner of pork stir fry, complete with fried rice, Joel started to talk about the call he'd received from DCI Karim earlier that day.

"So some good news, and he asked me to relay this information to you, Ada. They've made some connections to the case in Vancouver, but he couldn't go into detail. They're going to release the images from your dreamscape, Ada, and the one from that woman's attempted murder, to see if they can get the public involved."

Ada was taken aback by this news. "So they don't know who he is? But they think it's the same guy?"

"I don't know, sweetie, but they're going to ask for the public's help in identifying the man," Joel responded.

Ada listened to the rest of the conversations during dinner but kept quiet, thinking about the news from Joel.

Kira and Joel cleared up after dinner as Ada and Ramon had prepared everything.

"Are you okay, babe?" Ramon asked her as they went to sit in the living room.

"I am. I'm just a little worried that, if this guy sees the picture from my dreamscape, he will know it was me."

Ramon pulled her closer with his arm around her shoulders. "Well, I'm here now, and there's no need to go into our dreamscapes, so he has no way of getting to you. You're safe with me."

Ada felt more reassured by his presence and snuggled in closer to him. She still had no idea how she had landed such a kind, loving, and supportive man, but she wasn't going to argue with the blessing she'd received in him.

****

Earlier on Wednesday, DI Sandy Wilhelm had received a call from her colleague Dorina Keller from the Swiss Interpol office. After they caught up a bit on their lives, Keller said that she'd put the search parameters into the system, but nothing had come up just yet. They decided to keep in touch throughout the day while Keller searched all areas of Europe. Sandy decided to call Karim and see how his meeting had gone with the deputy chief.

"Hey, Sandy," Karim answered his phone. "We're green to go on the photo release! I'll let the Vancouver team know, and I've called Joel with the news so that he and his friend aren't surprised."

"That's great!" Sandy said. "Maybe someone will recognize him. Are we releasing at the same time as they do in Vancouver?"

"That's what I have to work out with them still," Karim responded. "I have to wait a couple more hours as it's too early for them right now. I'll let them have their rest."

Sandy decided to share the conversation she'd had with Agent Keller earlier, and said she would keep him posted throughout the day when she had updates from her.

At 5 pm, Karim decided to try Detective Julia Schmidt, who answered on the first ring. "Schmidt," she said abruptly.

"Hey, Julia, it's DCI Amir Karim. I just wanted to let you know that we have approval to release the photo we have of the suspect."

"Great news!" Schmidt replied. "I got approval late last night from my captain, so we can release them both. Do you have a time in mind to get these photos to the media?"

"I'd like to do it soon, so that it can be on the evening news tonight if possible," he responded. "Does that work for you?"

Schmidt laughed. "I've had the media team on standby since last night, so let's do it now. I'll give them the go-ahead to release both of the pictures together in one hour, does that work?"

"Brilliant! I'll get right on it here, thank you, Julia," Karim said before they ended the call. This was it; he knew this was the turning point he'd been waiting for. He let the deputy chief and Sandy know the plan, and then liaised with the media team to get both of the photos released in one hour's time with the caption "*Do you know this man? He is a person of interest in an on-going investigation,*" followed by the contact numbers for his department.

The whole department sat around the one television in the office and watched the *Breaking News* segment on the BBC with the photo from Ada's dreamscape and the one from Estella Crain's dreamscape right beside it. The news team was going over the basics of the investigation that had been made public from the Vancouver case, and then mentioned a potential link to the Arthur Millstone case from the previous month here in the UK. Karim sat there smiling, hoping that the killer or killers would see this and start to feel the net closing in around them.

Sandy's phone rang while they were watching the news, and she excused herself to take the call in the hallway.

"Hi, Dorina," she said.

"Hey, Sandy, so I think I might have a hit from Italy," Dorina said in a hurried and excited voice. She continued, "Back in September, a couple was found dead in their Naples mansion. Flora and Carmine Esposito ...."

Sandy needed a pen and paper. "Wait, wait, wait, I need to take notes," she said.

Keller laughed. She knew this was exciting. "Come on, DI Wilhelm! Be prepared!" she joked.

Sandy laughed and said, "Okay, I'm ready, go ahead with those names again."

Keller filled Sandy in on all the details that she had so far. Flora and Carmine Esposito from Naples had been brutally murdered in their home. The wife had her throat slit and the husband suffered grave injuries from a fall down the stairs, presumably during an altercation with the intruder or intruders. They were also robbed of artwork and other precious items, including jewellery, and the safe was broken into.

"So how does this relate to our case?" Sandy asked.

"That's the fun part!" Keller said. "It may look like basic murder and robbery, but they both had registered their chips, so it's automatic now for law enforcement to check the details of the downloads. Both of them had a deleted section. And I say section, because if the killer or killers were smart they would have taken the murder segment right to the end—but they didn't. They deleted a section but left a small bit at the end before all brain function had stopped. So we can tell that it was removed!"

Sandy was speechless. She knew she had to tell Karim immediately. "Thank you, Dorina! Can you share the files with us and the Vancouver team?"

"I'm working on that and getting the approvals. Hopefully I'll know if I can by tomorrow," Keller responded.

Sandy was too excited, "Okay, thank you, again! I have to fill in my team, we'll speak soon." And with that, the call ended. Sandy rushed back into the room where Karim was talking to the deputy chief. Perfect, she thought. She couldn't wait to fill them in on this new connection.

Forty-One

Andrei and Gustav were staring mindlessly at the television screen as the news kept repeating itself. There was Andrei's face, staring through Ada's window and beside it, the image of him standing in Estella's wine cellar with his mask on. The reporter kept repeating that the authorities believed that these two images belonged to the same man allegedly stalking women.

Gustav had already lost his temper with Andrei when they first saw the pictures. The poor kid had never seen that kind of anger explode from him before, and in fear of what he might do, Gustav left the house and drove away for a few hours to cool off.

Gustav now just shook his head. "They don't want to say stalking women *in their dreamscapes*, though. I'm sure the legal team wouldn't allow it."

Andrei glanced at him, looking dejected. "What are we supposed to do now?"

He knew this was all his fault. Watching Ada had become an obsession for him, and not realizing he

271

hadn't killed Estella had turned the tide on their whole operation.

Gustav stood up and headed into the kitchen. Andrei could hear the fridge open and two bottles clinking together. When he reappeared, Gustav was carrying two beers and handed one to Andrei.

"There's nothing we can do about the pictures now, kid. They're on every news channel and all over the internet. We're just lucky they haven't announced that there are any connections to other cases."

Andrei took a swig of his beer and said, "They might not be saying it, but they've made one connection. Otherwise they wouldn't have the photos from Ada's dreamscape and Estella's beside each other."

Gustav knew he had a point, but as far as the general public was concerned, these images had nothing to do with the attempt on Estella Crain's life. Their biggest concern was that the police were starting to connect cases together, but Gustav and Andrei had no way of finding out what they knew.

César Thiago Gomes hadn't been in contact again, and was likely assuming that Gustav would be hatching a plan to murder Estella.

"We need to sort some things out, Andrei. How quickly can you pack to travel?"

"I can travel light if I need to. Are you thinking we should go into hiding?" Andrei replied.

Gustav took a few deep breaths and tightly pressed his lips closed before saying, "I have a guy ...." Andrei waited for him to continue, but Gustav seemed lost in thought. "I have a guy who can quickly get us some fake passports. Start figuring out what you need to take or if it's all here already. I'm going upstairs to make a call."

With that said, Gustav got up off the sofa and climbed the stairs in a slow deliberate manner as if he was still deep in his thoughts.

Andrei was sorting out his own thoughts, and how he would access his money in the Caymans, when Gustav came back down the stairs.

"He'll be here in an hour with his equipment. He already had the fake passports made with the names and identities we set up for the offshore accounts, and just needs our photos. Do you have a suit you can put on for the picture and change your hair a bit?"

This all took Andrei a minute to process. Finally, he said, "Yes, I'll go get one from my place and be right back." He took Gustav's car keys and set off immediately to gather his things and what cash he had stashed away.

When Andrei returned, Gustav's 'friend' had already arrived. He was setting up a backdrop and the camera for the photos. Andrei headed right upstairs to change and fix his hair. He used some gel to slick it back and tied it in a half bun, then applied some foundation he had picked up at the drugstore on his way back to cover any blemishes and freckles on his face. The final touch was a pair of fake glasses that he had picked up as well. With the white dress shirt and jacket, he looked like a different man in the mirror.

As he headed downstairs he saw the flash of the camera go off, and when he turned the corner into the living room, he saw Gustav in a polo shirt and sport coat sitting in front of the backdrop. The biggest difference was that he had cut his grey beard to almost stubble, but in a tasteful way, and was wearing a brown hair piece that was also peppered with grey to make it look real for his age. Andrei couldn't help but smile at this transformation from a bald headed man with a long grey uncared for beard to the man sitting in front of him.

"Don't laugh," was all Gustav said as he had a few more pictures taken. When done, he stood up. "You're up, kid. Look at you … you clean up nice."

Andrei smiled. "Thanks," he said as he sat down in the chair to have his photos taken.

As Gustav's 'friend' was processing the passport sized photos, they helped him take down the backdrop and clean up the rest of his equipment. He still had his kit out that would adhere the photos correctly to the passports so that they wouldn't be detected, as well as the infrared light to check all the holograms were still there. Andrei motioned for Gustav to follow him into the kitchen.

"Should we go to the Caymans first to take out some funds?" Andrei asked. "I only have about twelve grand of free cash to use."

"Don't go to the Caymans. Use what cash you have and buy a plane ticket at the airport. I don't want to know where you're going, just go somewhere and I'll find you if I need to. Stay away for as long as you can, I have some things to sort out here first," Gustav replied. He added, "If you run out of funds you can wire yourself some from the offshore accounts to where you are. Just don't be lavish about it or it will set off alarms, okay?"

Andrei nodded his understanding. He was a 24-year-old secret millionaire and didn't really want to go into hiding, but was also smart enough to understand that it was necessary.

With their new passports in hand, Gustav and Andrei packed their remaining things into some luggage and backpacks.

"What about all the equipment here?" Andrei asked.

"You're leaving tonight, especially with your makeup already on. Head to the airport and buy a ticket, with cash, remember. I'll find you if I have to, but I don't want to know where you are." Gustav continued, "I'll leave tomorrow once I extract what information I need and wipe the database. I'll also have all the printouts with me about Gomes, so you just stay hidden."

Andrei agreed and they headed out to the car so that Gus could drop him at the airport and say goodbye.

Once at the airport, Andrei looked around at all the different airline counters, thinking about where he wanted to go. He spotted a counter for British Airways with some staff and headed that way. Dressed in his suit still and hair slicked back, he said, "Hello there, would you have any flights leaving late tonight to Heathrow?"

The agent smiled at him and started typing on her computer. "We have a flight leaving at 10:35 pm."

"Excellent," Andrei said. "Would you have any first class seats available?"

"Yes, sir, we do have some available. Would you like a window seat?"

"That sounds delightful," Andrei said in his fake businessman voice.

"May I have your name and passport, sir?"

"Yes, my name is Anthony Moretti, and here's my passport for the rest of my details."

Once the price was settled and paid in cash and his luggage checked in, Andrei had four hours to kill in the VIP lounge. He was already two whiskeys in when they announced the boarding for his flight and he headed in the direction of the gate. He boarded first with all the other businessmen and people who could afford first class. Once he was seated, the flight attendant came over.

"Welcome, Mr. Moretti, can I get you something to drink before takeoff?"

What's one more? he thought as he asked for another whisky. Once in the air he took a sleeping pill so he wouldn't be disturbed and would be refreshed and aware when he got to London. He was in hiding now and had to watch every move he made going forward.

Forty-Two

Andrei exited the plane at 11:17 am local time in London and headed for the customs lines. He knew that his picture had been on the BBC as well, so he stopped at the bathroom before entering the queue to reapply some foundation and fix his hair with some water. He needed to look like the picture in his passport to get through customs security without being detected, as he was sure they'd have alerts watching for him. Once he was safely through and had collected his baggage from the carousel, he found the Terminal Five train that would take him to Paddington Station in central London. He still needed to find a place to stay and get something to eat as he hadn't eaten on the flight after taking his sleeping pill.

Upon arriving at Paddington Station, he took the Praed Street exit. It was a chilly November day, but no-where near as cold as Detroit had been. The sun was shining and from the map on his phone he could see that Hyde Park was within walking distance. He stopped at a small cafe along the way to grab a sandwich and a coffee to take with him to the park while he planned his next steps. Finding a bench to sit on near the Italian Gardens with their fountains, he began to search for suitable accommodations that wouldn't question him paying in cash instead of giving a credit card.

****

Ada and Ramon had decided to go touring around London for a day and a half. She wanted to show him some of the sites in London, being a larger city than her own, and have a little privacy for themselves. They booked a suite for one night that overlooked Hyde Park. When they arrived at 11 am for early check-in, they stood in front of the window in their room in awe of the view. The trees were mostly barren due to winter coming on, but with the nice weather that day the fountains were going in the gardens. They'd brought a picnic with them and decided to head out to find a nice spot around the fountains to have their lunch before continuing on with their sightseeing tour.

The grass was dry and they laid out their blanket about twenty metres from the far end of the fountains so they wouldn't be in the way of people strolling around. They had hidden the Prosecco in a thermos and brought travelling mugs to hide what they were drinking.

"I feel like an outlaw," Ramon said. "This is what we have to do in Toronto if we want to sneak a drink in public."

Ada laughed. "We can drink outdoors here, but not in a park like this."

They shared their lunch together and watched people as they passed. There were couples holding hands walking around the fountains, people taking selfies, and a few people just sitting by and admiring the view, like they were. The sounds of the city seemed to fade away with the gurgling and dripping water of the fountains.

"I can imagine that people do their wedding photos here," Ramon said as he was taking in the whole view.

"They do! It would be so gorgeous with that background, so serene," Ada replied.

After they finished their food, they packed up the carryall they had brought with them and decided to walk the paths through the fountain area. Ramon was mesmerized by the layout of the garden area and kept stopping to stare at different artistic characteristics and statues, while Ada—who had been here before—was still admiring the other people who were out enjoying the park.

Ramon stopped. "Here it is!"

Ada looked around confused. "Here's what?"

He stepped away from her and smiled. "This is where I want to take your picture, sweetheart."

Her heart melted and she blushed. Ramon took out his phone and started taking pictures of her. She could only maintain the sweet smile for so long before she started making faces and funny poses until he stopped acting like a paparazzi.

"There, see? The start of our 'Ada the tourist' photos. I think the silly ones are the best," Ramon said as he pulled her closer for a kiss.

****

Andrei couldn't believe what he was seeing. He thought it had to be fate, that of all the places to sit down in this enormous park, he was within view of Ada. At first, he wasn't sure it was her sitting on the blanket with a guy, but once they started to walk around and got closer, he could see that it was definitely her. In the flesh. He had picked up a book at the airport and taken it out of his bag to appear as if he was sitting on the bench reading while he peered at her over the top.

This must be that same guy she was with in her dreamscape, he thought. He couldn't remember the name, but he looked like the same guy. Ada was smiling and laughing while this guy took pictures of her. "Stop already, man. I think you have enough," he muttered.

The couple kept walking in his direction, so he pretended to be engrossed in his book while snatching the odd glance at their approach. He was looking at Ada, at her eyes and smile, and then in one glance, their eyes met before Andrei could quickly look away. His heart was pounding in his chest. He knew he had gotten too close and had to make a move before they approached him further. He turned his back to the couple as he gathered his things, but in his hurry some items fell out of his bag onto the ground. Still with his back to them slightly, he picked up the stray toiletries and electronics that had fallen out but not broken, and again tried to calm himself before making his move out of the park.

****

As Ada and Ramon were walking hand in hand, she kept noticing a man on the bench reading a book. She noticed him because she could feel him staring at her and it seemed odd.

"Don't look directly at him, but the guy just over there reading a book keeps watching us," she said to Ramon.

His face lost the award-winning smile and became serious. "Okay, time for another photoshoot. Stand there and, yes; let me zoom in a little." Ramon snapped a few photos of Ada and a few of the man, now behind her, who was watching them.

"That should do it. Always be safe and have evidence," Ramon said.

Ada laughed and felt a little less creeped out. "Always thinking like a lawyer."

As they approached the man in their circuit of the fountains, he began to fidget and turned away from them. They weren't staring at him, but noticed his action in their peripheral vision so it would appear as if they hadn't noticed him at all. After he fumbled around with things, he immediately got up and started to walk away from them. However, in his hurry he bumped into another couple and got jostled around, and in that moment he looked directly at Ada and then hurried away again.

"That was odd," Ramon said and, looking at Ada, noticed the confused look on her face. "What is it? You're thinking about something."

Ada's mouth moved but no words came out until she finally managed, "I'm not sure, but he looked familiar."

They decided to not let this odd experience in the gardens bother them and continued on their sightseeing tour of London, hitting up London Bridge and Tower Bridge for more paparazzi photos of 'Ada the tourist,' as well as a pub just outside of Shakespeare's Globe Theatre. They toured old churches and went to see Big Ben and the Parliament Buildings all in a swift seven hours before they decided to retire to their hotel for some dinner. Once they were back in their room with another bottle of Prosecco, Ramon went into the bathroom and started to fill the jacuzzi tub for them to enjoy together. As Ada waited for the water to fill up and Ramon to let her know when it was ready, she popped the cork to the bottle and filled two of the glasses ready for their romantic night.

Ada had never been in a hot tub or jacuzzi before, let alone with another person, and as she sat with her back leaning up against Ramon's muscular chest and his one arm around her waist, she couldn't help but think this was the best thing in the world. They each had their glass of Prosecco and just sipped on them in the hot water and humming of the jets. No words needed to be spoken, just the simple intimacy in the silence of two people who enjoyed being connected. After the water had lost its warmth, they dried off and headed off to bed to connect more intimately in another way that didn't need words.

Forty-Three

Gustav had spent most of the previous night and that morning wiping the databases and transferring any files he would need onto smaller hard drives that he could travel with easily. He made sure to have everything they had found about César Thiago Gomes, including the printouts, placed in secure travel bags for his carry-on. What he wanted most of all was to go hide away in his Colorado cabin, but he knew that if he didn't make it look like he was going to carry out the last job given to him by Gomes, then he would likely be sought after. He knew that Gomes had immense wealth and was tech savvy enough to deal on the black market as well as hide himself so well. Gustav could only assume that Gomes would be able to find him if he tried to hide away.

He secured the windows on the main floor with a make-shift grate that he screwed into the framing and added some plank boards to the second floor windows that he had removed previously. It was an abandoned neighbour-hood, but he wasn't willing to take any chances with all his equipment there. Although erased, it was still worth a lot of money. He decided to take a break and have a beer on the couch. Flipping on the news and waiting to see any new developments in the story, Gustav saw the breaking news as the reporter spoke.

Vancouver detectives announce connections in the Estella Crain case to murders in Nottingham, UK, Naples, Italy and New York. It has been said that there may be others, but no sources have confirmed. DreamScape Ltd. has not provided any comment in the ongoing investigation, aside from saying that their platform and chips are safe for all users. Reports have come in that people are concerned with the level of access that the company holds on the implanted chips, and some have even asked to have them removed. Detectives on the case won't comment on any links directly to DreamScape Ltd., as it is only speculation at this point that any connection exists.

"Shit," Gustav said aloud. Now the authorities had linked four of the jobs together, and he knew it was only a matter of time before they expanded their scope and included others. He pulled out his phone and called an old contact from his IT security days.

"Hey, Mel, it's Gus, can I get a favour?"

Melton Grimly had been in on Gustav's antics when he was stealing information, but he never mentioned having a partner, and Mel got to keep his job. They distanced themselves after he was fired, but Mel had helped Gus set up his system and did the odd favour for him.

"What can I do you for, Gussy?" Mel replied.

Gus wanted to be brief. "The names of the detectives working that Estella Crain case in Vancouver. Call me back when you have them."

The call ended as it always did—no goodbyes, no confirmation, just a statement, and eventually a call-back.

Gustav knew what he needed to do when he reached Canada, and he understood the consequences. He didn't know how long he would be detained or what would happen once he shared his information. What he wished most was to get in touch with Estella and see if she could help him, but when he searched for any activity from her before shutting the system down, he couldn't find anything. No bank transactions, no credit card transactions, no emails. It was like she'd disappeared. Gustav assumed they had her in protective custody, and if he had actually been going to murder her, it would have been damn near impossible to do so. His best bet was to turn himself in and hope for leniency with the information that he could give them about Gomes.

His phone rang, and he opened the call but didn't say anything. On the other end, Mel said, "Julia Schmidt and Chris Hill."

"Thanks," Gustav said and ended the call.

He wished he had thought of this before clearing the system, but he started to search on his phone and learned that the precinct they worked out of was the police station in downtown Vancouver near the art gallery. He also searched for any news stories that mentioned any commendations and awards they'd been given. He then powered up his encrypted laptop and did a search for more detailed information about each of them, so that he knew how to approach them and whether they had any weaknesses he could use to soften his arrest.

Julia Schmidt was a psychology major and had decided to take her talents into policing. She had one son who was eight years old and a husband who worked in finance. Chris Hill was a generational detective. His father was in the force and his grandfather had been too. His two brothers, however, had decided on other careers in business and law. He was divorced and had no children, but had two nieces and one nephew.

"So she'll try to outwit me and the guy will be more by the book," Gustav mused from what he saw. They were both very capable detectives, so he would have to watch how and what he said to them.

With one last look at their pictures and the afternoon waning, he decided to grab his things and head to Detroit Metro Airport to find his flight to Canada. With the high alerts that Vancouver was on with the attempted murder of Estella Crain, he didn't think it was wise to show up at their airport. He had searched flights and knew he could fly into Victoria, British Columbia, but the flight would get him there around midnight Pacific time, and he would then need to find a place to sleep. There was no pre-booking when you were on the run, so he hoped to be able to find a cheap motel that would take his cash.

Gustav paid for his flight in cash, when he arrived, for a 6:45 pm flight to Victoria, BC. He was lucky to have made it and that they had seats still available, but after securing the ticket under his assumed name of Jonas Pedalton and disguised as his passport photo indicated, he became just another man like all the rest in the airport as he waited for his boarding call. The last thing he wanted to do was stand out. As he waited, his thoughts drifted to Andrei. He wondered if he was all right and where he had ended up. He assumed back to Mexico for the sunshine, but that might have been too predictable.

Over the last year Gustav had become closer to him, like he was a son, and the information on the news with his photo had made Gustav feel uneasy. The last thing he wanted was for the kid to be in danger or to end up in jail when it was Gustav, himself, who had recruited him. As he maneuvered into his seat, waiting for the flight to take off, his only thoughts were on how to save Andrei from this mess, and how he was going to do it all when he finally got to Vancouver. He had eight hours to work out a plan, and it all had to be in secret. No news media could be involved, because if Gomes knew what Gustav was up to, he would go into hiding, even more than he was now. Gustav had decidedly become the sacrificial lamb and was prepared to bleed for this.

Forty-Four

With the cases coming together worldwide, the Vancouver team decided to split their resources over two shifts that overlapped in the middle. Detective Julia Schmidt had opted for the very early start of 3 am Pacific Time so that she was available for conference calls, but mainly so she could see her son after school and have dinner with her family. It was the start of her Friday morning shift, and she already had a missed call from DCI Amir Karim, who had become the leader in this multi-departmental task force. She decided to call him back on her way to make a strong black coffee.

"Good morning, Julia!" DCI Karim cheerfully answered his phone.

"Yes, very early morning to you too," she responded in a rough, still somewhat sleepy voice.

She let Karim carry on excitedly while he told her of the new connections they were making and that one more murder seemed to fit the profile. He described the details of the blood spatter and demonic symbols, then ended his oration with, "it took us a while to really connect this last case in San Jose, but with the FBI's help we established links to the Naples crime scene and robbery. Also, the main thing, after the information went out, was that they checked his chip and it also had information deleted from it."

Schmidt was trying to process all the information that Karim was giving her. "Hold on, hold on, I haven't even had my coffee yet. Are you saying that a satanic looking crime scene is our guy?"

Karim got even more excited. "Yes! If he's going into their chips from a secure location, he would have to have a huge setup. He couldn't then just travel and stage crime scenes like this and Naples. We're leaning towards a team of people now."

Schmidt wasn't sure what to make of all this, as her brain was still waking up. "Have you seen any hits on the pictures, or any credible calls? I know we haven't had any here, just the regular spooks that call in."

"No, nothing has proven useful for us either," Karim said.

They ended the call so that Schmidt could catch up on information and they would regroup later in the day when Detective Chris Hill started his shift. Schmidt started to download the San Jose case file and print anything that was needed for the bulletin boards in the room that they had set up. Five cities now, she thought as she kept hitting the print button and preventing herself from thinking whether there could be more.

****

Ada and Ramon had spent the morning in the hotel, enjoying the amenities before checking out and heading back to the train station. Everything had been amazing for them, even though they hadn't got through everything on their list of things to see. Just the joy of exploring together was enough for them both. By the time they arrived back in Nottingham it was just after one in the afternoon, and with Joel still at work, they had the place to themselves.

"I feel like we've been going non-stop," Ramon said. "How about sweatpants, some tea, and a movie on the sofa?"

"Oh, that sounds like heaven to me," Ada replied.

They got themselves unpacked and into comfy clothes, ready for a movie marathon all afternoon. Ada turned on the television. It was on the BBC channel, so she watched for a bit while Ramon put the kettle on and popped some popcorn in the microwave.

The story about the murders came onto the screen and Ada saw that there were more cases added. In her shock she almost called out to Joel to tell him, but remembered he wasn't there and anyway likely knew about it. She and Ramon hadn't been paying attention to the news the last couple of days.

Ramon came in with the popcorn and set the bowl down, and Ada said, "Look! There are more cases. Five suspected links so far."

Before Ramon could say anything, the kettle began to whistle, so he got up to turn off the burner and pour the tea. Ada continued watching the news attentively. When the reporter started talking about a person of interest in the case, the screen changed to two large photos. They were the ones she had seen displayed before on the news, and one was hers from her dreamscape, but this time they struck her differently.

"Ramon!" she yelled, and he came rushing back into the room. She looked at him with wide eyes and said, "That's him! That's the guy we saw in the park who was acting all weird and staring at me. He's the same guy who was staring through the window in my dreamscape!"

Ramon had Ada pause the screen so he could look at the pictures. Then he took out his phone and scrolled through to find the photo he had taken of Ada and zoomed in on the guy in the background. He looked at each one, over and over. "It's hard to tell, but you may be right. Maybe that's why you had a weird feeling afterwards."

Ada looked at the picture on his phone as well. It was a bit grainy with the zoom, but she knew it was him. She could feel it. "I have to call DCI Karim and tell him he's here."

Ada tried to get hold of him, but after the third call, she decided to leave a message for him instead. "Hi, DCI Karim, it's Ada Carpenter. I just wanted to let you know that I saw the man from my dreamscape in London yesterday, in Hyde Park while I was there. I have a picture. Call me back, please."

Ramon brought the tea into the living room and sat down as he watched Ada pace back and forth. He could clearly see that she was agitated by this revelation, so he stood in her path and opened his arms to welcome her in for a hug. She melted into him and began to cry. All her fears had become real. She had thought she was safe by not going into her dreamscape, but now this man was a reality and he was near. Once Ramon's hug had created the desired effect of calming her, they returned to the sofa to find a comedy to watch while Ada waited to hear back from DCI Karim.

****

DCI Amir Karim saw the three missed back to back calls from Ada and the voicemail, but didn't have the chance to get back to her right away. I'll listen to the message later, he thought to himself as he downloaded another file from Interpol about a possible link. He was the go-to detective for making the link, so whenever another agency had a file they wanted to compare it came to him. He had already rejected over twenty other cases, but wouldn't turn the agencies away when they asked. Sandy had been helping on the cases as well, but he knew that they needed to direct their time and energy into finding the people responsible. The FBI and the Vancouver team had their digital forensic experts

294 ~ H.M NEWSOME

scanning the nights leading up to the murders to see if there were any hints of the victims being watched. The difficulty was that the chip only recorded what the person was looking at, so unless they saw but didn't notice someone hiding, it would be tough to come by results.

After another long day, Karim decided to head home and get some rest. "Are you okay to keep going, Sandy?" he asked before packing up his belongings.

"I've got a few more hours in me because I started later than you. Go get your rest," Sandy replied.

Without further urging, he packed his laptop away, grabbed his grey pea coat off the back of his chair, and headed for the parking lot. As he was driving away in the 5 pm rush hour traffic, he remembered the voicemail from Ada. He pulled out his phone and listened to the message. Then he played it one more time and called her back.

"Hi, Ada, I'm sorry to get back to you so late, we've been busy with all the cases."

"That's ok, DCI Karim," Ada said in a soft voice. "Can we meet to let you know the details?"

He smiled. "I was thinking the same thing. I'm in the car, and I'll head your way. I should be there at about half five."

As Karim was changing direction to head to Joel and Ada's place, he called Sandy to let her know about the lead and to inform the other teams as well.

"Oh, boy! This could be it!" she said.

Karim laughed. "Keep your hat on, Sandy. She may just be seeing things. I'll let you know once I've spoken to them and seen this picture."

As he pulled up to the house, he felt a sense of anticipation rush over him. He wanted to contain his excitement in case this information didn't lead anywhere, but also wondered if it was the break they needed.

****

A knock came at the task force door and an officer poked his head in to say, "Hey, detective, there's a guy out here who wants to speak to you about the Estella Crain case."

Schmidt looked up at him and said, "He's going to have to wait, or talk to someone who can take down his information."

The officer nodded and closed the door as Schmidt went back to staring at the crime scene photos laid out in front of her. She knew that Hill would arrive in a couple of hours and she had almost everything prepared to brief him. He likely would have seen the news before coming in and found out about the new case that had been connected, but the details would be something else.

Schmidt's phone rang and she could see that it was Sandy calling her. "Hey Sandy," she answered.

"Heya, Julia!" Sandy said, still full of excitement. "I just wanted to let your team know that we may have a lead happening here. The picture that we provided you from Ada Carpenter's dreamscape, of the guy watching her—well, she thinks she saw him in London yesterday."

Schmidt was taken aback by this new information. "Wait, you may have a sighting?"

"Yes! DCI Karim is out at her place now to verify the information and take a look at the picture that her boyfriend took with this guy in the background," Sandy said.

Schmidt was speechless, so Sandy continued. "As soon as we have all the information and the picture, we'll send it to you and Chris."

"Uh yeah, that sounds great, Sandy, thank you." Schmidt was still in shock as the call ended and another knock came at her door.

"Sorry to bother you again, detective, but this guy says he'll only speak to you or Detective Hill," the same officer said.

She took a deep breath. "Put the guy in a room for now, and I'll get to him when I can. Maybe he'll change his mind while he waits. Give him something to drink too, we don't need any complaints."

With that the officer left the room and Schmidt stood up to stare at the boards they had created. There were so many pieces to this puzzle still missing, and she really didn't know where to start. If the UK team could apprehend the guy from the photos, then maybe they could figure things out. She remained hopeful, but still confused about this whole mess.

Forty-Five

Gustav sat in a windowed interrogation room and watched the officers walk by with their coffee and files. They had provided him with a cup of stale black coffee and a bottle of water. He had been waiting for Detective Schmidt for almost four hours now and wondered if this was a psychological tactic of hers, or if she was just busy with the case. He hadn't had a chance to see any more news about the cases before arriving at the station, but assumed they were making progress.

I hope Andrei is doing ok, he thought to himself as he continued to watch people go by the windows. His travel to Vancouver had not been easy. After he landed in Victoria, it took him a few hours to find a motel that took his cash for the night—or what was left of it. The next morning he took the ferry from Victoria to Vancouver, staying warm inside for the hour and a half trip, and once he arrived, he had taken a taxi to the station. He had begun to pace the room again when he heard the door open. "Hello, sir," a female voice said.

Gustav turned around and saw a woman of medium height in her early forties with a somewhat stocky build. He thought that if she took off the sports jacket, maybe she would look different, but her emerald eyes and dyed blonde hair made her a striking figure.

Knowing he couldn't show any intimidation, he said, "Hello. Detective Schmidt, I presume?" though he realized full well that she was the woman from the pictures online.

The woman smiled at him. "Shall we sit?" she said, as she started towards the chair closest to the door.

They took their seats. Gustav could tell that she was sizing him up, just as he was doing to her, so he decided to make the first move.

"Thank you for seeing me today, Detective Schmidt. I believe I have some information that may be of use to you regarding the cases you've been working on."

Gustav stopped there, and as soon as he saw the corner of her mouth turn up in a slight smile, he knew that she probably wouldn't believe him at first, and that she had many people saying they knew something.

Finally she spoke. "That sounds interesting, sir, but can I start with your name, please?"

"Of course, my name is Jonas Pedalton. Would you like to ask me more questions or should I just lay out the information that I have?"

After he said this, he felt he had shown too much of his hand already, giving her time to assess him and his intentions.

She opened her notebook and Gustav could see her write down his name before she pulled it closer to herself and put her left arm over the paper. "Why don't you tell me why you're here, Mr. Pedalton," she said.

Gustav opened his attaché and pulled out a folder with all his information to begin. As he did so, he could see her eying it and what it held. He didn't want to offer himself up on a platter to the detective right away because he wanted her to listen to the information he had gathered. However, he knew that, either way, he was going to be arrested at the end of this disclosure.

"I've found the mastermind behind these killings that you are investigating," he began. He noticed her eyebrows rise and her head cock to one side slightly, at his opening statement. He continued, "I am willing to hand over all the information that I have regarding this individual, in return for a better deal for myself."

Gustav paused, as he could see that she was taking in all that he was saying.

"Would you excuse me, Mr. Pedalton? I would like my partner to be in the room for this as well," she finally said.

"Of course, please invite Detective Hill to join us," Gustav replied, and she slowly got up out of her chair, smiled at him, and exited the room.

Gustav took a deep breath. He didn't know how this would go, but he hoped they could all remain civil while he presented the information to them. He fully understood that he was guilty in all these murders, as he was the one who had committed them, but they needed the psychopath behind the curtain. He began to pace the room again to get his brain cells flowing and ready for their return.

****

Once Schmidt had left the vicinity of the interrogation room, she half-jogged the rest of the way to the task force room, where she found her partner, Hill, going over the files that she'd left for him.

He looked up as she came breathlessly into the room. "So another crazy?" he asked.

She shook her head as she tried to form words. "This guy says he knows who the *mastermind*—his words—is behind all the killings. Call the other teams and let them know what's going on. Then I need you to come back up with me to interview him."

Hill was a bit stunned, but immediately tried to call DCI Karim and DI Wilhelm to let them know about this new development. "Shit, Amir must be sleeping," he said after trying him, so he tried Sandy and she picked up on the second ring. After he'd told her about this Mr. Jonas Pedalton who was waiting to give his information, he asked her if she could inform the other teams so that they could head up to the interview.

"Of course!" Sandy replied, and with that he hung up the call.

"Do we have a plan here, Jules?" Hill asked.

Schmidt had had some time to think while he was on the phone. "I think we let him tell us everything he feels we need to know. He seems very eager to get it out, but mentioned a deal for himself as well, so I'm wondering if he's involved."

Hill understood the assignment. Listen first and digest the information, then ask questions.

****

Gustav had been pacing the room for almost forty minutes when the door opened again, this time with both detectives entering. The man was over six feet tall with light brown hair cut very short, and walked into the room with a confident energy. He held out his hand to Gustav.

"Hello, I'm Detective Hill. Nice to meet you Mr. Pedalton."

Gustav shook his hand and smiled as they all sat down again at the table.

"Would it be all right if we recorded this interview?" Detective Schmidt asked.

Gustav, knowing full well that the evidence he had couldn't be changed, responded, "Recording will be just fine."

Schmidt pressed the record button on a small device and placed it in the centre of the table. "Interview dated November 27th, 2026, with Detectives Julia Schmidt and Chris Hill present, along with Jonas Pedalton who would like to give evidence. Please go ahead when you're ready, Mr. Pedalton," Schmidt said, notebook open and ready.

Gustav eyed both of them, lifted his chin slightly and, placing both his hands on top of the folder, began.

"I would like to begin by telling you that I am fully aware that I will be incriminating myself during this interview. I do not seek legal advice just yet."

The detectives looked at each other quickly and Schmidt said, "Understood, please continue."

"I was employed by a man who went by the screen name *theVoyeur*, who paid me as a hitman," Gustav said. "When I wanted out of the situation, I knew I had to find out who he was, so that I had material to help myself in a situation such as this."

Gustav maintained eye contact with each of them as he explained.

"The man who paid me is César Thiago Gomes, aged 56, of Brazilian descent. His current whereabouts are unknown to me, but I'm guessing that he is on his yacht somewhere in the Mediterranean, hiding out. He has a large home in San Jose, California that he hasn't seemed to be at for over a year. He was also a sitting board member at Varcity Telecom and DreamScape Ltd.."

Here Gustav paused to watch their reactions. Detective Schmidt kept a calm face, but he could see a sparkle of recognition in her eyes at both those company names. However, Detective Hill was less careful and placed a hand over his mouth to try to cover his reaction, then scratched at his chin to make it seem like an involuntary movement.

"I have all the details in this folder here," Gustav continued, "but what I've come here for is to save the life of Estella Crain."

This time Detective Schmidt couldn't hide the surprise. "What do you mean, save Estella Crain?" she asked quickly as she leaned forward.

"I have been contracted to kill her," Gustav began, "and I do not wish to do so. If I don't do anything, he will likely hire someone else. I'm willing to cooperate with everything, but I want to make sure that none of this information is given to the media yet, and I would like to help you work out a plan to catch this bastard."

They all looked back and forth at each other. Detective Hill slumped back in his chair with his arms crossed. Gustav thought this meant this guy didn't want to work with a criminal.

Finally, Detective Schmidt took the lead. "Mr. Pedalton, the things you have said here today are going to have you arrested at the end of this conversation. Perhaps we can listen to some more of your ideas once we have had a chance to go through the file."

Gustav knew this was coming. "I'm sorry, detective, but I need to know now that you'll work with me, and not just lock me away while you try to catch this guy. Estella Crain needs to be in protective custody until you find him. I have a deadline of November 30th to have her killed, and if he doesn't hear from me, he will go into hiding."

"I understand," Detective Schmidt said. "Interview paused," she said for the benefit of the recording, then addressed Gustav. "Please give us a bit of time to confer with our captain about this and we'll come back. We'll place an officer outside the door so we don't have to cuff you to the table."

Gustav nodded his agreement, and the detectives left the room and flagged down an officer to watch the door. Gustav had played his hand, but he wasn't sure at this point if they were going to cooperate with him or not. His chance for calling this off had come and gone, and he sat there thinking of further ways to convince them to listen to his ideas.

About an hour later, the two detectives came back into the room and started the recording again. "Interview resumed," Schmidt said. "Mr. Pedalton, we're very interested in the details that you have about your employer, but we would like to ask you some questions regarding the murders. Do you want a lawyer now?"

Forty-Six

Gustav had hired a lawyer the previous Friday morning after doing his research before leaving Detroit. He had paid a $10,000 cash retainer to Aimee Chen, a top defence attorney with Brooks, Weinberger and Associates. He had explained what he was about to do and assured her that he had the funds to pay her more. He could see that she didn't like the idea, but agreed to be his lawyer throughout him turning himself in and to come to the station when she was needed. She had tried to insist that she be there from the beginning of the interview, but Gustav had told her that he wanted to see how things went first and not pose a threat by having his attorney there from the start.

The police had been kind so far, and Aimee had been called to come in for 8 am in the morning to continue the interview. Gustav had been given food, water and access to a bathroom as well as a cot and blankets that were brought into the interview room for him to rest overnight. There was always a guard at his door, but it seemed to him that they were keeping him on friendly terms because they needed the information that he had.

By 6:30 am an officer came in to wake him up. Although he hadn't gotten much sleep, he was grateful for the rest. They allowed him some time in a bathroom, under guard, and then brought him some breakfast and coffee while he waited for his lawyer to show up for their pre-interview.

****

After leaving Mr. Pedalton the evening before, Detectives Schmidt and Hill had made sure that he was comfortable before heading back to the task force room to alert all the teams to what was happening. They could barely contain their excitement in sharing this break. Knowing they had until the next morning, they arranged a conference call for 4 am their time to explain the situation to everyone. Before Schmidt left for the evening, she helped Hill put together an email to everyone with the details and the downloaded recording from the interview so far so that they were all prepared.

"I'll leave my phone on in case anything happens, but be here for the teams if they have follow up questions," she said to Hill, who nodded his approval. "And don't stay too late if you're going to be here in the morning, we need to be fresh for tomorrow," she added before she walked out of the room.

The next morning, Hill walked into the task force room with an extra large coffee and sat at the table with Schmidt and their captain, waiting to start the call. Once everyone had dialed in, the excitement was perceptible.

"Ok, ok, everyone," Schmidt began. "I know this is a big break, but we still have to see what information he has today. DCI Karim, were you able to work with Dorina at Interpol for information on this Gomes person?"

Dorina Keller spoke up. "Hi, Julia, yes, we worked together on that, and we're still gathering information about him. We've shared what we have so far regarding his financials and business connections to the Interpol teams around the world, and we've released his picture to airports and law enforcement agencies."

As they discussed the upcoming interview some more, Schmidt let the team know that they were going to press Pedalton for the identity of the man in the pictures and had prepared a folder of their evidence for the interview. With the meeting concluding, and everyone having jobs assigned to look into Mr. Pedalton and Mr. Gomes, DCI Karim piped up.

"Should we also be looking at Walter Dumas? What if the CEO of DreamScape Ltd. has a role to play in all of this?"

They all agreed, and left that to Karim and Sandy to follow up.

"Also, Amir, can you work with the FBI to try and get their lawyers to allow us to release the information about the murders and that they were done in their dreamscapes?" Schmidt asked.

****

Gustav saw the detectives walk past the window of the interrogation room and open the door. He noticed Detective Julia Schmidt was carrying a file folder much like his own, placing it on the table as they both calmly sat down.

"Good morning, detectives," Gustav's lawyer began. "I am Aimee Chen and will be representing and advising Mr. Pedalton."

With all the introductions made, Detective Schmidt placed the recorder on the table and started it. "Interview dated November 28th, 2026, with Detectives Julia Schmidt and Chris Hill present, along with Jonas Pedalton and his lawyer Aimee Chen. Mr. Pedalton, would you like to start with the information in your folder?"

"Before my client starts," Aimee said, "we would like to work out the terms of the deal for Mr. Pedalton."

Schmidt and Hill looked at each other. They had discussed this possibility with their captain before the interview. "Depending on the information that we receive, we're willing to work with Mr. Pedalton to capture the alleged Mr. Gomes," Schmidt said in a calm voice. "We have placed Ms. Crain in a secure location with marshals, as suggested, while we sort out the details of how we can go about this," she continued.

Detective Hill jumped in for the next part of the deal. "We can also offer Mr. Pedalton a shorter sentence depending on his cooperation. He has already admitted to his involvement in the murders, so jail time was already a given. But it can be significantly less, depending on his help."

Gustav nodded his agreement, and his lawyer said, "We agree," for the sake of the recording.

Having discussed with his lawyer what he was going to share that day before the detectives arrived, Gustav knew that he would be formally arrested at the end, but wanted to give them everything they could use to help find Gomes. He opened his folder and looked at his lawyer, who nodded at him to proceed.

After having gone through all the murders and how he had planned them and carried them out, he also gave the detectives everything he had on Gomes, including the black market antiquities deals and the snuff films that he had purchased on the dark web. The detectives had let him talk the whole time while he went through all the details, but as he finished and closed the folder, Detective Schmidt spoke.

"Thank you, Mr. Pedalton. That was a lot of information that we didn't have. If we had a forensic technologist come and sit with you, would you be able to help them go into the information you have provided?"

Gustav's lawyer nodded at him that it was okay, so he said, "Yes, I can help with that. Maybe we can locate Gomes."

He saw a smile on Detective Schmidt's face after his agreement. Then she spoke again. "We just want to ask one question before we break for lunch."

He saw her open her file folder and retrieve two photographs that she held up to show Gustav.

"This young man, who attempted to murder Estella Crain, has been spotted in London, UK," she said.

Damn, Andrei! Gustav thought, as he worked to keep his face neutral and continued to maintain eye contact with the detective.

"Would you happen to know who he is, Mr. Pedalton? You made it sound in your statement that you worked alone on all the murders, but we have video proof of another man, not you, attempting to kill Ms. Crain."

Gustav was at a loss for words. He had wanted to keep Andrei out of it, and had thought by giving them so much information that they would leave the kid alone. His lawyer spoke up when she saw her client wasn't reacting.

"Thank you, Detective Schmidt. Please allow me some time to discuss with my client over lunch and then we'll continue."

****

Detective Schmidt had a smug smile on her face as she closed the folder again and they exited the room. Their first step was to download the interview to share with the teams, and then grab lunch for them all.

"Think he'll give up his partner?" Hill asked as they walked back to the task force room.

"I don't know, I almost think he's sacrificing himself, but yet he really wants justice. Maybe he feels remorse at what he's done. I can't quite figure him out yet," Schmidt responded.

During the second half of the day they would get to ask their questions, and see what Mr. Pedalton's plan was for Estella and Gomes, and if it all made sense.

After they had all finished lunch separately, the interview resumed with the detectives asking more detailed questions about how Mr. Pedalton was hired each time, and how he was able to access each individual's chips.

"As I mentioned, I'd worked in IT," Gustav said, "and I've always had a knack for finding information, which is what got me fired from my job. When DreamScape Ltd. came out with the chip, I thought it would be fun to see if there was any way into their system. As a hacker, those ideas become little projects. Like a person who decides to paint a picture, it's my creative outlet. So when I found a way into the main system, I knew I would be able to access people's chips, but I didn't have the technology to go into them at the time. That became my next project, creating the head gear that I used to allow myself access into the chip as well."

"So," Detective Hill continued his line of questioning, "how did this Mr. Gomes know that you had accessed the chips to be able to commit these murders and hire you?"

"Here's the thing about Mr. Gomes, as you call him," Gustav began. "He seems to have invested heavily in tech companies because he's quite tech savvy himself. He deals a lot on the black market, as I showed you, and he found me. He saw that the mainframe had been hacked and tracked me down. He's far superior in his skills than me, frightening as that may be. Which makes me think now that he still may have access to Dream-Scape Ltd., even though he's been booted off the board for a while."

This idea stumped them all.

"Please excuse me," Detective Hill said, and left the room to call DCI Karim and have him immediately coordinate with the FBI about this new lead. If they could track who had been accessing the DreamScape Ltd. mainframe, maybe they'd be able to track Gomes down.

Meanwhile, Detective Schmidt decided to press the issue of the other man in the pictures again until her partner returned.

"Mr. Pedalton, we know that you couldn't have been working alone because the attacks on Ms. Crain and Mr. Newbury were carried out at almost the same time." She held up the pictures again for him to look at. "Who is this man?"

She could see that Pedalton was making no gestures of recognition, and he finally said, "No comment."

She put the pictures down on the table. "Ms. Chen, please help us out here and advise your client to reveal the identity of this man."

Aimee Chen smiled at the detective, sensing her frustration. "Detective, my client has pretty much solved your case for you and provided you with all the information to convict whilst also turning himself in. Please do not pressure him to comment on things he doesn't choose to."

Before Schmidt could respond to the lawyer, Detective Hill came back into the room and gave a nod to his partner to let her know that it was all taken care of and the team was on it. Schmidt continued, "Okay, Mr. Pedalton, what exactly is your plan for catching Mr. Gomes, and how does it involve Estella Crain?"

Forty-Seven

César Thiago Gomes had been watching the news for the last three days in case he saw anything about that bitch Estella being murdered. Instead, all he saw were the connections being made to the other betrayers that he had eliminated. He laughed to himself as the news reporters talked about how great these people were and what a loss it was to society. "Blah, blah, blah, cheers to their death!" he would exclaim at the screen.

His plan was to head inland for his crew to grab supplies to last three to four weeks at sea in international waters, where he felt the safest, but they had to be careful of oncoming weather systems and choose their position wisely. For the month of December, tropical storms were less likely off the coast of Morocco, so he spent the morning with the captain of his yacht, whom he called Skippy, out of playfulness for their long-standing professional relationship.

"We're heading to Barcelona to dock and get supplies for the next month. I know the crew have been wanting some shore leave, but we cannot right now," Gomes said.

"I understand, sir. Will we stay the night at least and head to the Straits of Gibraltar at first light?"

Gomes thought about it. He knew he could trust his crew with the amount he paid them, but worried about docking overnight in the Marina Port Vell.

"We'll get there about midday, and they can wander the area and head to the beach while a few of them gather the supplies needed. I want everyone back on the yacht by 9 pm so we can get an early start," Gomes replied.

With the agreement made, he made a few calls to arrange for a security detail to be present overnight. He had made some connections on the dark web, not only finding Gustav as a hit man, but also some worldwide protection to be paid for when he needed it, all discreet.

Opening his safe, he took out a few thousand euros in cash and began to walk around the yacht to talk to the crew. He handed each person a six hundred euro bonus for their short shore leave, and explicitly advised them not to speak to anyone about the vessel or whom they worked for. The faces that lit up from the extra cash, he knew he didn't have to worry about, but with the two crew members who gave him a skeptical look when they took the cash, he decided to have them followed just in case.

With the security arranged, and the crew paid, they made it to Marina Port Vell around three in the afternoon. The crew disembarked with laughter and towels under their arms for those who were heading the short distance to the beach for a picnic, for it was far too chilly at this time in November to be sunbathing. Others left with their purses under their arm, ready to hit the shopping not too far away near the Plaça de Catalunya. Gomes saw the security detail waiting to board, and having given the two photos of his crew that were to be followed, he noticed two of the men break off from the group in order to follow them at a distance. Having met with the security team, and leaving the yacht to them, Gomes headed to the restaurants that lined the marina to find a place to eat amongst the crowds.

The day was waning, and he decided to take an evening stroll up La Rambla. He had always been a person who was well aware of his surroundings, and while he walked, he couldn't help feeling as if he was being watched. Many times, Gomes would stop and look at a stall to check his peripheral, noting the people who were behind him, but he didn't notice anyone in particular who was always there. The uneasy feeling was still there as he approached the Gothic Quarter, so he turned right and headed into the winding streets for a better opportunity to see if he was being followed.

He knew that his name had not been on the news and couldn't think how the police would know about him, seeing as he hadn't had any hands-on dealings with the murders. Only that kid's picture had been on the news due to his utter failure at the job. Even if they'd caught him, *theVoyeur* couldn't be traced, he assured himself as he took a few more turns, winding his way back towards the marina as he went. Each turn was an opportunity for him to give a slight glance back, but he didn't see anyone consistently. He had seen the same couple laughing together twice, but they had gone into a shop and he didn't see them again. No one else lasted more than a turn or two.

With the paranoia creeping in, he boarded his yacht and asked the security team to watch their surroundings in case he was followed. These men were essentially hired guns and he paid them very well, so they stood guard, and would do so all night if they needed to. Gradually the crew began to return. Some of them found him in the seating room and thanked him again for their bonuses. Skippy came to Gomes and advised that all the crew had been accounted for and they would head to bed.

"Wait, Skippy," Gomes said. "Can you take us out to sea a bit and anchor there for the night? I would feel much better being away from the city."

"What about the security detail, sir?"

Gomes hadn't thought about that. "Right, give me a moment to talk to them." So he went in search of the team lead.

Having explained his need for leaving the marina, he asked the team lead if any of them wanted to stay on and be shuttled to shore a bit further up the coast the next day. Four of the men left the yacht, while two stayed on with extra pay and an agreement to be shuttled to shore at Valencia. Once everyone who was staying on board was accounted for, Skippy set out for the open sea to anchor overnight.

While they were ferrying away from the Marina, Gomes logged into the secure satellite link he had onboard and hacked into the Interpol main server. His arrogance led him to believe that he wouldn't find anything, so when he saw his picture listed with his full name as a person of interest, his blood boiled. He couldn't press Skippy to keep going tonight as it was unsafe, but he desperately wanted to get out into international waters and safe from prying eyes as soon as possible. Searching some more, he couldn't seem to find why he was a person of interest, and began to doubt his abilities at hacking until he realized that there were also encrypted folders he could not access.

"They wanted me to find this," he muttered to himself.

Now in a rage, he went to Skippy and asked him to anchor close to any port and shuttle the two security men ashore so they could leave first thing in the morning without having to do it then.

"But, sir, it's dark and—" Skippy began.

Gomes cut him off. "We can't be far from Tarragona. Drop them there and I'll hear no more about it. Just get them off the boat!"

Gomes went to let the two men know that they would be disembarking that night and to get ready. He was feeling slightly better having a plan, but needed to get Skippy to agree to alternating shifts with his back-up pilot so they didn't waste any time getting through the

Straits of Gibraltar. It would take them almost two days to get there.

With Skippy arriving back at the yacht after he ferried the security team to shore, Gomes had a meeting with him about the alternating shifts to keep the vessel moving and not lose time.

"We'll have to increase the speed to 20 knots if we want to make it there by tomorrow evening, so we're cruising through the night," he said to his captain. He headed back to his seating room and poured himself a glass of whisky. He knew something was going on, but he wasn't sure how Interpol had any information about him or whether they had connected him to the murders or not.

"I bet it was that bitch!" he said aloud.

Estella Crain had caused his downfall from two companies, and all he could hope for now was seeing news of her murder. He logged into the secure satellite again and sent a message to Gustav through their encrypted chat.

theVoyeur: You have 2 days left, keep me posted.

Gomes hadn't seen Gustav online for many days now and assumed he was working on his plan for this murder he was contracted to do, but now he was wondering if that was really the case.

"They don't know who I am, or my real name, they proved that to me," he mused. "Plus I have the video of good old Gustav murdering Arthur. He wouldn't dare jeopardize himself, he has too much pride."

With those last confident thoughts in his mind, and the yacht cruising at 20 knots towards international waters, he headed to his cabin to get some sleep.

Forty-Eight

Ada had enjoyed the last week off with Ramon, and was dreading going back to the office.

"Are you sure you'll be okay on your own while I'm at work, babe?" she asked him as they were taking a walk through her favourite forest.

Ramon squeezed her mittened hand and said, "Of course I will be, silly. I have some calls to make this week too, because I'm doing part-time work while I stay here a while longer."

They had both agreed for Ramon to extend his stay after they'd seen the guy from her dreamscape in Hyde Park. Ramon didn't want to leave just yet, not only to be protective, but also because he couldn't imagine going back and not being able to see her again for so long. It had only been a week, but they had become so comfortable around each other that it was as if they had been dating for years. Joel felt it, too. They had become a little family in such a short amount of time.

That night they were having Ada's family and Kira over for dinner, and she could tell that he wasn't the least bit

322 ~ H.M NEWSOME

concerned with meeting them all. Everything just felt so natural and easy. She was blown away each day. They met up with Kira for lunch at a pub and shared some laughs and drinks to enjoy this last full day together before life returned to a bit more normal with work.

"We should really get going to help Joel with the dinner prep before my family starts to arrive," Ada said to them as Ramon was asking for the bill.

"Oh, the family meet and greet! Ramon, watch out!" Kira jested as they stood up to put their jackets back on and walk back home.

Ramon put his arm around Kira's shoulders and said, "I was more worried about meeting you than her family." He winked at her and they all laughed.

"The best friend is the most important person. That's where the impression lies," he said.

They continued to joke with each other as they walked until Ada became extremely silent and didn't hear the last joke that Kira made.

"Babes! Didn't you hear me? I said wouldn't it be great if Ramon just got a job while he was here ... huh? Are you okay?"

Ada came out of her distraction and replied, "Sorry, honey, I thought I saw someone, but he's gone now. Yes, that would be amazing!"

She squeezed Ramon's arms a little harder and smiled up at him, but she could see the concern on his face.

"What did you see?" he asked.

"Oh, it's nothing," she said, "just a man in a hat who looked like that other guy we saw in London."

This alerted Ramon immediately. "Where?"

Ada tried to calm him and brush it off, because she wasn't sure if her mind was playing tricks on her now.

"He's gone. I'm sure it was just my imagination. Let's keep going," she urged.

****

Andrei couldn't stop thinking about Ada after seeing her in real life in London. Part of him knew that it was rash for him to go to Nottingham, but he wanted to see her again, desperately. He convinced himself that it was a good idea not to stay in any one place too long, so leaving London was sound judgement. He booked a train to Nottingham early Sunday morning, and arrived around half ten to explore the city. With some notes from when he was looking her up before, he knew the general area in which she lived and worked, but didn't want to head there straight away. He found a cheap hotel that took cash and left his belongings there while he went out for a walk.

After having lunch at a pub, he continued on his walk. He couldn't help his luck. He saw Ada with two other people, arms all entwined, walking and laughing down the opposite side of the street. He ducked into an alley between two shops and watched them until he noticed Ada looking at him. "Shit!" he muttered and retreated down the alley a bit further so that he wasn't in view if they passed by. He could still hear the other woman's voice and the deep laugh of that guy she was always with now, as they were getting closer, but then the talking stopped for a moment. He ducked down behind a garbage bin until he heard their voices again and they receded into the distance.

He approached the opening of the alleyway to see if they had gone, and saw only their backs as they headed off in the opposite direction. He knew he would be risking things if he followed, but was confident in his abilities and kept a good distance on the other side of the street from them to see where they were going. Eventually they all entered a house with a small gate at the front of the garden. Looking around, he found some hedges just a few houses off from that one and decided to keep watching.

"Just like in the forest," he thought.

****

Ada shook off the illusion of seeing that man on the street and joyfully helped Joel in the kitchen, while Kira opened some wine for all four of them.

"Big day!" Joel said and nudged Ramon in the arm.

"It's not, would you guys stop pestering him," she said. "You're making too big a deal about this."

Kira gave her a side-eye look and whispered in her ear, "You dated Frederic for longer and he never met your family, so it's a big deal, babes."

Ada gently shoved her away and took a sip of her wine. Ramon was in good spirits and she felt excited for him to meet them.

Her mum, Helen, and Davey arrived and the greetings started. Ada laughed when Ramon hugged her mother due to the height difference, and then gave a handshake and half hug to Davey.

"Come in, come in," Ada said, so they wouldn't all be bustling around the front door.

She stood in the front room to get people to sit down and, as she glanced out the window, she saw the back of a man walking; wearing a hat and jacket similar to the man she thought she saw as they were walking home. "Stop it, Ada," she said to herself, realizing that her paranoia was getting out of hand now.

She heard her mother say, "Joel must be cooking tonight because it smells so good," and her brother laughed.

Ramon piped up in her defence. "I can never tell anymore because Ada makes wonderful meals. We make them together sometimes."

Ada's mother looked a bit shocked, but took the comment with grace.

Kira mouthed, "Here we go" in Ada's direction and rolled her eyes.

Joel and Kira were used to this put down sort of jesting that her mother did, but it would be new for Ramon, and they were all ready for it.

"Let's not let this wonderful meal go to waste. Everyone take a seat and I'll bring out the starters," Joel said.

They began with a winter salad of mixed greens, shredded veggies, roasted squash, and pecans before Joel brought out the main course of braised lamb shanks, done in a red wine gravy with mashed potatoes and asparagus. Ada was seated on the side of the table that gave her a full view of the front window and, as the conversations continued, she couldn't help but glance over her brother's shoulder to the window, where the curtains hadn't yet been drawn. It was dark outside, so she couldn't really see anything except the light from the street lamps, but she watched for shadows and movement, knowing full well that from the outside, someone could see everything that was going on inside their house.

****

Andrei had walked up and down the street a few times so that he wasn't in one place too long, but when it got darker he found a nicely hidden place opposite the house to conceal himself in. They were having a dinner party and hadn't closed their curtains, so he could see everything that was going on inside. Sometimes it felt like Ada was staring right at him as she looked out the window from a distance, but he knew that she couldn't see him. Knowing that this would go on for a while, he decided to stretch his legs again with a walk, instead of continuing to watch them eat.

As he was coming back around the corner, an hour or so later, he saw people exiting the house and assumed the party was over. Ada was hugging people in the front garden and he didn't want to be seen, so he hopped a small wooden fence to a neighbouring yard across the street to stay out of view. As he backed up to get into the shadows, a motion-sensing light came on and he saw Ada turn her head in his direction. They locked eyes for only a moment, but even at a distance he could sense the alarm in hers, so he hopped the fence again and ran in the opposite direction. Realizing he might have blown his cover, he headed back to the hotel for the night.

****

"Please tell me you saw that!" Ada said to Ramon and everyone else. Ramon had seen it and was ready to give chase when Ada stopped him by grabbing his arm firmly. Her mother and brother didn't know anything about what was going on with this man, or that Ada even had a chip, so Kira said, "Some creep out wandering. Don't pay him any mind, sweetie."

They finished their goodbyes to Helen and Davey and went back into the house, where Joel immediately handed Ada DCI Amir Karim's card and said, "Call him."

Ramon sat Ada down on the sofa and held her hands, looking right into her eyes. "Sweetheart, I think you were right in what you saw earlier. Don't ignore your intuition. You've been off ever since the walk back from the pub. If you believe it was him following you, then call this detective and tell him."

Ada knew they were all right in what they were saying, so she grabbed her phone and dialed the number. She wasn't sure he would answer so late on a Sunday night, but he did.

"DCI Karim," she heard on the other end of the line.

"Hi, DCI Karim, it's Ada Carpenter again. Sorry to bother you so late, but that man that I saw in London ... I think he's here in Nottingham."

There was a pause before he responded, "Hey, Ada, thank you for calling me. Why do you think he's here?"

She then proceeded to explain everything that had happened that afternoon and what had just happened that evening.

He had said he wanted to put a patrol outside her house, but changed his mind and asked her very slowly, "Ada, if this is the guy, he may be very dangerous and linked to a bunch of murders. I'm not saying this to scare you, but I'm wondering if you would be willing to help us catch him?"

Ada asked for a moment and put the phone on mute while she conferred with the rest of the people standing around her in the living room. When she unmuted the phone, she asked for the details of how she could help.

"Uh huh ... yes ... oh, okay ... is that safe? ... tomorrow?" was all that anyone could hear as she continued on the call.

"I have to work tomorrow, but we can do it in the evening," she finally answered before ending the call with him.

Everyone was staring at her and she leaned into Ramon as he wrapped his arms around her. She explained the plan to them all and felt a rush of fear and nervousness wash over her, but she knew that she had to help the police catch him.

If it really was him, she thought as she began to doubt herself.

Forty-Nine

On Monday morning, DCI Amir Karim and DI Sandy Wilhelm got word from their Interpol contact Dorina Keller that there had been a possible sighting of César Thiago Gomes in Barcelona. The visual wasn't confirmed, but a man fitting his description had disembarked from a large yacht and was followed into the Gothic Quarter, where they'd lost him. Wanting to inspect the yacht further, the local police had arranged for a team to head to the port, but when they got there, the yacht had already left.

Keller continued, "We have teams searching for the yacht along the nearby coastlines, and a helicopter searching the area. Unfortunately, no one took note of the name on the yacht, so it's harder for them to figure out which one it is."

Karim was dismayed, but still hopeful. "If I had to guess, he'd be heading away from the area. Can they search for any yachts that are continuously on the move?" he asked.

Keller understood the idea and let them know she would get back to them with any news. Before they hung up the call, Karim expanded on the search for the guy in the photos in London, and how they had had no luck in tracing his actions. They had seen him entering and leaving Paddington Station and believe he's now arrived in Nottingham, as their witness, Ada Carpenter, had called the previous night to let them know she thought the same man was following her. He told them about the plan to try and catch him that night with Ada's help. Having everyone on the calls with the Vancouver team and the evolving plan regarding Estella Crain and catching Gomes, there was nothing else new to discuss. All of them had their own roles to play in this worldwide effort to catch these men.

Karim turned to Sandy after the call and asked if she had heard from Ada yet. The plan was for Ada to keep in touch with Sandy via text throughout the day to see if she spotted the man, in the hope that he wasn't spooked from last night. In addition, Karim had a team going through CCTV for the areas of Nottingham train station and those where Ada thought she saw him. They wanted to see him on camera, get an idea of his movements, and possibly find out where he was staying. Karim had gotten rush access to the footage due to the high profile of the case and the possibility of catching the man who had attempted to murder Estella Crain.

"I'm going to check with the tech teams and see if they've found anything yet, Sandy. Let me know if you hear from Ada," Karim said as he grabbed his coffee to head to the second floor.

****

Ada was feeling nervous that morning before heading to work and really didn't want to leave Ramon's side. He gave her one last hug and some words of encouragement before she and Joel headed out to work. "You've got this, sweetheart! You've got me here and Joel by your side. Not to mention DI Wilhelm via text. Just be aware of your surroundings, and we'll hopefully get him tonight. I love you."

Ada had her face snuggled into his chest as he said these last few words. She pulled away from him with a surprised look on her face and saw him smiling down at her.

"I love you, too," she finally said as they kissed, and she headed out the door with Joel.

"I can feel your anticipation and excitement, Joel, so spit it out," she said as they walked down the street.

Joel couldn't contain his smile any longer. "Oooh, honey! If you hadn't finally said it to him, I was going to!"

They laughed and gushed about her budding romance all the way to work, not really paying attention to people around them. Joel's last piece of advice before he went to his office was to keep checking out her office window throughout the day and scanning the streets. As she sat at her desk, she felt she should update DI Wilhelm that there were no sightings on her way to work.

Ada's phone went off immediately. *Ding, ding.*

It was DI Wilhelm advising her to be seen during the day in case it would lure the man out, so she sent Joel a message that they were going out for lunch today on police orders.

As they walked to their favourite bistro, Ada kept stopping to window shop, but really it was to check the reflection to see the surrounding area behind her. Every time they stopped, Joel would stand facing her side and scan the area as well.

Once seated at their usual table, Ada confirmed with Joel, "I didn't see him, did you?"

Joel simply shook his head as the server came up to chat with them before taking their orders. After she left, Joel asked, "What if he doesn't show up today? Will you have to keep doing this?"

Ada wasn't sure how to answer this question. She hated the *what if* cycle, but from what she had seen, this guy wasn't giving up.

"Well, I'm hoping that his stalker vibe is so strong that he can't resist. I mean, he came from London the very next day after he saw me in the park," she said.

Joel agreed. This guy did seem to be a bit unhinged, and had even followed her home to watch the house.

The afternoon was drawing to a close and they hadn't spotted him yet. She stood in front of her office window looking up and down the street, knowing that there was no way he would know which floor or window was hers. She glanced in both directions, looking intently at the people walking, but he wasn't one of them. Just before she sat down again, she caught some movement outside the cafe across the street. Someone had bumped into one of the tables set outside for their customers. The man sitting there dropped his paper to see what the commotion was, and that was when she saw him. She grabbed her phone off her desk and tried to take a picture by zooming in, but it just kept getting grainy. She still took a couple of shots and sent them to DI Wilhelm, Ramon, and Joel. Her phone rang as Joel was bursting into her office, and she ushered him to the window and pointed as she answered DI Wilhelm's call.

****

DI Sandy Wilhelm alerted the team that was going to assist with catching this guy that he had been seen. She sent one person to do a walk by and then to sit at the cafe as well, so they could get some video to confirm that it was the right person before making the arrest. She hated the red tape part of the job because, if it was up to her, they would just grab him now. An hour later she got a call from the person who was to go to the cafe saying that he wasn't there anymore, and that they had checked the surrounding areas and couldn't find him.

"Dammit!" she muttered as she hung up the phone.

She had heard from Ada that the man hadn't been spotted again, and that Ada was at home now.

She walked to Karim's desk and said, "Do we really do this tonight? She saw him once and it's not been consistent, nor do we have confirmation that she's not just seeing men who look like him."

Karim understood her concern. "We need to see him ourselves. Do you think it's better to just have her watched by one of our own and they can see if he reappears?" They decided to huddle up with the team and then call Ada with what was going to happen that night.

With their decisions made, Karim called Ada. "Hi, Ada, this is DCI Karim. We just wanted to let you know about some changes to the plan."

He advised her that they had sent someone to the cafe earlier, but the man was gone already, so they couldn't see who he was. He reassured her that they weren't doubting her, and they were still searching the CCTV for Sunday and now for today, around her work. They were going to set up a surveillance team, very discreetly, to watch her house, but if she still wanted to attempt a walk this evening, alone, someone from his team would be there to follow her from a distance. He also reassured her that they didn't think him to be dangerous, but that he simply wanted to meet her, and there would be undercover officers nearby.

With her agreement that she would still go out on her own that night, Karim sent his team out right away for surveillance, with a car down the street from her house at all times. They were mobile now, and he wanted constant communication from his team.

"I told her she would be safe, so let's make sure that she is! Eyes open, everyone," he said before they were dismissed to their posts. Ada had told them the route that she would take, so he sent officers out along her path beforehand to stay hidden.

****

Joel and Ramon didn't like this idea at all, but nothing could sway Ada from her determination.

"I have to see if this helps," she pleaded with them. "I can't live in fear that he's watching me all the time. And I know he may not even show, but I have to at least try."

She could see the looks on their faces, wrought with concern, but she headed out on her own at the agreed upon time of 7 pm, giving the officers enough time to get into place.

Walking in the opposite direction to her way to work, she tried not to hurry or rush her pace, and appeared to be just going for a casual stroll. She stayed vigilant on her walk, as she would have any other time, walking alone at night, and made sure to look at any man on either side of the street. She wasn't sure what the undercover officers looked like, so she couldn't pick them out of the people she saw as she headed past the pubs. People were in a jovial mood for a Monday evening, and she remained friendly as she passed them with a hello or a laugh. She was just supposed to make a loop, so she took a left and continued down the sidewalk as she headed into a subdivision of houses and parks.

For a moment she thought she heard footsteps behind her and stopped to tie her boots, turning slightly to the side so she could glance to her right, but she didn't see anyone there. Maybe it's one of the undercover officers, she thought as she stood up and kept walking. As she approached the entrance to the park, she could feel her hesitation building. It was darker here and she wasn't sure what to expect, so she told herself to be calm and brave as she hit the entrance.

She couldn't immediately see anyone in the entrance, and knew that this pathway led back to her street, but DCI Karim had instructed her to not go through the park and to stay on the lit streets. She remembered that the park entrance she passed as she left her home was clear, but this entrance was poorly lit. She quickened her pace a little and tried to not let her fear consume her. Just as she was under a streetlamp again, she heard shuffling footsteps and quickly turned around in fright.

The man was standing in the shadows still, but she knew it was him, the man who had been watching her in her dreamscape. She wasn't sure if it was fear or bravery that made her say something.

"What do you want?" she asked with a forceful tone.

He stepped closer, slowly, into the light of the streetlamp she was under. "Ada, I just wanted to say hi, and that I think you're a very interesting and talented person."

She could tell that he felt awkward, but she felt more shocked being addressed by her name. The whole walk she had had her phone in her hand, with DI Wilhelm on the other end listening to the walk as she went, so Ada's one sense of security was that the detective would hear this conversation and send someone right away.

"Umm, thank you," she hesitantly said, her body rigid with unease. Where are they? Was all she could think as time ticked on.

The man took another step forward and she took one step backward to keep the distance between them, but he was more in the light now and she was positive it was the same man.

He spoke again. "I hope I haven't frightened you. I just really wanted to talk to you, but you're always with someone else."

As he said this, he looked down at the ground shyly. Ada could see a car park quietly down the street, with its lights off, so that he wasn't alerted. Two people got out of it without closing their doors, then began to slowly approach the man from behind. She knew she had to keep him distracted while they came on. "You know my name, but I don't know yours."

He almost seemed delighted that they were talking. "I'm Andr ... Anthony. My name is Anthony. It's nice to meet you."

Just as he said this with a smile on his face, an officer grabbed him from behind, and the look of shock and sadness on his face was palpable. Another car came down the street from behind Ada and told her to get in. As she stood there in awe for a moment watching him being taken to the other vehicle, she felt a hand on her shoulder and screamed.

"It's okay, Ada, it's me, DI Sandy Wilhelm," the woman next to her said.

Ada crumpled into the woman's arms and began to cry, letting out all the fear she had held in for the last couple of days. Finally, she got into the back of the unmarked car, and they drove her around the block to her house where she was consoled by Ramon and Joel.

Fifty

Gustav had been waiting for the detectives for a couple of hours with his lawyer, feeling the money just drip away with every minute that ticked by, since she would charge him to sit in this room and wait. It was almost noon and they still needed to sort out the rest of the details for faking Estella's murder. Eventually, Detectives Schmidt and Hill entered the room, bringing with them some fast food for all four of them.

"I figured this could be a working lunch," Detective Schmidt said to him. Gustav didn't mind the treatment he had received here, and they had been working together so far.

The female detective continued, "Before we begin our lunch, Mr. Pedalton, I just wanted to let you know that the man from those pictures I showed you has been caught in Nottingham while stalking a young woman. He will be charged with the attempted murder of Estella Crain and the stalking of Ada Carpenter. Is there anything you would like to add now?"

Gustav realized there was no point in hiding his reaction any longer. He closed his eyes and shook his head no. He felt a great sense of disappointment in Andrei, that he would let his obsession with that girl allow himself to be caught. Questions were circulating through Gustav's mind as he ate his burger. *Why didn't he just go off-grid? Why would he go somewhere where there's CCTV everywhere? Why would he stalk this girl? Where was his brain?* Gustav just couldn't understand.

After they finished eating, the detectives wanted to interview him some more, but Gustav was frustrated by this point and blurted out, "Estella must die today!" That seemed to get everyone's attention, so he continued in a calmer voice, "Gomes will be watching the news and may even message me on our secure messaging system to confirm that it's been done. That was how I communicated with him in the past."

The detectives assured him that only a few trusted media outlets had the story ready for the breaking news just after 4 pm, and the smaller media channels and internet would follow along, assuming it to be true. They had a statement prepared to give a press conference, and Ms. Crain had been cooperating with the ruse by agreeing to the staged crime scene photos that would be leaked.

Gustav was hoping that it would be enough. "He'll still expect communication from me, stating that it's completed. I need access to my laptop and other materials that I arrived with."

The detectives stared at him in silence for a moment, when his lawyer piped up. "I'm sure Mr. Pedalton agrees to doing this in your presence and with a tracker attached, to help locate Mr. Gomes."

Gustav nodded his approval of this suggestion.

"I will need a VPN so he can't access my IP address and know that I'm in police custody. I will work with your teams and you can monitor the entire conversation," he said to them.

With the agreement made, the detectives left the room to get someone from the IT department to help Gustav set up his laptop and make it untraceable, as well as set up their own systems to try and track Gomes' IP.

"Do you think this will work?" his lawyer asked him.

Gustav wasn't completely sure, but it was the only way he could think to make it plausible to Gomes. "I can only hope," he replied.

****

Gomes and his crew were almost at the Strait of Gibraltar, having taken a bit longer than expected with the helicopters flying around. Every time they spotted one they would lessen their speed or stop altogether so that they didn't appear to be moving quickly away from the area. So far, they had gone undetected, as the helicopters had flown over and kept going. Gomes figured that they were on the lookout for the yacht that had docked for only a couple of hours before leaving the Barcelona port again, as he was sure that he had been spotted.

Interpol is relentless, he thought as he sat in his cabin shuffling through his passports to figure out which one he would use if he needed to make landfall.

He headed up to the main sitting area with the large television set into the wall and turned on the news to see if anything about Estella Crain was being mentioned. To his despair he saw no mention of her death yet. It was dark out now, and they had slowed their speed for safety at night, but he was not going to bed until he knew she was dead. He opened his laptop, connected to the secure satellite, and sent an encrypted message to Gustav.

> *theVoyeur:* Is it done? Your time is up.
> I'm not liking this silence.

He left the connection open and kept the news on the television while he poured himself a glass of Glen Fiddich.

"Sir," Skippy said as he came into the room, "the crew are going to close down the kitchens soon, would you like anything?"

Knowing it might be a long night, Gomes said, "Yes, have them put together a platter of different things for me to graze through."

With a nod, Skippy exited the room to relay his message. Gomes leaned back on the comfortable sofa, awaiting word from Gustav.

****

Gustav and his lawyer were moved to another room where officers had brought all the equipment that he had arrived with. He was directed to sit down at the table so that he could set it all up. The young officer assigned from the IT security team was watching him closely.

"How long until the news breaks?" he asked the detectives.

"Just under two hours," Detective Hill said.

Gustav nodded, realizing he had to say something now. "Are you all set up to track and trace?" he asked as he looked at the young officer beside him.

"Yes, sir."

He logged into the secure messaging application and saw that he had a notification already. "See, he's already looking for confirmation."

Upon opening the application, they all saw two missed messages:

> *theVoyeur:* You have 2 days left, keep me posted.
> *theVoyeur:* Is it done? Your time is up. I'm not liking this silence.

Gustav sighed before typing his reply:

> *SilentIsTheNight:* It's done. Transfer the rest of

the funds.

theVoyeur: Excellent. Do you have proof?

SilentIsTheNight: I didn't stand around to take pictures to incriminate myself.

theVoyeur: Fair enough, but how do I know you're telling the truth?

Detective Hill laughed. "This guy is paranoid for a psychopath."

Gustav shook his head and continued:

SilentIsTheNight: You'll just have to wait for the news to come out.
I'm sure she will be found soon. It was hard to get in there between check-ins with the cops.

theVoyeur: When I see the news, I will pay the remainder.
Until then, be available.

Gustav looked around the room at the detectives, waiting for them to say something. Detective Schmidt spoke up. "We'll just have to get comfortable here then."

SilentIsTheNight: Ok.
theVoyeur has signed off.

The trace didn't prove to be useful, as Gustav had known it wouldn't be. Gomes' IP address was bouncing around to different countries the entire time. He heard the detectives whispering and made out a few words: *sighting, Barcelona.*

"Is there news about Gomes?" he asked. "We're supposed to be a team here so we can catch him."

They looked at him and then at each other, and Detective Schmidt filled him in on the sighting in Barcelona and about the yacht likely being on the move.

Gustav sat back and thought for a moment. He was the only one who really knew how this guy operated. "A couple of questions," he said. "Did you leave breadcrumbs for him to find on the Interpol database if he hacked in?"

The detectives nodded, and Gustav continued, "If he's found out and is on the run now, I would assume that he would head out to international waters for a sense of safety. Did you leave that tracker in the system to know if he had been in?"

At this, the young officer spoke up. "Yes, there was a suspicious search performed for his name, and from his reaction in Barcelona, if that was him, we think he found the pictures of himself on the site. But nothing else was accessed, because they encrypted it all with your suggestions."

Gustav decided to tell them about how unstable the man was, based on the messages that he'd received after the failed attempt on Estella Crain's life. "If he's on the run, he may become unpredictable," he said to the team in the room.

A knock came at the door to let them all know that the press conference was getting set up, and the story would hit the waves in twenty minutes.

"You stay here with this officer, and if you need a private moment with your lawyer, he can be excused for a moment," Detective Schmidt advised before she and her partner left the room.

His lawyer looked at Gustav and said, "I have to get back to the office. Don't say anything or do anything for them until I get back." And with that Aimee Chen grabbed her briefcase and left the room as well. So Gustav sat there with the young officer, staring at his screen, waiting for another message to come through, if it would that night.

Fifty-One

Ada called the managing director at her office on Tuesday morning to explain what had happened the night before and said she was taking a mental health day, as she was still quite shaken. Before Joel left for work, he showed Ada and Ramon where the Christmas decorations were and explained that it was tradition for him and Arthur to start decorating on December 1st. Since this was his first Christmas without him, he would love it if they could help uphold the tradition.

"Of course, Joel! We'll start decorating and put the tree up so that we can decorate it when you get home tonight," Ada said.

Joel hugged them both before he left. Ada hadn't realized that he might be struggling with the upcoming holiday, with all that had been going on with her, as well as Ramon's visit.

Ramon carried the boxes out from under the stairs where they were stored, and placed them all in the living room. As they started going through the boxes, Ramon said, "You know, since this is your first Christmas at this house, maybe we should get you some of your own stuff to add to Joel's?"

Ada smiled at his suggestion. "That would be lovely."

They started opening the boxes and put out some random decorations, including a garland on the stair banister with holly and berries in it, then wrapped a gold and silver ribbon through it.

By lunchtime, Ramon asked, "How about a lunch at the pub under the castle and then some shopping?"

She adored the fact that he enjoyed making plans and agreed, so they went to get ready before heading out for the afternoon. After lunch they went to the main street with all the shops and began browsing for Christmas ornaments. In one shop they went into, Ada lost sight of Ramon until she saw him at the register paying for something and coming back to her with an opaque bag.

"What's in there?" she asked.

"Nothing for you to see yet," he smirked back at her. She found some items for the tree and a couple of decorations for her room to make it more festive before they started to walk home.

The weather had turned a bit colder and Ramon held her hand as they walked, each with their own bags in the opposite hands. "Are you feeling better, love?" he asked.

She squeezed his hand and said that she did, and that being with him that day made all the difference. She started dinner for them all as Ramon struggled with the fake tree and putting all the pieces together, while making a mess on the floor with the small bits that had fallen off in the tussle. When Joel came in the door and saw the banister, the undecorated tree, and the boxes of ornaments waiting for him, he smiled and his eyes began to water.

"Thank you both, so much. This is absolutely lovely."

Ada hugged him and poured him a glass of wine while they waited for dinner to be ready.

****

DCI Karim had sat across the table from Anthony Moretti, so named according to his passport and the ID that they'd found on him. As he wasn't from the UK, he didn't have a lawyer already, and although he asked if he could find one, they said that he could have a public defender assigned to him and be present for the questioning. Karim could tell from the sullen look on Mr. Moretti's face that he did not enjoy that option. Mr. Moretti had been in the lockup overnight, and that morning been brought into an interrogation room and offered some breakfast, but he had declined and opted only for coffee.

Once the public defender arrived around 11 am, DCI Karim went to ask DI Wilhelm to join him in the questioning while he gave the lawyer some time with his new client. After thirty minutes, they came back in and Karim pressed the recording device on the table and started with introductions.

"DCI Karim and DI Wilhelm are present with the accused, Anthony Moretti, and his lawyer that has been assigned to him, Gregory Ives. The date is Tuesday, December 1st, 2026, time 11:37 am." Karim opened the folder that he'd brought in with him and continued, "Mr. Moretti, can you please confirm that this is you in these photos?"

Andrei looked at his lawyer, and Mr. Ives gave a slight nod of his head, so Andrei responded with, "Yes, those are me."

DCI Karim went on, "Can you tell us who hired you to kill Estella Crain?" He saw with every question asked that this young man was looking for guidance from the lawyer that he didn't know. With a shake of his head, Mr. Moretti answered, "No comment."

The next few questions received the same answer and Karim began to feel that this interrogation was going nowhere, aside from Moretti admitting to being in the photos, which was enough for the attempted murder.

"Let's take a break for some lunch, shall we?" he asked the accused and his lawyer. They all agreed and, for the recording, DCI Karim said, "Interview paused at 12:56 pm." Food was sent for, and Karim and Sandy left Mr. Moretti and his lawyer alone in the room.

After lunch was over, they continued with the interview as DCI Karim opted for a new tactic. "Interview resumed at 13:45. Mr. Moretti, I'm not sure if you are aware, but your partner is being held at the Vancouver

352 ~ H.M NEWSOME

Police Department, having willingly turned himself in. A Mr. Jonas Pedalton?"

The only reaction this sparked from the young man was a bit of a smile before he corrected it, but he still didn't answer anything.

"He's been most cooperative in this case and many others. Are you aware of the other cases?" he asked, and received another "No comment." Sandy touched Karim's arm, signalling that she wanted to try.

"Anthony, may I call you that?" she asked, and Andrei nodded. "For the record, let it be known that the accused has nodded his head in assent. Anthony, we are concerned here. We have you on video attempting to kill Ms. Crain in her dreamscape, and we know that Mr. Pedalton has advised he was responsible for many other murders. How would a smart young man such as yourself get mixed up in this?"

Karim knew what Sandy was trying: the softer approach. He watched the young man's body language and facial expressions intently as Sandy was talking. It was as if he wanted to say something, but had been instructed, either by his lawyer or Mr. Pedalton, not to say anything.

Karim was caught off guard by Sandy's next question. "Is your name really Anthony Moretti?"

This got a surprised look from the young man, and his lawyer spoke up. "Are we here to determine who this individual is, or what his crimes are?"

They knew they had struck a chord, so Sandy continued, "I only ask because just before you were arrested, when you were talking with Ada, you sounded like you were going to give her a different name."

Getting nowhere with Mr. Moretti, they decided to conclude the interview and put him back into lockup. Essentially they had what they needed, his confession to being the person in the photos, which would get him attempted murder and stalking. Karim said he would update the other teams with the information and that Sandy should go home, as she had been working some late nights recently.

As he was about to call the Vancouver team, his phone rang. It was Dorina Keller from Interpol. "Hey, Dorina," he answered.

"Hi, Amir, I just wanted to let you know that a potential yacht was spotted heading through the Strait of Gibraltar earlier today towards international waters. Our helicopters were keeping an eye on this one, because it seemed to be moving quickly in bursts. We aren't positive it's him, but we have notified the United Nations to coordinate with local authorities to send a boat out that way for an inspection."

"That's great news, Dorina," Karim said. "Fingers crossed it's him and I'll let the team know. I was just about to call them with an update of our interview with Mr. Moretti, which went nowhere aside from him admitting it was him in the pictures."

"Well, you've got him on something," she replied as they ended the call.

****

Ada, Ramon, and Joel were trimming the tree to some Christmas carols and having a grand time singing and decorating.

"I bought a couple of ornaments to add to the tree," Ada said to Joel as she showed him. "I hope they go with your decor."

Joel laughed and said, "Honey, you could put strings of popcorn on the tree if it made you feel at home. They're lovely, go ahead and put them on."

As Ada hung her decorations, she asked Ramon if he had anything to add to the tree, seeing as he'd bought something in the store when they were there.

"No, nothing to add just yet," he replied slyly and she shook her head. He was up to something, but she wouldn't push; it was obviously a timed surprise.

"Time for hot chocolate and a Christmas movie, I think!" Joel said as he went into the kitchen while Ada and Ramon cleaned up the boxes and stored them again under the stairs.

Fifty-Two

Detective Chris Hill had heard from DCI Amir Karim that they'd caught the man in the photos and media was being arranged for release later that evening. The headlines were already filled with speculation about Dream-Scape Ltd.'s involvement in the murders, but nothing could be confirmed. Regardless of confirmation from the company itself, their stock prices were plummeting, and CEO Walter Dumas was trying to quell the fervour by reasserting the safety of the chip implants.

"This media circus is getting out of hand," Hill said to Detective Schmidt as she walked into the task force room with more coffee for them.

Schmidt placed the steaming mug in front of him and replied, "People are afraid. They don't want to think that this implant can be hacked and they can be murdered, any more than they want a computer virus on their electronic devices. We live in a world that is promised privacy, and yet our information is out there for those bastards to attack."

Hill filled her in on the developments from Nottingham and Interpol's sighting of the yacht headed out to international waters.

"In your last talk with Mr. Pedalton, did he mention any further bits of wisdom to help catch this guy?" he asked her.

Schmidt smirked. "He had a few ideas, but right now he's just waiting for Gomes to respond to him. The news has been reporting Estella's death, and we haven't heard back from him yet."

"What kind of ideas?" Hill pressed.

Schmidt rolled her eyes. "None that really seem viable. He did mention that we should keep eyes on Dumas, being the CEO of the company and all."

Hill nodded his head as he processed that thought. "Wait, we have the hit man here, how is anyone else in danger?" he asked.

"I don't know," Schmidt replied, "but it's always unpredictable when dealing with psychopaths."

The television was on mute in the room, but they could see all the headlines scrolling across the bottom of the screen of the news channel. Hill looked up for just a moment to see where he'd left his coffee mug and saw a live feed of Walter Dumas on the screen.

"Jules, look!" And he unmuted the television as Walter Dumas stood on the front steps of DreamScape Ltd. and continued his press conference.

"... understand that many of you feel afraid. But in no way are these murders connected to DreamScape Ltd. The security of our systems is our utmost priority, and we have not detected any privacy breaches."

Hill gave a chuckle. "Either he's lying or they have really shitty security."

"... number one concern is your safety, my safety, everyone's safety. I have a chip and still enjoy my dream-scape every night. Do not fear what the media is trying to persuade you to believe. Trust in the technology that has remained faithful and secure to you for years."

"Well, that was a load of bull," Schmidt said as Dumas exited the podium.

Walter Dumas came across as a grandfatherly type, looking out for his children's—the general public's—best interest. His silver hair almost matched his grey suit, with a red tie and red pocket square. The look was topped off with his round framed glasses to give the right impression to the crowd. Intelligent, caring, old rich grandpa nerd who wanted the best for you. Rarely did CEOs speak publicly anymore. It was always a public relations person or lawyer giving the details, so the impact of him doing the press conference would be meaningful.

Hill watched Schmidt as she stood in front of the bulletin boards that had all the connecting pieces of the

358 ~ H.M NEWSOME

puzzle and asked, "Did we ever look at the connection between Gomes and Dumas?"

She turned around and replied, "Interpol was looking into that, and the last I heard was that Gomes was one of the first shareholders in Dumas' new company when DreamScape Ltd. was created. Let's follow up with Dorina on that and, in the meantime, I'm going to ask our friend Mr. Pedalton if he found anything out. I didn't see anything in the folder he provided, but maybe he knows something."

When Schmidt returned to the room about thirty minutes later, Hill asked her, "So?"

She shook her head. "He stopped looking into connections when he found Gomes, and then he was asked to murder Estella and decided to end all this by coming here. But he did offer a nice bit of policing in case we weren't smart enough."

Hill laughed. "And what was that?"

"That maybe we should talk to Dumas," she said and smiled.

Hill couldn't control himself at that remark. "As if we haven't been trying to arrange that for the last few days."

They shared more laughter and went back to the evidence they had. The case seemed to be dragging now as they waited on other departments to get back to them.

****

César Thiago Gomes had been watching the news all day and evening. The yacht crew was asleep and they were drifting ever so slightly, with the night pilot at the helm keeping watch and checking that their current coordinates were accurate. He felt relief that Estella Crain had been murdered and was celebrating solo with half a bottle of gin. He hadn't seen any more helicopters and there were no other vessels around, but he wasn't prepared to make himself feel comfortable here in international waters just yet. Simply knowing that Interpol had his name and picture was enough to have him still living with a sense of unease. He needed to plan the just-in-case scenarios.

Morocco was the closest landfall and he knew his money would go a long way there if he needed transportation. He set aside payments for his crew in case of emergency, having checked with Skippy earlier about the lifeboats and inflatable rafts for everyone on board. Instead of keeping his valuables in the safe, he now kept a go bag with everything he would need for a quick escape.

Just as he had decided to get some sleep and shut off the news, he saw the headline 'Breaking News' and decided to see what it was about. There were pictures on the screen of Gustav's accomplice, Andrei (he remembered the name); one picture from Estella's dreamscape; and a mugshot. He turned up the volume to listen.

"Last night in Nottingham, United Kingdom, this man, Anthony Moretti, was arrested under the suspicion of being the man who attempted to murder the CEO of Varcity Telecom, Estella Crain, in her dreamscape. Mr. Moretti is being questioned by the local police, and we await more details."

Gomes could feel his blood pressure rising. "This idiot!" he said aloud and threw his half-full glass of gin against the wall, sending the ice cubes and wedge of lime to the floor with the broken glass. He sat there thinking for a moment. Andrei and his partner didn't know who he was, so it wasn't like they could say much about him. However, Andrei knew that someone was paying them for the jobs, and they had his screen name, *theVoyeur*. He pondered some more about what this kid could tell the police and if he was in any real danger. Finally, he decided to message Gustav and find out why the kid was in Nottingham in the first place.

> *theVoyeur:* Your partner has been arrested.
> How stupid can you be?
> Why was he in Nottingham in the first place?
> And where are you?

Gomes's escape to land under an assumed name was looking more like the outcome at hand as he waited for a response. His thoughts turned to what he would tell the crew, and what he would do with his yacht. He couldn't just leave it at a port; there were too many watchful eyes and cameras around. Finally, a message came back through.

> *SilentIsTheNight:* We decided to go into hiding. I didn't know where he was going or what he was doing, but he messed up.
> *SilentIsTheNight:* After Vancouver, I'm headed to my cabin in Colorado.
> *theVoyeur:* He is now a lost cause, I hope you know that.
> *theVoyeur:* Stay hidden and don't get any fancy ideas.

Gomes signed off, and was still fuming when he stood up to get another glass and he poured himself one more drink. He thought of all the contacts he had made and wondered if any of them could act in the UK. Looking at the time, he knew it wasn't a job for this late hour and that he'd think more clearly in the morning. He had to act fast and plan ahead from here on out. Somehow, he had to get back to North America.

Fifty-Three

César Thiago Gomes awoke at 9 am the next morning when the automatic blinds went up in his cabin, as they were always set to do. He knew his crew would have breakfast waiting for him shortly. He had only managed about three hours of sleep, as his mind had been swirling about the possible outcomes from the arrest of that imprudent young man, Andrei. Still feeling uneasy, and now on edge on top of it, he wasn't sure what he was going to do. He got up and put on his robe over his briefs and went out to enjoy an espresso in the open air, hoping it would refresh him and get his brain working.

"Good morning, sir," the lovely brunette crew member said, greeting him with a tray of his usual breakfast: eggs, sausages, avocado slices, pineapple, and some other fresh fruits they had on board.

"Would you like some toast as well today?" she asked him.

Knowing he might need the extra strength that day, he nodded and said, "Please."

He ate his eggs and sausages while he waited for the toast to arrive, and picked away at the fruit as he contemplated his next move while staring out at the open waters before him. His first thoughts were, "How far are we from land? And what part of Morocco is the closest?" He made a mental note to go and talk to Skippy after he'd finished eating and getting dressed.

As he headed for the helm to see his captain, a plan began to formulate in his mind. He smiled as he went along the corridors and said to himself, "Never doubt yourself, César."

Opening the door, he greeted his captain. "Good morning, Skippy! And how are you on this fine day?"

"Um, I'm well, thank you, sir. How can I help you?" was the semi-shocked reply he received.

"Very well, I'll get right to the point. I need to know how far we are from the coast of Morocco and whereabouts along the coastline. Can you get me that information?" Gomes said to him.

"Of course, sir," Skippy replied. "Just give me a few moments. Are you planning to head inland? It would be a nice stop."

Gomes smiled at his captain. "Not exactly, my dear friend. But the crew may be permanently inland soon."

Having left Skippy with a confused look on his face, but attaining the information he needed, Gomes headed to his cabin to make a private satellite call to a contact in the United Kingdom. With all the details given to his contact, he felt a sense of calm come over him now that one problem had been dealt with. Andrei would be eliminated. Next, he grabbed his dry bag and put in a couple of suits, travelling clothes, and other necessities, along with bundles of cash and his Italian passport under the name of Marco Bianchi, his Spanish passport with the name Jorge Morales, and his French passport under Charles Dubois. He counted out bundles of cash for each of the crew members, giving them each 5000 euros to keep quiet about what had and would happen.

The crew had assembled at the stern of the yacht for the meeting that Gomes had told Skippy to arrange, and when he arrived, he could see the confused looks on their faces.

"Good afternoon, my dearest friends," he began. "I know that the last week has been a bit confusing for all of you and I appreciate your adaptability to the changing course of our journey. You will be thankful to know that you will all be on land in Safi by this evening."

This last statement brought smiles to his crew and some clapping.

"Yes, yes, I know you want to feel the earth beneath your feet, as do I. However, we will not be docking at a port to get there, and I won't be coming with you."

The confusion returned to their faces and, before a few of them were about to ask questions, he put his hand up to stop them.

"I understand that you may have questions, but please know I will tell you very little for your own safety. What you do need to know is that I have here beside me 5000 euros for each of you."

The crew members began getting excited and talking amongst themselves, so he had to reel them back in. "Ladies and gentlemen!" The silence resumed so Gomes could continue as he checked his Patek Philippe & Co. watch.

"You have exactly five hours and 36 minutes to prepare everything you need to take with you, and remember that not all of your belongings will fit into the lifeboats. So only the necessities, please. I'm sure you can buy replacement items."

He gave a nod to Skippy to start handing out the cash to the crew. Just as he was about to leave the room, he turned around to them and said, "I appreciate all of you for your hard work and dedication to me over the last year. I hope that I have your trust, as I trust you."

He turned to leave again when he heard a soft female voice. "Sir? Why are we taking the lifeboats?"

Gomes plastered a smile on his face before turning to address her. "My dear, the life of this yacht has come to an end, and for your own safety and mine, we are abandoning her." Then he made one final address to the group. "If you're not off the yacht in time, you will be left behind. Thank you."

With that taken care of, he strutted away from the stern and continued with his own plans.

Back in his cabin, he opened the safe to take out the remaining item in there: a bundle of C4. The previous year, when his only thought was to take out DreamScape Ltd. in one swift blow, he had learned from an unsavoury individual how to create a bomb using C4. While he'd never used it, he had felt safe having it nearby just in case he ever needed it, and today was that day. He buzzed Skippy on the intercom, hoping that he wasn't frantically packing but still at the helm. After a few moments, he heard his captain's muffled voice come through.

"Skippy, can you come to my cabin, please?"

"Right away, sir," was the reply.

He didn't want everyone knowing about his plans, but if there was one person he really could trust, it was Skippy.

On entering his cabin, Skippy gave the appearance of being distressed.

"What is it?" Gomes asked.

"Sir, I was about to buzz you. The radar is showing a large ship approaching us, moving slowly, but it looks like a direct course unless they correct."

Gomes nodded as he thought. Probably the UN looking for the yacht. He said aloud to Skippy, "How long until they intercept?"

"At the speed they're going, sir, probably four to five hours, but if they pick up speed at all ..." and he trailed off.

Gomes bit his lower lip and sighed. "Okay, tell the crew they now have less time to gather their belongings. What I asked you here for was to let you know the plans.

I'll be placing a bomb in the engine room and I'm going to give you the detonator."

He was interrupted by his captain. "But, sir!"

"No, no 'but sir,' Skippy," Gomes continued. "I'll be leaving the yacht in about an hour in one of the boats. I'm not telling you where I'm going, but it is not to Safi like the rest of you. Please take this extra 10,000 euros to show my appreciation. Once everyone is safely away in their lifeboats and heading a good distance from the yacht, press the button, here, and then toss it into the water, all evidence gone. Can I trust you with this?"

Skippy nodded. "Yes, sir. I'll get everyone into the boats and do as you ask. Please be safe."

After ironing out a few more details about his plan and how he would get to where he needed to be, Gomes put on a wetsuit over his clothing and grabbed his dry bag to head for the lifeboat that would take him most of the way to shore. He didn't want to take the boat all the way in and was aiming for a quiet beach in Oualidia where he could come out of the water, a mellow village with less tourist activity, especially in December. Once on shore he would ditch his wetsuit and head to the nearest road to flag down a car to take him into the village, where he would hire a car to drive him the two and a half hours to Casablanca. From there he needed to somehow bribe his way onto a cargo plane headed for the United States, but he knew that would all be determined when he got there. "One step at a time," he reminded himself as he revved the tiny engine in the boat.

368 ~ H.M NEWSOME

He was thankful for a large breakfast and lunch when he stopped the boat about a mile from shore and jumped in the water with his dry bag on his back. He was fit, but still knew that swimming to shore was a large undertaking. He started out at a good pace and hoped that, as he got closer to the beach, the small waves and current would drive him forward.

Once on the beach he hid his wetsuit in some tall grass, put on his shoes from the dry bag, and headed for the road. He had planned which direction he needed to walk and, as he went, he kept his eye peeled for any vehicles he could flag down. Not being able to see the yacht from the shore, he only hoped that by now the crew were safely in the lifeboats and heading away from it. Just as he was gazing out towards the ocean, he heard a *beep beep* coming from behind him, and a man in a small three-wheeled truck asked, in Arabic, if he was lost. Having studied many languages, Gomes understood him perfectly and asked if he could ride in the back of his truck to the Crystal Palace Hotel in Oualidia.

"Naeam tabean," the driver replied, giving his consent to the request.

At the hotel, Gomes went to talk to the concierge about hiring a car to take him to Mohammed V International airport in Casablanca. He communicated in Arabic the entire time and, although he wasn't a guest at the hotel, the concierge agreed to call him a car. He was about to give him a large tip for his services, but then thought it might stand out too much, so left him with thanks before waiting at the front of the hotel for his car to arrive. The black Mercedes-Benz W123 pulled up and they began their drive out of Oualidia, heading up the coast to Casablanca. About an hour into the drive, as Gomes was peering out the window at the ocean, he saw the explosion of his yacht.

The driver started to speak fast, a little too fast for Gomes to understand him, and then he pulled over to the side of the road and called someone. From the sounds of the conversation, it sounded like the local police, to let them know about an explosion on the ocean.

"Asaf alaa al-intizar" the driver said, apologizing for the wait, and they got back into the car to continue their drive.

Once they reached the airport, Gomes had himself dropped off at a distance so that he could find the freight area and get to the tarmac. Keeping a watchful eye on the security guards around, he managed to spot an employee about to enter a secure key-card locked door. He spoke in Arabic to the young man and showed him some money. This was either going to get him arrested, or given access to the area. Thankfully, the young man was happy with taking the money. He let Gomes enter with him and showed him where the loading area was for the cargo planes. Gomes remained in a darkened section of the warehouse loading area to watch who was best to try and persuade.

After about twenty minutes, he felt a tap on his shoulder. Alarmed, he spun around, ready to fight, but all he saw was the young man who had let him in. In hushed tones the young man told him that he knew who to talk to and if Gomes had money he could get him on a flight.

"Yes, thank you," Gomes replied, and the man ran off to talk to a large man standing on the tarmac by the cargo bay door of an aircraft.

Remaining in place, Gomes waited for the young man to return, with the conversation looking favourable. The young man came back and said that he could fly for 2500 euros—2000 for the man out there and 500 for himself. Gomes agreed to the terms and said, "I'll pay when I'm onboard." The young man nodded, said he would get him a uniform to wear, and took off again.

After about an hour, Gomes wondered if the young man had abandoned the plan, but he shortly returned with a coverall uniform in grey and an orange vest to wear over it. After Gomes put the coverall on over his clothes, he was escorted to the cargo bay door, where the young man and his large superior walked inside him. Once inside he paid them both, and was directed to seat himself in the open area away from the cargo and given instructions for safety. They would leave in ten minutes, he was told, headed for New York, JFK International airport.

Fifty-Four

Twelve hours had elapsed since Gustav had replied to *theVoyeur,* saying "Don't hurt him, he doesn't know anything!" but he hadn't seen Gomes back online since and his message was never read. Gustav was panicking and needed to speak to the detectives, but since he had been moved to a secure location with armed guards and a tech team, he hadn't seen them. The good part was that he had a regular bed and a shower to use now, in thanks for his cooperation and help with the case, but his thoughts remained on Andrei. Gustav asked one of the tech operators they had placed with him if he could again call Detective Schmidt to warn her about the danger to the man they'd arrested in Nottingham. The young tech operator was nice enough to comply and stepped out of the room, leaving the condo unit to place the call.

On returning, the tech operator advised Gustav that the detectives would be on their way shortly, as they had some news of their own and wanted his take on it. An hour later both Detectives Schmidt and Hill arrived at the condo, where Gustav was anxious to talk first.

"Please, I need your help before we get into your new information," he spat out as soon as they had taken off their jackets.

"Okay, Mr. Pedalton, what's so urgent?" Detective Schmidt answered, seeing his agitation.

Gustav calmed a bit and continued, "That young man they arrested in Nottingham, I fear for his safety. Gomes sent a message yesterday saying that this young man is a 'lost cause' and I know that means he's going to try to have him killed."

Detective Hill answered, "He's in lockup, in a cell, and because he hasn't been cooperating, he will stay in that cell. He is perfectly safe, Mr. Pedalton."

Gustav shook his head in dismay. "You still don't understand the scope of this guy's abilities. All I'm asking of you is to let the police in Nottingham know that there may be an attempt on his life. Please! If I wasn't being watched by all these folks here, I would hack into their database and connect with the detective in charge over there. But seeing as I'm cooperating and all, I am asking you two to do it the right way."

The more reasonable of the pair, Detective Schmidt, answered him. "I'll make the call right now to the team in Nottingham. Okay, Mr. Pedalton?"

"Yes, thank you," Gustav replied, finally feeling heard.

Schmidt left the condo to call the Nottingham team and Gustav was left with Detective Hill, who kept eyeballing him as if he had some hidden agenda.

"Look, detective," Gus began, "I know you don't really like dealing with me, but let's see if we can wrap this business up soon. Coffee?" And Gustav went into the kitchen to make a fresh pot of coffee for them all.

When Detective Schmidt arrived back in the condo, she assured Gustav that the team was now aware and they were stationing a guard to monitor him.

"Now, onto our news," she said as she sat down at the table where there was a fresh steaming cup of coffee waiting for her. "We have been notified that a yacht matching the description of Gomes' yacht has exploded off the coast of Morocco."

Gustav was intrigued by this information, and began to play out some theories in his head while she continued to speak.

"The crew were located in Safi, but none of them will confirm why they left the yacht, or if the owner was aboard at all, or if he got off. His picture has been shown to them all, and not a single one is identifying him as the owner."

Gustav gave a slight chuckle at that. "You find this funny, Mr. Pedalton?" Detective Hill abruptly interrupted his colleague.

Gustav smiled at him and said, "Not at all, detective, I am merely amazed still by his ingenuity. He must have paid them all very well for not one of them to confirm that it was his boat."

"Yacht," Detective Hill corrected him.

"Yacht, yes, sorry. You must be a boat man yourself."

"Gentlemen! May I continue?" Detective Schmidt intervened. Eyeing them both with a stern look, she finished with the information she wanted to share. "Gomes is in the wind, and we don't know if he disembarked from the yacht at an earlier stage or somewhere in Morocco. We have Interpol doing searches, but it's a large area to cover, and with his resources, we don't know how far he has gotten. The question I put to you, Mr. Pedalton, is where do you think he would go?"

Gustav sat and pondered this for a moment before saying to them, "If he could find a way, I would say he's heading back home."

"And what makes you think that, Mr. Pedalton?" Schmidt replied.

Gustav stood up from the table where they were sitting and walked over to the window to gaze out at the downtown Vancouver skyline.

"From my research, he was one of the first people to invest in DreamScape Ltd. when it was brand spanking new. He and Walter Dumas funded it, basically, and his thanks for all that was to be kicked off the board by being voted out, like some sad Survivor episode. He hired me to eliminate the people who wronged him, and as they were all board members of DreamScape Ltd., I would guess that he isn't done. He may try to contact me again to do something for him, but I haven't seen him online for almost a day. What would be left for him in his revenge?" This question he posed to the detectives, and they looked at each other and then back at him.

"His remaining revenge, detectives, is either the betrayal he feels from Walter Dumas or DreamScape Ltd. itself. It will depend on which one he wants more. To ruin the company, which he's already been doing with the help of the media, or to take out Dumas?"

Gustav fully turned around now to face them, and saw that Detective Hill was sitting with his arms crossed, likely not having believed him, while Detective Schmidt seemed deep in thought.

She was the first to speak. "So if you're correct, then we need to put eyes on Dumas and DreamScape Ltd. My one issue with this theory is that he's done everything online and through you, so why would he get his hands dirty now?"

Gustav smiled at her. "That one is easy. He's unravelling. He blew up his super yacht and is on the run. He can feel the pressure, but wants to finish what he started. He may still reach out to me to see if I'll help him in this, so it's best if I stay active online for that. He thinks I'm hiding out in my cabin in Colorado."

Detective Hill gave a grunt and said, "You really think he's just going to lose his mind and try to kill Walter Dumas? With all the media attention going on? Come on."

Again, Gustav smiled. "Psychopaths tend to have a mission, and I've seen him unravel before. I even gave you a copy of the chat when he lost his shit on me. Yes, it's preferable to capture him before he does anything else, but until we have a better idea of what that is, it will be hard."

Detective Schmidt spoke up before Hill could answer him. "Thank you, Mr. Pedalton, you've been a great help. Please let us know if he contacts you about anything. We'll get his picture out to the FBI to monitor the San Jose International airport, and to give to the teams that will watch Dumas and his company."

With all the details sorted out, and the detectives leaving, Gustav went back to the tech operator and asked, "Any chance you want to do a little digging? You can put it on your resume as solving a major crime."

The young man looked at him, unsure of how to respond. "I ... I don't think we can hack using police computers, sir."

Gustav sat down beside him and laughed at his naivety. "Son, you can hack using any computer. Here, let me show you."

He pulled up the picture of César Thiago Gomes that had been distributed and began to code into the system to find similar photos of him on government databases. His first thought was that Gomes would have a fake passport, like himself, and if he could find that, it might help them in their search.

The young tech operator had a concerned look on his face, so Gustav reassured him, "Just tell them I forced you to do it," and smiled at him. The first thing to come up was Gomes' Brazilian and US passports, both with his real name on them.

"Well, we're getting somewhere. Let's figure out what's on the dinner menu tonight while the search continues."

Gustav couldn't help but feel like he was working with Andrei again, but knew that this kid didn't want to break any laws. From the kitchen, where they were looking at that night's takeout menu, they heard the computer chime with more results.

Fifty-Five

Ada had decided to work from home on the Thursday and Friday because she wanted to spend as much time with Ramon as she could before he left on Sunday. So there they were, both sitting at the table on their laptops, working together. She learned quickly that Ramon talked to himself about his cases while trying to figure things out and what the next actions would be. She even caught herself answering him at one point, thinking he was asking her a question.

"Sorry, sweetheart, I was asking myself. If it's bothering you, I can work from upstairs."

She laughed at him and said, "Of course not, I'll just tune you out, and you can carry on your conversation with yourself," and they both laughed. Ada then added, "But if you do ask me something and I don't answer, it's because I'll assume it was for you," and she gave him a wink and blew him a kiss across the table.

She couldn't believe that it had already been a week and a half with Ramon here, and didn't know how she would cope with him being across the ocean again. This was the life she wanted, who she wanted, and she knew it in her heart, even though there was still a part of her wondering if it was all real and true. She kept stealing glances over the top of her laptop at Ramon working in deep concentration. He would make this really adorable gesture when he was deep in thought of covering his mouth with his hand and staring intently at his screen as if the information in his head would just transfer to the computer.

Her next thoughts after admiring him were of how she could be with him. How easy would it be to find a job in Canada? Would she like Canada? Maybe he could move here? Ada knew she wasn't going to get any work done with her mind cluttered with thoughts of a future that she didn't even know would happen. Trying to focus, as she knew she was getting carried away with herself, she repeated an affirmation in her head: "I focus on the present and enjoy the now." With that shifting her mind, she began to focus on the document she was editing for the director.

In the afternoon, Ramon went upstairs and changed into a suit. "Where are you off to, handsome?" she asked him.

With his bright smile, he assured her, "One of my clients happens to be here, so we're going to meet in person. I'll be back in a couple of hours."

And with a kiss goodbye, he was out the door. Ada thought it was odd that one of his clients would just so happen to be in Nottingham, but when you're a fancy lawyer at a big Toronto firm, she guessed that you have all sorts of people with money and influence to attend to. She continued her editing, and around 3 pm took the steaks out of the fridge for a moment to add some spices for them to marinate in before dinner.

Ramon arrived back before Joel, all smiles. "Good meeting, I presume?" she asked him.

He hugged her and said, "It was a great meeting. You can get so much accomplished in person rather than on the phone with these people."

Instead of logging back on for work, Ramon started preparing some potatoes and green beans for them to have with their steaks while Ada finished up her work day.

When Joel arrived home he could smell dinner already simmering in the pan. "Okay, so you two need to stay at home and work more often. I love coming home to the smell of good food cooking."

Ada shoved him away as he tried to bear hug her from behind. "Yes, I'll just be your stay at home wife, and Ramon, well, he can be the cook or the cabana boy." They enjoyed the jokes and worked as a team to finish the dinner together.

****

DCI Amir Karim had held a meeting with some officers late on Wednesday, offering some overtime to anyone who wanted to help guard an important prisoner. He didn't mention who it was, but he was sure that the team knew who he was talking about. They only had one important case right now. A few officers volunteered for the job and the extra pay, and amongst them was Officer Geoffrey Storri.

Officer Storri had been on the Nottingham police force for ten years and still hadn't made detective inspector, which left a bad taste in his mouth. So when the opportunity came up to watch over the Moretti prisoner, he volunteered, as he had been contacted the night before by a third party offering a nice bonus to have him eliminated.

He had always wanted to work for the police, but after not passing his DI exam for the third time and seeing that justice wasn't being done, as criminals were continually being let go, he developed a sense of contempt for the police force. Storri hadn't been shy about his complaints either, which is why, he assumed, that he had been contacted for this worthy cause. "Justice," they called it.

His first shift on the watch had been the night before, overnight, but that day he was on the afternoon shift. Someone had given Moretti some reading material, a book and a magazine, items he wasn't supposed to have, but Storri understood why. Even last night, the kid wouldn't shut up. He kept asking questions about policing and the computer systems that the building used, and then telling him that their jobs would be easier if they just did X, Y, and Z. Storri just shook his head, thinking to himself: If you're so smart, then how did you end up in here, behind bars? With the prisoner occupied, Storri relaxed in the chair across from the cell and watched his prey.

He knew where all the CCTV cameras were placed and had a few ideas for getting the poison into Moretti's food, but it was all about timing. He had the vial that had been given to him in a secret meetup the previous night after his shift; it was tasteless and odourless. He knew that the food would be delivered around half five, and since Moretti was the only prisoner being held that day, there would be only one tray.

As Storri was contemplating the process, Moretti spoke up. "Do you have another book? I'm done with this one."

Storri rolled his eyes. "You shouldn't even have that one."

Moretti gave a sly smile and said, "Well, I could talk to you instead."

Storri wasn't going to have that, so he took the finished book and quickly left to grab another one from the break room, where they kept some novels for the officers to enjoy on their lunch breaks. As he was about to choose another book, he was detained by a fellow officer wanting to talk about their weekend. Realizing that he didn't have time for this, he tried to exit the conversation a few times, to no avail.

After fifteen minutes he finally said, "Look, Johnny, I'm supposed to be on guard right now," and quickly left for his post with the new book in hand.

As he was heading back to the cells, he saw the dinner tray waiting in the hallway. Now having an obstacle in his hand, the transition wouldn't be as smooth, but he had to try anyway. Having taken the vial out of his pocket and palmed it in his hand, he made it look awkward for the cameras by juggling the book and the tray, finally turning his back on the camera to place the tray on the floor to readjust. As it sat there, in a quick four seconds he added the liquid poison to Moretti's soup, and then picked the tray back up with two hands, the book tucked under his arm as he entered the holding area.

He felt confident as he walked down the aisle towards Moretti's cell, which was the third on the right. As he got there, he said, "Double treat for you, a new book and your dinner."

But as he looked up to see where Moretti was, he panicked and dropped the tray of soup and bread on the floor as well as the book while he shouted for help. He wasn't expecting to see a dead body when he came back; that was *his* job. The other guards and officers rushed in and unlocked the cell to check for vitals, but there were none to be found.

Did this kid just commit suicide? he wondered. The shiv was in his hand and his throat was slit. This just can't be, he gave no indication of wanting to die, Storri thought.

With all the bustling bodies and DCI Karim being called for, Storri shrank into the background and just watched the chaos of the scene.

Fifty-Six

Friday morning, Detective Schmidt arrived alone with some breakfast for everyone. When Gustav saw her, he said, "Are you the delivery person now, too?"

She gave a half smile filled with sympathy and replied, "Deliverer of bad news, more like it."

Gustav knew in an instant what she was going to say. He just stood there and shook his head, waiting for her to confirm his thoughts. She put the food down on the table and allowed everyone to grab theirs and leave the room so she and Gustav could speak privately.

"Go ahead," Gustav said curtly.

"I'm so sorry, Mr. Pedalton, Anthony Moretti died in his cell yesterday evening by what looks to be his own hand. They had officers stationed to watch him, but he asked for a book and the officer on duty left for fifteen minutes to fetch him a new book to read, and when he came back, Moretti was dead."

Gustav stood there in disbelief. There was no way that Andrei would kill himself. Absolutely none.

"He wouldn't have, not in a million years, committed suicide."

Detective Schmidt gave that same sad smile again, and Gustav's temper went through the roof. "Don't you dare give me that look! That kid was murdered, I'd bet every cent that I have on it. What has been looked at? I'm sure there's CCTV. This guard just happened to be gone for fifteen minutes? Does it take that long to get a book or was he dawdling for a reason?"

The detective held up her hands against the tirade. "I understand you're upset, Mr. Pedalton. I get it, I do. And the Nottingham police who were working on the case are looking into those things as we speak."

Gustav excused himself and went to the bathroom and cried as silently as he could. Once he was done crying, he was filled with rage again, and this time not directed at the incompetence of the police but at Gomes. He'd done this. Gustav knew it in his bones.

Coming back out of the bathroom, he grabbed his coffee and said to the detective, "Seeing as I'm going away to prison anyway, I decided to use this equipment you've so nicely set up here to do a bit of espionage myself." His tone was curt; he had given up caring now. "To get this over with quicker, I found a couple of passports that Gomes may use in his travels. Yes, it's illegal, and I'm done giving a shit."

Detective Schmidt seemed taken aback by his tone and what he had done. "Mr. Pedalton, are you telling me that you hacked into multiple government databases to find these?"

Gustav shrugged his shoulders. "I'm not telling you anything. Just letting you know some information."

With Gustav considering this the end of the conversation, he gave her the information that he had gleaned from his searches. So far he'd come up with two names: Marco Bianchi and Jorge Morales.

****

Having driven for almost eight hours from Las Vegas, César Thiago Gomes was starving, having only eaten some snacks since a short break four hours before. He had flown into Harry Reid in Las Vegas from JFK in New York under the name Jorge Morales. His rental car, a plain four-door sedan, was rented under Charles Dubois to keep anyone from connecting his whereabouts. Wanting desperately to stretch his legs and find some real food, he pulled into a strip mall about a twenty-five minute drive from his home in San Jose. Putting on his baseball cap and a sweater over the dress shirt he had flown in, he headed for the diner on the edge of the plaza.

After eating some food and planning his next steps, he realized he couldn't just show up at his house, especially dressed as he was. He found a thrift shop in the plaza and went inside, something he had never done before and didn't want to do, but he needed a disguise. He wandered around and found some hideous looking charcoal grey sweatpants, though he cringed at the idea of putting them on, then found a black woollen hat to cover his hair. The finishing touch was a reversible vest that was bright red on one side and black on the other.

As he was checking out, he joked with the cashier, "Running gear, now that it's not as warm."

She eyed him with a look of *like I care, mister*, and finished ringing in the items for him to pay.

He went back to his rental car to sit for a few hours until the sun started to go down. He was torn in his decisions about where to go next, realizing that anywhere he wanted to go would likely be watched by the police. His home, Walter's home, the DreamScape Ltd. building—all would be under surveillance. What he really needed was a good night's rest, which he hadn't had since before he learned of Andrei's arrest a few days earlier. He'd been running on adrenaline ever since. He decided to have a quick nap in the car, and to be sure that he didn't oversleep, he set his alarm for one hour.

****

Detective Schmidt had decided to stay at the condo and use the equipment and computers there to work from. She didn't like what Mr. Pedalton was doing, but it was certainly going quicker. She logged into the police database with her credentials and put in the two names that she had been given to search for flight registrations. There was one hit. Jorge Morales had flown from JFK

THE DREAMSCAPE MURDERS ~ 389

International Airport in New York to Harry Reid International Airport in Las Vegas, Nevada.

"He's here!" she said aloud. She looked at Mr. Pedalton, who simply shrugged his shoulders and smirked, telling her, *I told you so.* She got on the phone to Detective Hill and let him know that Gomes was in the US and that he had landed in Vegas twelve hours ago. She told him to alert the FBI and get the teams ready.

She soon got a call from the head of the FBI task force, saying that their tactical and undercover units were in place at all possible locations. He asked her to keep them informed if she found out any new information, and if they knew where he was heading.

"My guess, sir, is that he's already in the area of San Jose. He landed over twelve hours ago, and no matter what form of transportation he took, he would be there by now. We'll keep each other updated," and she ended the call. "Okay, Mr. Pedalton, I don't want to do this, but I need your help. As legally as possible, can you search for anything that would help us with his whereabouts?"

The response she received wasn't entirely what she was expecting.

"If you call that FBI guy back and give me access to their network, I can use any street cameras or other security footage available to do a facial recognition search for him. But I'd guess they'd have already done that, no?"

She didn't want to bother the FBI lead with such an inane question doubting his abilities, but she also didn't like assuming that everyone was doing their job, so she placed the call to confirm. Once done, and feeling a little deflated from the conversation, she turned back to Gustav and said, "Yes, they're already working on that."

She could see the wheels turning in his head and was astonished at how intelligent he was, but backtracked her thinking, realizing what he had done: hacking into people's dreamscapes and murdering them.

Finally, he came back with a solution. "I'm guessing he would take a car so that there were fewer eyes on him. If he rented one in Vegas, then they would have scanned his passport or ID that he used to obtain the car."

"But we checked the names you gave us and there were no more matches with rental car agencies, trains, or smaller planes," she retorted.

"Yes, but maybe we don't have them all. We need to check all the rental agencies for cars leased late yesterday or earlier today by the picture on the ID," he said.

"That will take a long time," she replied, but Gustav just nodded his agreement.

She called the FBI lead again, asking for system access so they could help in the search, and gave him the idea of what they were looking for. An hour later, Gustav had the access he needed and began the searches, starting with the rental car agencies at the airport.

****

The sun was setting and Gomes' alarm had gone off to wake him from his nap. Feeling slightly more refreshed, he leaned up from his reclined seat and glanced out the windows. Seeing that the parking lot was a bit more empty, he decided to change into his sweatpants and flipped the vest to the black side. He pulled out his phone and called for a taxi to meet him outside the diner where he'd eaten. They advised him that one would be there in about ten minutes. He grabbed his dry bag, walked over to the edge of the diner, and waited for his taxi to arrive.

Once inside the cab, the driver asked him where he wanted to go. "Colleen Street," Gomes said, "and I'll let you know when to stop." Colleen Street was one street over from Walter Dumas', and he was going to see if he could sneak in through the backyard. As the driver passed James Street, where Walter's house was located, Gomes looked out the window and saw a couple of black SUVs. Not very camouflaged, guys, he thought, smiling to himself.

Once they turned left onto Colleen Street, the driver asked where, and Gomes responded, "Keep going." There were no black SUVs on this street, but he didn't know if any other undercover cars were around.

At the end of the street, he asked the driver to pull over and got out, paying in cash and putting his bag on his back while exiting the vehicle. He looked in every direction and didn't see anyone suspicious, so he crossed the street and saw an unfenced yard that he decided to go into. Hoping for no motion-sensing lights, he walked close to the house until he reached the opposite side that had no lights on it, and then headed for the rear of the yard. Climbing the corner of the partition wall, still under cover of darkness, he slid down into the yard that was diagonal from the one he had been in. There were bushes here along the wall, which gave him a chance to get the lay of the backyard before moving forward.

Counting in his head how many more yards he would have to traverse before reaching Walter's—he figured it to be four more. He also knew there would likely be police in the yard surrounding Walter's house, so he would have to stop in the neighbour's.

By continuously climbing the back partition walls, he made it to the yard next to Walter's and paused to listen. As he sat there in the neighbour's yard, he wished he could fly so that he didn't need to be on the ground with the police. As the thought entered his head, he looked up and saw a large oak tree in the yard that he was in, which had branches reaching close to Walter's second floor windows. He decided to climb the tree and took refuge in one of its larger branches, flattening himself down along the limb to watch the police crew in the backyard of Walter Dumas' house.

Fifty-Seven

Gustav had searched all six rental car agencies one by one. As they say, it's always in the last place you look. He finally found a photo on Aviva for a Charles Dubois, which looked the same as the other passport photos they had. He told Detective Schmidt, who immediately placed a call to the FBI to have them get the tracking information for locating the car. Gustav watched her pace the floor as she waited for the call back to see what they found out. After about thirty minutes they called to say that the car had been located in a strip mall in San Jose, about twenty to thirty minutes from where the FBI had been waiting at Dumas' house.

When Detective Schmidt ended the call, she told Gustav, "They found the car and are sending a tactical team there now to surround it," finishing with a sigh of relief.

Gustav could feel the relief too. It would soon be over, and no one else would be in danger. He thought of Andrei's family and decided, when it was all over, that he would tell them Andrei's real name so that they could contact his family and disperse his estate, if they let them have the money. He wasn't sure on that point, as it was funded from criminal activity, but it would remain to be seen.

"You want another coffee while we wait?" he asked the detective.

"No, thank you. My nerves are already shot as it is," she responded.

Gustav nodded and got up to go to the kitchen. His thoughts strayed to what would happen next for him and how severe his sentence would be. He had been keeping his lawyer updated with everything and, as he wasn't being questioned, she hadn't been needed for the last few days. He heard the detective's phone ring from the other room and went back with his coffee to see what it was.

"The FBI are letting us listen to the live comms with the tactical team," she said and put her phone on speaker.

****

Lead FBI agent Thomas Coombs had his team set and all exits of the parking lot blocked off. There was no use of flashing lights. The tactical truck dispersed the team on the roadside so they could slowly approach and surround the vehicle in a crouched position. With the dark of night, they couldn't be seen by an onlooker until they got closer to the lights of the parking lot.

"Sound off," Agent Coombs instructed.

"Eagle One: ready to approach the rear of the vehicle."

"Eagle Two and Three: driver side approach, 10 metres."

"Eagle Four: approaching the front of the vehicle."

"Eagle Five and Six: passenger side approach, 7 metres."

"Team in position, sir," responded Eagle One.

"Go, team leader," Coombs responded on the comms.

The tactical team rushed the car with their guns drawn and flashlights turned on, shouting, "FBI, stay in the vehicle!"

Agent Coombs felt satisfaction watching the team in action, but it soon dissipated when he heard Eagle One on the comms. "Sir, the vehicle is empty."

Ripping the earbud out of his ear, he stormed off to his car while shouting for one of the other agents to wrap this up and head back to Dumas' house immediately.

****

From his prostrate position on the large branch, Gomes had watched a good number of the officers leave the yard quickly and wondered what was happening. Now was his chance. He had been eyeing the Juliet balcony a couple of windows away from where he was. He knew that if he could get on the roof, he could hang down and land there.

Gomes looked up at the tree and figured out which branches would take him closest to the roof, so he began to climb. He would have liked to go higher so that he could drop down onto the roof, but the branches further up didn't appear stable enough to hold his weight and support a jump. He compromised on a thicker branch that would allow him, if he ran lightly, to jump the three or so feet to the roof.

Looking in both directions for where the officers were watching, he leaned against the trunk of the tree with his bag on his back and readied himself to be propelled forward. Pushing off, he did an acrobatic run, using the arches of his feet to balance on the limb and leap onto the roof. He tried to muffle the thud on the roof as much as possible, and lay still for a while so as to not raise suspicion if someone listened for more sounds. After a few minutes he slid slowly down to the eaves and starfished his way over to the window.

Once he was right above it, he shimmied his full body down to the eaves and sat on the edge for support while he glanced down to see if there were any lights on in that room. Grabbing the edge of the eave with both hands, he spun himself around and hung in the air above the small balcony. He looked down to make sure he was in a good spot and took a deep breath, then let go. He landed in the middle of the balcony with a soft-footed landing and again remained motionless while he listened for any disturbance from inside the house or outside with the cavalry. Having had one of these windows, much to his dislike, at his own home, he knew that they only had a latch between the doors. He opened his bag and took out the hunting knife that he had bought on the road trip to San Jose. He slid the tip between the doors and gently lifted the latch that secured them.

He knew that Walter Dumas was divorced and his kids had all gone on to have their own lives, so he would likely be home alone, with maybe a few police inside as well. Trying to regulate his heartbeat, Gomes slowly opened the doors and slid inside the dark room, closing the door behind him. He paused to allow his eyes to adjust to the darkness and confirm the layout of the room. He removed his shoes and started to walk softly in his stocking feet to eliminate any noise. Realizing this was a guest room, with a dresser and bed on opposite sides of the room, he made his way to the door to the hallway.

From the darkness showing underneath the door, he surmised that the lights in the hallway were off. He checked his watch, which illuminated to show that it was almost 11 pm. Walter was approaching seventy years of age, so he likely wouldn't be awake at this hour. Gomes opened the door and glanced out precariously into the hallway. No lights were on in either direction. He guessed which direction was the staircase, lit up slightly from the arching window in front of it that caught the street lights outside. Not detecting any lights on downstairs, he headed right and began slowly glancing into rooms. Two doors were ajar and he could see that neither was Walter's bedroom. What he hadn't seen in his quick glance was an FBI tactical member hiding in a dark corner wearing night vision goggles.

He approached the last room in the corridor and, not seeing any light from under the doorway, slowly opened the door and softly entered the large room. As his eyes adjusted again, he saw that the room had a four-poster bed, a long waist-high dresser, and drapes thick enough to cut out any light from outside. The drapes, however, weren't fully closed and a slit of light was cast across the room. Gomes paused before he decided to approach the bed with the human-sized lump under the covers. The person was lying on their side with their back towards him, so he crept closer to stare and ponder where to place his attack. He had never killed anyone himself before, as he always hired people to do it, but this one was more personal and he needed to do it himself. He could see Walter's silver hair on the pillow with the blankets tucked up close to his ears, so going for his neck wouldn't be wise. The hunting blade was sharp, but he didn't think it would be sharp enough to go through a duvet and inflict a mortal wound.

He made his final decision, lightly grabbing the edge of the duvet that was hanging off the bed to lift it and plunge the knife into Walter's back. Slowly, he moved into position, in one swift motion lifted the duvet with his right hand, and drove the knife into Walter's back with his left. When the blade struck, he felt a resistance that jarred his arm and hand, causing him to drop the knife on the floor before he could try again. With a shock, he realized that he had struck something metal. Just as he did so, the person lying in the bed spun around with a quickness that could not have been Walter and tried to grab him. Gomes fought this pretender off and with a quick turn headed back towards the door. It was now lit up from a hallway light, where he was met with an imposing figure blocking the way wearing combat gear and goggles on top of his head, pointing a gun at him.

"Hands on your head, get down on the floor!" he heard shouted at him, and then realized the trap he'd fallen into. Walter wasn't here. It was a setup by the FBI. Gomes raised his hands above his head, and with the light streaming into the room now, he could see in his peripheral vision where the knife had fallen. The person who had been in the bed—an elderly agent by the looks of him—began to approach him from behind. In an instant he decided to lunge for the knife as he pretended to get on his knees in a last ditch effort to escape.

One squeeze of the trigger was all it took for the FBI tactical member to bring Gomes down, landing the shot in his left shoulder as he lunged for his weapon. They radioed Agent Coombs to let him know the good news.

"Sir, César Thiago Gomes has been apprehended. Send in the medical team, he's suffered a GSW in the left shoulder while reaching for his weapon."

Coombs responded, "Put it in the report, agent. Thanks for the update. And good job."

Agent Coombs called Detective Schmidt to let her know, and asked if she could relay the information across the pond to the other teams while he cleaned up here. The news spread like wildfire. Even though it was the middle of the night in California, the media still released the breaking news online, which spread world-wide from there.

Fifty-Eight

Gustav knew his comfortable accommodations were over now that the FBI had arrested Gomes. The FBI took him to a cell to await extradition, since his passport with the name of Jonas Pedalton was a US passport and therefore the Vancouver team couldn't hold him. Detective Schmidt arrived at his cell with FBI Agent Thomas Coombs and they both entered to talk to him.

Agent Coombs began, "Mr. Pedalton, Detective Schmidt has told me how much you helped out with this case, and even though we are extraditing you, we would like to put you into witness protection so that Gomes can't somehow get to you while he awaits trial."

Gustav was confused. "So I'm not going to jail?"

"As a key witness in the case against Mr. Gomes, we need you alive. You will be formally charged with hacking the DreamScape Ltd. database, but the laws around what happens in dreams haven't been enacted yet. I know you murdered those people in their dreams, but I'm not sure how to enforce that as, technically, you didn't physically do it," Agent Coombs responded.

Detective Schmidt chimed in, "The extradition could take some time with the paperwork, maybe a week or so, but we'll keep you under close watch here until then."

Gustav grunted at that. "Yeah, like you kept a close watch on Andrei?"

The detective looked confused. "Who's Andrei?"

Gustav realized his mistake, but figured now was as good a time as any to tell them his real name. "Anthony Moretti was not his name. His name was Andrei Kuzmenski, and I would appreciate it if you could notify his family about his death."

"Oh, I see," Detective Schmidt said, "so you were close. I'd gathered that, but is there anything else we should know? Is Jonas Pedalton your real name?"

Gustav rolled his eyes and sighed. "Well, if I'm going to get a new name in witness protection, I might as well throw this one out too. My name is Gustav Lindenholst."

Agent Coombs pulled Detective Schmidt to the side and Gustav couldn't hear what they were saying, but the hushed tones didn't sound derogatory after the bomb he had just dropped on them.

When they came back over, Coombs said to him, "I'll update the paperwork, Mr. Lindenholst, but as you mentioned, your friend Andrei was not protected very securely in his cell in Nottingham, and I need you to testify. Detective Schmidt here has agreed to send you back to the secure condo, under guard again, but your IT equipment will not be available to you anymore."

Gustav agreed to that. A bed and shower and coffee was a lot better than rotting in a cell for a week. He made one request. "If I don't have anything IT related to play with, can I have some books to read?"

Before Detective Schmidt had a chance to leave the cell, Gustav called out to her. "Detective? Has there been any word on what happened to Andrei in Nottingham? Did they find the person responsible?"

Detective Schmidt turned around. "They discovered some corrupt officers in their employ who had been bribed to distract the guard on duty. When the guard went to get a book, he was held up on returning, which gave another officer a chance to go into the cell to murder Andrei. They discovered a few members that had been contacted to kill him, including the guard that went for the book. He was as shocked as everyone else when Andrei ended up dead. This crime is being added to the list of Gomes' offences. I'm so sorry we could not stop that from happening, Mr. Pedalton—I mean Mr. Lindenholst." With her apologies, she left the cell until Gustav could be transferred back to the secure condo.

****

Saturday, December 5th, first thing in the morning, Ada, Ramon, and Joel saw the news that a man named César Thiago Gomes, a 56-year-old native Brazilian and US citizen, had been arrested for the murders. They listed the names of Brian and Amara Adebayo, Flora and Carmine Esposito, Arthur Millstone, and Archibald Newbury, and the attempted murders of Estella Crain and the CEO of DreamScape Ltd., Walter Dumas. Joel was in tears, finally having closure on Arthur's death, and Ada held him in her arms as they all sat and watched the story continue. When they got to the part about a man named Andrei Kuzmenski being murdered while in Nottingham lockup and showed his pictures, Ada felt a sense of relief wash over her, knowing that he would not be bothering her any longer.

Ramon's flight was at 2 pm that Sunday. He would have to leave Nottingham first thing in the morning to catch the train to the airport, but just as they were going over their plans, Joel spoke up. "Don't be silly. I'll drive the three of us to Heathrow so you can have a proper goodbye. We'll leave here at 9 am tomorrow morning."

Ada hugged him again and said, "Thank you!"

With the details of the next morning sorted out, they got dressed and paid a last visit to Ada's mom and brother. They all had lunch together and Ramon got to see where Ada had grown up. After lunch they went to meet Kira at a pub for a drink and some more goodbyes.

Ada was feeling the weight on her heart growing with every goodbye for Ramon, and by the time they reached home, she was almost in tears.

"What is it, sweetheart?" he asked her.

As a tear rolled down her cheek, she said, "I don't want you to go. I don't know how to go back to having you so far away. I love you."

Ramon smiled that dazzling smile at her and wiped the tear from her cheek. "Sweetheart, I love you too, and the distance cannot stop that. Plus, now that everyone has been arrested, we can meet in our dreams again until we see each other once again in real life."

Ada knew he was trying to be reassuring, but it wasn't helping. All she wanted to do for the rest of the day was be in his arms.

Joel had cooked a roast dinner that night and Ramon decided to share his good news with them. He went upstairs to get the gift that he had bought Ada when they were out shopping for Christmas ornaments and came around to her chair. He sat down beside her and said, "I have a little something for you."

Joel smiled, all excited. Ada wasn't sure what kind of gesture this was, so she opened the bag. Inside she found a Christmas ornament that said, "Our first Christmas" on it. It was cheesy, but she loved it all the same. "But you won't be here for Christmas," she finally said to him with watery eyes.

Ramon put a quizzical look on his face. "Are you sure?"

Ada's heart leapt into her throat. "Do not toy with my emotions right now, mister!" Her statement brought out the biggest laugh from Ramon, while Joel kept watching with anticipation.

"Well, the second part of all this is that, while I've been here, I've been interviewing for a job at a law firm in Nottingham. Shelley, Winthrop and Associates. That's where I went on Thursday afternoon when I said I had to meet a client."

Ada was shocked, and so was Joel. "So you're looking to move here?" she finally said.

"Yes, sweetheart. I can't stand the idea of not being able to see you, either. Did you think you were alone in that?"

Ada stood up and hugged him, then asked, "When will you find out?"

"Hopefully next week, but if it's not that one, I will keep trying other law firms. There are a few exams I will have to take, but they will start me off in a generic role until I can update my credentials. I'll find a way, my love. But either way, I'll be here for Christmas. Living or just visiting. You can't get rid of me that easily."

Joel was so ecstatic that he stood up and rushed over to give Ramon a hug. "You've already made this Christmas feel so special, and it will be even more with you here." The trio enjoyed their last dinner together until the next time and Ada's joy was palpable.

The End

About the Author

Author
H.M. NEWSOME

To start, this is a work of fiction, any resemblance to places, characters, or names are completely from the imagination of myself, the author.

This book has been a long time coming, and I am so proud that it has finally arrived. I have always been a writer, whether it be poetry or articles, but this is the first novel. I had started many others, but they didn't take. Writing has been my outlet since I was a teenager and discovered my ease with words. Love what you do and you can live through it.